Finding April

FINDING APRIL

David Thear

Copyright © 2018 David Thear

The moral right of the author has been asserted.

Apart from any fair dealing for the purposes of research or private study, or criticism or review, as permitted under the Copyright, Designs and Patents Act 1988, this publication may only be reproduced, stored or transmitted, in any form or by any means, with the prior permission in writing of the publishers, or in the case of reprographic reproduction in accordance with the terms of licences issued by the Copyright Licensing Agency. Enquiries concerning reproduction outside those terms should be sent to the publishers.

Matador
9 Priory Business Park,
Wistow Road, Kibworth Beauchamp,
Leicestershire. LE8 0RX
Tel: 0116 279 2299
Email: books@troubador.co.uk
Web: www.troubador.co.uk/matador
Twitter: @matadorbooks

ISBN 978 1789015 355

British Library Cataloguing in Publication Data.
A catalogue record for this book is available from the British Library.

Printed and bound in Great Britain by 4edge Limited
Typeset in 11pt Adobe Garamond Pro by Troubador Publishing Ltd, Leicester, UK

Matador is an imprint of Troubador Publishing Ltd

For Katie

ACKNOWLEDGEMENTS

We know that an ugly duckling is unlikely to grow into a sleek white swan, but it might emerge as an attractive duck. This furry creature grew with the kind assistance of informed friends and emerged from the reeds fully feathered, paddling with new found confidence.

My heartfelt thanks go to Miriam and Gillian who read two early versions of the manuscript, making many invaluable suggestions. I am also grateful to Cressida, Abigail and Gwilym, who checked later versions, suggesting further ideas. Their final efforts were appreciated without ruffling any feathers.

After so much excellent guidance, any errors that remain are entirely my responsibility.

Finally, I should like to thank my late wife Katie who encouraged me to take the plunge.

PART 1
FATEFUL JOURNEY

ONE

Two girls hurried across the school field still wet from the early morning frost. April had made a decision and stopped to face her friend Mandy. She and James Fleming were going to get together and she was now ready to do something about it. James was eighteen, in his last year at school before leaving for university.

'That's impossible. And anyway what's brought this on all of a sudden? You know you can't make a move in this place without everyone knowing about it.'

She was right. Mandy had been keen on a boy last summer and had accidently dropped her books just in front of him, falling and 'twisting' her ankle. He was embarrassed and ran away. When word got around she became the butt of teasing and smutty humour.

The two friends had thrived at Milsham Grammar School. Both shared a love of English. Mandy Daniels was sixteen and thin with mousy hair. She planned to stay on to take A-levels. April Saunders was ash-blonde and fifteen. Her mature figure drew lustful looks from the boys, particularly during swimming lessons.

April frowned, hugging her coat around herself.

'I'll have to find a way to meet him.'

'You could try the school dance in a couple of weeks,' said Mandy. She shivered and turned to trot back towards the school.

'That's a thought,' said April, hurrying to keep up. 'But I don't think it'll work. We'll need a proper plan.'

April was proved right. James didn't dance until the end, when he homed in on Teresa Marshall who wasn't interested. April did her best, dancing with Brian Humphries and looking at James when they passed by. Brian had been a friend since primary school. It was no secret that he liked April, although he'd never said anything. Now he asked her out to the pictures during the Christmas holiday and, to Mandy's surprise, April accepted.

...

It was the beginning of the new year of 1959. The two girls were sitting on the rug in Mandy's bedroom playing records.

'Come on, you're good at organising things, what's your brilliant plan for me to meet James?'

Mandy rose and stared into the back garden. Her father was tending a crackling bonfire, where a coil of blue smoke joined the clouds from his breath. She closed the window to shut out the acrid smell, turned and sighed.

'I don't get this infatuation with James Fleming. He doesn't seem interested in you. Brian on the other hand is nice and good looking. You know he likes you. Why don't you go out with him?'

'I don't want to. You go out with him if you think he's so cool.'

'I never said that.' Mandy flushed and turned back to look into the garden. 'I was only thinking about you.'

'I've made my mind up about James. I really like him and I'm sure he likes me. I catch him looking at me from time to time, but when I look back he turns away. He's obviously shy, so it's going to be a challenge.'

Mandy stiffened as she put on April's new Elvis LP. It was a Christmas present and they had been playing it non-stop ever since. They sat on the rug with their backs against the bed, closed their eyes and listened again. There was a long period with both of them lost in thought until Mandy rose to turn over the record.

'I've never seen him around here. You'll need to find out where he lives and what he does in his spare time.'

'That won't be easy. We'll need help from your gang.'

Mandy's gang consisted of a group of middle school boys, former friends of her younger brother. They were often willing to do favours for her. April had never understood why and had decided not to ask.

At the beginning of term, Mandy briefed her gang who were sworn to secrecy. Before long they reported that James came from a village near Bishops Stortford and travelled to school each day by train. However, there was no information about his evening or weekend activities.

The following Saturday afternoon, the girls walked

through the woods and stopped at the wooden bridge above a stream. Mandy leaned over and dropped a small twig that drifted slowly underneath.

'Sometimes you can see small fish in here.'

'We still have no idea what James does at weekends,' said April.

'He could be with Teresa Marshall. We know he likes her and she lives in Stortford.'

She moved across the bridge to look out for the twig.

'He wouldn't do that. She's a tart.'

'She seems alright to me,' muttered Mandy as she watched the stick reappear and gather speed.

'I want James and I mean to have him!' shouted April.

Mandy looked up in surprise.

'You might not succeed. You have to accept that.'

'Why are you talking like this? I need your help and you're just trying to upset me.' April turned and stormed off towards the road.

Mandy called after her friend's retreating back.

'There's no need to get ratty. I'll try and help.'

Three weeks later they received an unexpected break when they learned that James supervised a youth club in Milsham for 12-16 year olds on Thursday evenings.

'This is it,' said April. 'We'll join this club, spy out the land and make a plan.'

...

James placed the needle carefully on the record and adjusted the volume of his new Frank Sinatra LP. He'd bought it with money from the Christmas bonus he'd received from his weekend job. The kids would probably prefer rock'n'roll, but he was in charge and would play his music. The church hall was bright and cheerful with the mixed voices and laughter in contrast to the cold February night outside.

At six-fifteen he had arrived with the vicar to put out the snooker and table-tennis tables and open the snack bar. After which the cleric retired to his house across the road. He would reappear around fifteen minutes before closing time and chat to the boys and girls before they left. James would help him clear up before closing for the night. The kids were usually well behaved and he didn't anticipate any problems.

He had won a game of table-tennis but not too easily. He leaned against the wall with a mug of coffee and listened to the gramophone, experiencing a twinge of pain when he remembered the row with his father who had torn up his revision notes and thrown them in the dustbin. He had retrieved them and a confrontation followed:

'You can't do this to my work.'

'I bloody can. If you don't get a job and bring money into the house, I'll burn the lot. We can't afford to support you at your age.'

'You won't have to. I'm going to university in the autumn.'

'No you're not. People like us don't go to university. You get yourself a job or you're out the door.'

'What do you mean? You can't throw me out. This is my home.'

'Not any more it ain't if you don't get a job.'

James couldn't believe his father would really throw him out. He had lived in this tiny cottage as long as he could remember. The sights and smells were so familiar he didn't notice them anymore. He looked with fresh eyes at the worn lino, the brown rag rug by the fireplace and the little pilot radio in the corner with its circular dial that glowed yellow when you switched it on. His father had paused, hearing a sound behind him. James's mother stood in the doorway clutching a handkerchief and was starting to cry. He rounded on James again.

'Now you've gone and upset Mum.'

His father had never supported his studies but this time he was really angry. He couldn't understand why this had blown up now until, a few weeks later revising at home, he noticed his mother was there more than before. She'd been put on short time at the factory. Why hadn't anyone told him?

His thoughts were interrupted by the sight of that pretty blonde girl April from the fifth year with her friend. He hadn't seen her here before and watched as she chatted and laughed with the others. Sometime later he was distracted by an argument at the snack bar and strode over to sort it out. He looked around afterwards but the girls had gone. Then a door at the other end of the room opened and April's friend appeared. He was surprised as he had always assumed it was locked. Mandy came straight towards him.

'There's some trouble out there. You'd better come and deal with it.'

He followed her through the door and along a dingy corridor before entering a dusty and dimly lit room. There were chairs stacked along one side except for one that stood in a pool of light facing the door. April sat there with her arms tied behind her. James stared as two younger boys pushed past him and ran back to the hall.

'Are you alright?' he asked.

'I'm okay,' said April, wriggling to give her impression of a damsel in distress.

'Do you want me to untie you?'

'Yes please.' She gave another convincing wriggle.

James turned to Mandy.

'What's been going on here?'

'The boys were messing about and they wouldn't let me untie her.'

'What's your name?'

'Mandy.'

'Okay Mandy. Go back to the hall and close the door there. Make sure no one comes through. April and I will be along in a few minutes.'

He didn't notice that Mandy had remained in the shadows near the door as he bent and studied April's face.

'If I'm to release you, you'll have to pay in advance. It will cost you one kiss.'

She smiled as he bent and kissed her. At last they stopped and drew breath.

'We'd better try that again,' he whispered and this time he cupped her upturned face in his hands and kissed her slowly and tenderly.

'I've wanted to do that for a long time.'

'I didn't think you'd even noticed me.'

After April had been untied, they stood together and kissed again as Mandy tiptoed away. They agreed to meet at April's house on Saturday afternoon.

Returning on the train that night, James smiled as he leaned back with his feet on the opposite seat, closed his eyes and listened to the rhythmic clacking of the wheels. Saturday couldn't come soon enough.

February 12th
Everything we planned worked perfectly. We kissed in the back room at the church hall. He said he'd always wanted to. I knew I was right. We're meeting again on Saturday. I'm really excited –

February 15th
It went great yesterday. We stayed in and played records in the front room. After mum and dad went out in the evening, we kissed and cuddled on the settee. He's quite shy and nervous but he obviously likes me –

TWO

James had a weekend job on Saturday and Sunday mornings, clearing out and tidying a warehouse. On Saturday afternoons he cycled into Bishops Stortford to catch the train which took him to Milsham. April's home was a 1930s semi with a shallow front garden which needed just three steps from the metal gate to the front door. If the weather was fine, they would walk along the river or through the woods. When it was cold or raining they curled up in her front room playing records and chatted or read together. He hardly ever saw her parents who usually went out on Saturday evenings and didn't return until after eleven, by which time he was on the last train home.

April's older sister Carol was unlike her. She was nineteen, dark-haired and serious. She had left home at sixteen and was a trainee nurse in London, returning for Sunday lunch every other weekend. On the only occasion when they had met, James had felt uneasy as she appraised him.

He was awkward with girls and often said the wrong thing as he struggled with his nervousness. His relationships with the opposite sex usually lasted for only one or two dates but this time it was different. He had been seeing April for three weeks and had never felt nervous in her company. They were happy just to be together.

He had been offered a place at Bristol University to read English and needed to get good marks in his A-levels. He loved History and English Literature, particularly the Romantic poets and would often carry a book of verse to read on the train. When they were together he would sometimes read to her.

March 1st
We're getting to know each other much more now. He talks a lot about the things boys usually go on about, but he's the first one I've met who loves poetry (apart from dear old Dr. Williams at school). He's doing English, French and History at A-level this summer so he has to revise a lot. When he comes he's often got a poetry book with him. He likes to read bits to me sometimes, so I've been hearing some Auden recently. I always enjoy his poetry. Everything's great between us except sometimes I feel he's living in a world of his own and holding me at a distance. I shall persevere though –

March 15th
It was wet yesterday. We lit the fire and sat making toast. James is unhappy at home and told me. He's

never spoken to anyone else about it, so I was glad that he felt able to confide in me. I wish I could explain my own situation. But there are frightening things that we cannot speak about even to ourselves.

One Saturday afternoon the couple were walking hand in hand through the woods with only the sounds of birdsong for company. James thought that it must be time to go back. When he turned to April, he saw how the low sunlight that streamed through the bare branches had turned her into a figure of shining gold. He had never seen anything so beautiful and that night he wrote a sonnet to her. The next morning he read it through and realised that it wasn't much good but he had put all his feelings into it. He could never show it to her.

March 29th
James is calling me his golden girl after seeing me in the sunlight. Boys can be silly sometimes. I don't want him to start putting me on some pedestal. We're reading Browning now. 'Oh to be in England now that April's here,' he said. I told him I'd heard that a zillion times and anyway he'd misquoted. It seems I know more Browning than he does but I didn't let on. I asked him whether he liked Dylan Thomas and he went quiet, saying something about it not being on the syllabus. I'm beginning to realise that his knowledge and understanding of poetry is pretty limited.

Although they were happy together, James was only dimly aware of his growing feelings for April. He was a timid lover but she didn't seem to mind. He worried that he might lose control if things went too far, then anything could happen. Suppose she became pregnant? Obviously he wouldn't be able to go to university or escape from home. The prospect was unbearable so he muddled on.

April 5th
Easter weekend. It seems funny not seeing James. Carol's home. She's doing fine at the London Hospital, although the work's hard and she gets very tired. Matron's a bit of a dragon too, it seems. She means to stick with it. Rather her than me… Went over to Mandy's house last night. We had some good laughs. She doesn't want me to get too involved with James. I have a nagging feeling that she knows something and isn't telling me. I'm so scared. I don't know what to do. I meant to speak to Carol but I couldn't. I will next time.

Walking together on the school field one lunch time, April told James that they wouldn't be able to meet on the following Saturday as she had to attend a family birthday party in North London. The news caught him unawares and he stopped.

'Perhaps I could come over on Sunday?'

'Sundays are no good. I help Mum with the dinner in the morning. After that we all sit in the front room. I usually go upstairs to catch up with my homework and revision. You're not the only one with exams. I've got my O-levels in a few weeks.'

'I'll miss seeing you.'

'I'll miss you too but it's only for this Saturday.'

The weekend without April found James in a predicament that he hadn't experienced before. Waking each morning he would think of her and a warm glow would spread through him. During their walks together, they said barely a word all afternoon. It was so easy and perfect. April was his first sweetheart and he didn't know what came next. One day he felt happy and told her so. She had rewarded him with a smile that melted his heart.

April 11th
My birthday! We're off to Gran's for tea and Carol's coming over. There's to be a cake and presents. Sixteen at last! I've asked Mum to get me that blue dress with the little daisy flowers from the 'Pretty Things' shop in Edmonton (I tried it on last Saturday). I told James I had to go away. He thinks its Gran's birthday. He was upset. I was too, but I daren't admit it's my birthday as I told him I was already sixteen two months ago. Oh what a web we weave. HELP. Mandy says that James may be seeing Teresa Marshall. It can't be true. Please God it isn't.

The following Saturday afternoon the couple walked along the river. A gentle breeze rippled the surface of the water. The trees and hedgerows wore the bright green leaves of springtime and they passed a blackthorn hedge with its dazzling white blossom. Then the sky darkened and large raindrops fell, increasing steadily in intensity. There was a flash and rumble of thunder. Casting round for shelter, they ran to a footbridge about forty yards ahead and arrived panting beneath it. April leant against the brick wall and shivered. James put his arms around her and drew her close. He could smell the dampness in her dress and felt her breasts against his chest. He kissed her fiercely as the storm broke around them. Eventually she pushed him away and spoke in his ear above the uproar.

'Be gentle with me, James.'

He felt confused. He was full of things to say but the words wouldn't come. She sensed it and kissed him tenderly. He began to pull up her dress. She slipped it off and folded it on the ground. He fumbled with her bra strap as she lifted his shirt and ran her hands over his back. April placed her bra on top of her dress and they kissed again as he fondled her breasts.

'I love you April.'

'Do you really?' she whispered, nibbling his ear.

He undid his trousers and pulled down his pants, then stopped.

'Perhaps we shouldn't …'

'It's alright. There's nothing to worry about.'

He thrust at her. It wasn't easy trying to do it for the first time, standing up. She reached down to guide him into her but at her touch he climaxed with a shout and a long moan of pleasure as he gradually subsided.

'I'm sorry. I'm so sorry.'

'It's alright, it's too difficult here. But we've made love together and that's special for both of us.'

After a quick clean up, she turned around and asked him to brush off any dirt from her back that had come from the wall. He did so then slid his arms around to hold her breasts firmly in his hands. She reached up and removed them.

'My breasts are sensitive, my love, so try not to grab them like that.' She turned and smiled at him as she dressed.

'Tell me how you're feeling. Say you love me again.'

'I do, April. I think I always have.'

The storm was over. After a final hug they walked hand in hand into the sweet smelling air.

As April's parents had decided to stay in that evening, they went over to Mandy's house and sat around and listened to records. When April left the room for a few minutes, James was startled when Mandy stared intensely at him.

'If you hurt April, I'll kill you.'

He couldn't understand it. What was she on about? He knew he could never do such a thing. He felt hot with indignation but couldn't say anything as April returned at that moment.

April 19th
Yesterday we got caught in a thunderstorm and sheltered under one of the river bridges. We made love together. It was wonderful. James is forgetting his inhibitions and says HE LOVES ME! I hope it's true as something serious is happening to us. Later Mum and Dad decided to stay in so we went over to Mandy's place. I feel happy and excited and am filled with hope –

The following Saturday afternoon was cold and windy and the couple stayed in and played records. James sat on the floor with his back against the settee and April laid full length along it. Her right hand periodically stroked his hair or just rested on his shoulder.

The record finished and James rose to remove it. When he looked back at April he found everything was quiet. He could hear birdsong outside but something was missing. He realised that the constant commentary in his head had gone. He felt light and as carefree as a child. It had happened before but this time the significance of it was clear. He felt happy because they were together. He gazed at April and was overcome with tender feelings for her; he felt deeply touched as he recognised her vulnerability for the first time. He wanted to sweep her up in his arms and protect her from the whole world.

The experience had left him both elated and anxious. He tossed in bed that night realising things were out of control. He had fallen in love with April. How had it happened? He hadn't expected it. How could they continue together?

He rose and stared out at the silent moonlit countryside. He had originally assumed that their relationship would finish at the end of term. That was only seven weeks away and he'd already organised his summer with full-time work on a building site to earn some much needed money. He had also fixed up a three week hitch-hiking holiday with his mates. When school finished, he wouldn't have his train pass that gave him free travel to Milsham. Back in bed he stared at the ceiling, afraid that when he saw April on Saturday he wouldn't be able to stop his feelings for her pouring out.

The following week, unable to cope with the rush of his feelings, he stayed in the library during the lunch periods to avoid seeing her but he found it difficult to concentrate. At night he was pulled in two directions. His fear, rationalised by his mind, told him that he should never have become serious about April. There was no future in it. She was just an ordinary girl and wasn't good enough for him anyway. His overwhelming priority was to go to university. Once there, he would meet lots of clever and attractive girls. April was all wrong for him so he should end it straight away. At the same time, his longing for her that knew no words lay deep inside him.

The following Saturday he managed to get through their meeting without mishap. He forgot his fears and relaxed in the warmth of April's company and couldn't bear the thought of being without her. If she had noticed his inner conflict, she hadn't said anything.

May 3rd
Something is bothering James. It could be that he's worried as his exams are getting close. I hope he isn't having second thoughts about me as I've become fully committed. I can't face the prospect of losing him as I love him so much and I need him. I am certain that something is growing inside me. Carol's here the Sunday after next. I have GOT to talk to her then.

THREE

He cried with frustration on the way home. He sat curled up in the train compartment, unable in his misery to decide what to do. He needed help but there was no one to talk to except Evelyn. He didn't know whether that would be alright, but there was no one else.

One evening a week, James spent a couple of hours discussing his A-level English studies with Dr. Evelyn Watkins, a retired academic from Cambridge. She shared a cosy cottage in the next village with a tabby cat and was ten minutes away by bike. She had been his English teacher's tutor at university and the two had kept in touch. Evelyn looked forward to her weekly tutorial with James. He was bright, not Oxbridge material, but he should do well enough. James admired Evelyn's wide range of knowledge and incisive intelligence. During their discussions she had helped him to understand better the work of the writers he was studying and encouraged him to read more widely. That evening, after nearly an hour spent on Thomas Hardy, Evelyn disappeared to make a pot of tea. She returned with it on a tray with a plate of biscuits. It was their usual routine and signalled a break from the academic discussion. James hunched forward, staring into his cup. Evelyn sensed his mood and enquired if everything was alright.

'You've got three weeks before the exams. Are you getting worried?'

All at once he poured out the details of his present plight. She listened patiently, sipping her tea until his story petered out.

'I'm sorry. I shouldn't have said all this but I can't decide what to do.'

Evelyn put down her empty cup and refilled it. She had seen so many students struggling with the pain of their emotions and burgeoning hormones. She assured him that she was glad he had brought it up.

'You need to resolve this as soon as possible. Either you share your feelings with this girl or finish the relationship. You don't need all this worry now.'

'I can't tell her about my feelings. I could make a fool of myself.'

'James, you need to grow up and take some responsibility for your life. I can't tell you what to do, that's for you to decide. If you resolve to end this relationship, try to be considerate towards her. You need to use your head. Make your decision and carry it through without being distracted by your emotions.'

'But that would be so difficult.'

'Some things in life can be difficult. You need to find the courage to deal with this. Now, if you've finished those biscuits, we'd better get on to Blake.'

. . .

In spite of Evelyn's advice, James had no clear plan. On his way to see April the following Saturday he stared out of the train window at the passing fields. He had a provisional idea. When he arrived she would ask him what he would like to do. It was a fine day so he would suggest a walk in the woods. Once there, he would find out whether she had feelings for him. If she had, then he would say that he cared for her too. It would be difficult, but he would risk it. On the other hand, if she saw their relationship as just a friendship, he would tell her that it had no future and they should finish it. He had doubts about whether any of this would work but it was all he had.

Walking up the familiar road towards her house, he felt butterflies in his stomach and his confidence draining away. As he came through the gate, April swept open the front door and stood there radiant and smiling. His legs felt wobbly and he was consumed by a rising panic as he followed her into the front room.

'What shall we do this afternoon?'

He couldn't look at her. Staring at the clock on the mantelpiece he heard a voice shouting:

'We're not going to see each other anymore. It's over. I don't want to go on with this!'

He realised in horror that it was his voice. April went white and stepped backwards. One hand clutched the armchair and the other flew to her breast. Her mouth opened but no sound came out. James turned away and found himself looking at the small brown flowers on the wallpaper and the ornaments on the sideboard. After a long silence, he heard what sounded like a little girl's voice.

'James?'

He turned slowly and stared down at the swirling pattern of the rug.

'I thought you loved me.'

'Well I don't and I never have.'

He had to get away. He blundered his way into the hall, ran out through the front door and strode up the road. He was afraid that she might come after him so he kept going, threading his way through the Saturday crowds in the High Street until he reached the end of the shops. Finally he stopped and, turning round, was relieved to see that she wasn't there. Although part of him wished she had been.

His thoughts and emotions rose in a confused torrent.

I've done it. It was the right thing to do. I'll soon get over it. What have I done? Why did I say those things? I could go back and apologise. Perhaps we could talk it over.

Then he remembered her stricken face and knew that he couldn't go back. He walked slowly along the road until he came to the turning for the railway station. He couldn't face sitting on the station platform, so he plodded on. After nearly an hour, he found himself passing the open air swimming pool at Hoddesdon. April loved swimming and they'd planned to spend a day there when the weather was fine and the exams were over. Now that wasn't going to happen.

Trudging along the main street, he felt tired and thirsty and climbed up to the noisy upstairs room of a cafe. He slumped down at a table next to the window with a drink and stared at the passers-by. Some were strolling along smiling and laughing. What had they got to laugh about? He remembered April laughing as they raced each other down to the river a couple of weeks ago. They had been so happy. They should be together this evening. He could feel her body against his, the smell of her hair and the softness of her lips. He stared out at the busy street and noticed a passing bus. That was it. He could catch a bus and be back at her house in half an hour. He would apologise and tell her that she was everything to him. But he knew he couldn't do it.

Eventually he left the cafe and continued his homeward journey. Blind to the balmy evening, he walked on until his legs ached and he needed to rest. He sat on a bank and listened to a blackbird. Then he remembered that he'd left his book of Shelley's poems in April's house in his rush to escape. He thought about the poet's short life and tragic death at sea. What were those lines he wrote on the beach?

I could lie down like a tired child and weep away this life of care …

Yes, Shelley knew all about despair. He finally reached home where his mother immediately put the kettle on. After struggling to eat a sandwich, he went to his bedroom and stayed there.

...

April sat trembling in the armchair with her head down and hands over her face, unable to take in what had happened. After a while, she jumped up and flung a cushion across the room. It thudded against the wall, narrowly missing the picture of a shepherd and his sheep. Rubbing tears from her eyes, she ran upstairs to her bedroom, slammed the door, threw herself face down on her bed and cried.

Shirley Saunders was in the kitchen and heard the bedroom door bang and her daughter's howls. She dried her hands on her apron, hurried up the stairs, knocked gently on the bedroom door and opened it. April turned her face away.

'Whatever is wrong, dear?'

'Nothing.'

'Is there anything I can do?'

'No. Leave me alone.'

Shirley withdrew and returned to the kitchen. When April's father came in from the garden and washed his hands at the sink, he stopped and listened as the plump figure of Shirley skirted round him with a boiling kettle.

'Is that April crying upstairs?'

'Yes. James was only here for five minutes. I don't know what was said, but she ran up to her room afterwards and has been crying on and off ever since.'

'How long ago was this?'

'About half an hour. I went up but she wants to be left alone. It's best to let her have a good cry. She'll come down when she's ready.'

Drying his hands, he glared.

'That sod. God only knows what he said. I'll have him for this.'

'Sit down Ron and have your tea. I'll take her one up.'

An hour later Shirley returned to April's bedroom. The tea lay cold and untouched on the bedside table. April had taken off her dress and lay snuggled down in bed.

'We're just going to have tea, dear. Are you coming down?'

'No thanks, Mum. I'm not hungry.'

'Perhaps we'd better stay in this evening as you're upset. We could talk about it if you're ready. It might help.'

'No. You go out and enjoy yourselves. I'll have an early night.'

'Alright, dear. If you're sure. I'll look in before we go.'

At half past six Shirley returned with some bread and jam, a slice of cake and a fresh cup of tea on a tray. April had washed, put her nightie on and was in bed fast asleep.

She woke in the early hours of Sunday morning. She didn't want to remember what had happened, but the pain wouldn't go away. It must have been her fault. What had she done to make him behave like that? She tried to remember what had been said during the last few weeks. She must have put him off but couldn't think of a thing. Could there be someone else? That didn't feel right, she was sure that she would have sensed that. Maybe he was just bored. He had seemed distant last week. Whatever it was, he couldn't face her and talk about it. He'd got himself worked up before he arrived, but why? She remembered that he said that he'd never loved her. That couldn't be true after what they had shared. He was her whole world. She loved him and didn't want to go on without him. She sobbed quietly before falling asleep again.

...

Later that morning Mandy wondered what had become of April, who always came over to her house after breakfast on Sundays. It was nearly eleven so she decided to seek her out.

Fifteen minutes later she breezed in through the back door of the Saunders' kitchen.

'Where's April this morning?'

'Hello dear. I'm glad you're here. She's still in bed. I can't get her up. Perhaps you can persuade her. You'd better be prepared though. She had a bust up with James yesterday. I said to Dad …'

But Mandy had gone, racing up the stairs two at a time before bursting into April's room. She found her sitting on the edge of the bed. Her face was red and swollen from crying. Mandy sat and put her arm around her.

'Tell me what happened. What did he say to you?'

'He said … he said we're finished. Then he said that he'd never loved me. I love him Mandy and I was sure he was starting to love me. I can't believe what's happened.'

'The bastard. I warned him. I'll kill him for this. He won't get away with it.'

April stood up and turned to face Mandy, her puffy face set with determination.

'No. You mustn't do anything. I have to deal with this, although at the moment I don't know how.'

'Alright. You're feeling hurt now but I promise you it will pass. Get dressed and come downstairs. We're going for a walk. The fresh air will do you good.'

'I can't go out. Everyone will see I've been crying.'

'No they won't. Off you go now.'

April shuffled into the bathroom. Mandy returned to the kitchen, took a loaf out of the breadbin, cut a thick slice and put it under the grill.

'She'll be down in a minute. We're going for a walk, but she's got to have something to eat first.'

'Well done dear. I'll make some fresh tea. I'm so glad you came. April's lucky to have such a good friend. What did she say exactly? What happened?'

'She and James have broken up. It's good riddance as far as I'm concerned. Don't worry. She'll be fine.'

FOUR

April rose early, crept downstairs and quietly closed the kitchen door. She wasn't hungry but put the kettle on. Her mother's handbag was in its usual place by the door. She extracted a ten shilling note from the purse and scribbled a note. She drank her coffee and saw it was already after eight-twenty and time to go. She was wearing her new daisy dress and a little light makeup. She paused to look at herself in the hall mirror, pushed a stray hair aside, picked up her shoulder bag and eased the front door open.

'Where are you off to so early?'

Her mother was coming down the stairs in her dressing gown. In spite of April's precautions, Shirley had heard the faint sounds from below. Her daughter never rose before nine on Sundays so she was suspicious.

'I'm going to see James. I must run or I'll miss the coach.'

'You never said you were going dear'

'Sorry Mum, I only decided yesterday. I'll be back a bit late for dinner. Bye.'

It was already eight-thirty two when she turned into the High Street. Thank goodness there was still a queue at the coach stop.

The High Street was quiet at this time on Sunday morning with only a few people walking dogs or visiting the newsagent. April joined the queue and shortly afterwards an elderly couple arrived, greeting her in a friendly manner. An old man in front of her was agitated about the coach being late and was complaining to anyone who would listen:

'Drivers today can't be bothered to get up in the morning. No pride in the job, that's the trouble these days. It was different before the war. You were lucky to have a job then. You'd have been out on your ear if you came in late.'

Soon afterwards the coach drew up and everyone began to climb inside. They were all old people, thought April. Maybe it was their outing. The argumentative man got on and started to harangue the driver, who'd had enough trouble getting the coach started that morning. He ordered the old man to sit down or he would put him off. This threat made matters worse and as the two continued to argue, April felt a nudge from behind.

'Go on, dear, push past and we'll follow,' said the old lady behind April.

'What about a ticket?'

'Never mind about that. On you get. Go right down the back.'

April did as she was told and found herself in the rear corner seat with the two pensioners beside her. The argument at the front had been settled and the coach set off. As it cleared the suburbs and rumbled along the arterial road, she looked out of the window as the town receded from view. It had been a week since James had walked out. She had been so sure of their growing love but, when they had come face to face in school on Friday, he'd looked away. Perhaps he'd never loved her after all but today she would find out. It was no use talking to mum who didn't understand how she felt and would have said not to go. Mandy had already said she shouldn't go but she had never liked James. She didn't have a clear plan. When she got off at Bishops Stortford, she would find her way out to his house in Cooks Green. It was a gamble but she needed to talk to him. She should be back in good time to see Carol. Opening her bag, she took out the small book of Shelley's poems that James had left behind.

'Wine gum, dear?'

It was the old lady. April accepted the offering.

'I'm Betty and this is George. What's your name?'

'April.'

'That's a lovely name isn't it George? I bet your birthday's in April. Am I right?'

April nodded with a smile.

'What's your book dear?' asked Betty, her curiosity getting the better of her.

'It's a book of Shelley's poetry.'

'Oh.' Betty looked confused for a moment. 'What brought you on this trip then?'

'I'm just going to visit someone'. She turned to look out of the window again.

'Lincoln's a lovely place for an outing, although it's very hilly I'm told.'

'I'm not going to Lincoln,' said April, beginning to feel uneasy.' I'm getting off at Bishops Stortford.'

George and Betty looked at each other.

'I think you're on the wrong coach dear.'

'Isn't this the Greenline?'

'No dear, that left just before you arrived.'

The horror of what had happened dawned on her. She had never been on the Greenline coach. She was on an old people's outing to Lincoln. It was so unfair.

'What am I going to do?' she cried. 'I can't go all the way to Lincoln.'

She stared out of the window. The passing countryside which had seemed so beautiful in the May sunshine now looked strange and menacing. As she dabbed at her eyes, Betty reached across and squeezed her hand.

'Don't worry dear. You come to Lincoln with us. You can phone from there and we'll all be back this evening.'

April's anxiety increased as the coach sped northwards. She had no intention of spending the day with the old people in Lincoln and thought if she should speak to the driver; but she stayed in her seat and wondered what to do. Perhaps she could catch a train back from Lincoln but she might not have enough money. She decided to get off at the first stop and get a lift back.

•••

The Wansford Service Station and Cafe between Stamford and Peterborough on the A1 was situated on both sides of the road. It had been built alongside a major crossroads and roundabout. The coach wheezed to a stop and, after a warning from the driver about being back on board in no more than thirty minutes, the old people poured off in the direction of tea and the toilets.

Betty turned to April with a smile.

'You come and have a nice cup of tea with us.'

'No thanks. I must try and get a lift back.'

'You be careful, dear. If there isn't a bus or coach, try and find a nice family. Keep away from lorry drivers.'

April thanked her, ran lightly across the road and entered the cafe. There was an aroma of fried food and a low hubbub of voices, punctuated by the excited chatter of children. She looked around. All these people were going south. It should be easy to get a lift. Two women in white aprons were dispensing food and drinks from behind a long counter and a steaming tea urn. There was another woman at one end on the till, taking the money. April approached her.

'Excuse me. Are there any buses or coaches that stop here that I can catch to go south?'

The woman eyed her suspiciously.

'No, of course not. The only coaches that stop here are for petrol or a short break. We're not a bus stop.'

April supposed that must be true. They were in the middle of nowhere surrounded by fields. She looked at the tables that were occupied and decided to ask around.

She selected a young couple in their mid-twenties. He looked friendly with a wide open face. He'd already given her an approving look when she'd come in. His companion was a thin, pinch-faced woman in a green blouse. April approached them and asked if they could give her a lift. The young man smiled and turned to his companion who gave April a stony look.

'Sorry,' said pinch-face. 'We're not going your way.'

April retreated and tried a table with a young family.

'Sorry miss, but we're chock-a-block as it is.'

Next she tried a middle-aged couple.

'I'd like to help you,' said the man, 'but we're not going south. We're turning off here and going to Leicester.'

This wasn't going well. Looking round, she became aware that pinch-face and her friend were having a noisy argument. Suddenly the woman jumped up and screamed at April.

'Why don't you stop pestering respectable people? Lorry drivers are more your sort.'

With that, she flounced out followed by her embarrassed companion.

April froze, speechless with indignation. Unfortunately the outburst had its effect. People looked away and no one would meet her eye.

She felt hungry and went to sit by herself at the end of the room with a cheese sandwich and a lemonade. Across the road she saw her coach setting off again. Alone in this strange place, April found her hands shaking and her confidence ebbing away. The underlying fears she had tried so hard to suppress were coming to the surface. Desperate for some distraction, she fumbled in her bag for Shelley's poems. No, there wouldn't be anything useful there. She struggled to slow her rapid breathing. After a while she felt calmer and realised she no longer wanted to visit James. She needed to go straight home to speak with Carol. If only they had a phone at home.

'Scuse me miss. I saw what happened. Can I help?'

April glanced up at a heavy looking man in a white t-shirt, with a ruddy face and short cropped hair.

'It's alright, I don't need a lift.'

'Course you don't.' He sat opposite her and slurped his mug of tea.

'You remind me of my daughter. She's fair like you. Don't know what I would've done without her after my wife died.' He passed a hand over his eyes.

There was a period of silence as April watched the passing traffic before looking up at him for the first time.

'What happened to your wife?'

'She got run over crossing the road a couple of months ago. She dropped some shopping and stopped to pick it up. A bloody car went straight into her. She didn't stand a chance. God knows what I would've done without Lorna.'

'How old is she?'

'She's fifteen and clever like her mum.' He sighed. 'It's hard for a man to bring up a daughter when he has to work all hours. That's why I'm here on a Sunday, going south to collect carpets. They've got to be in Sheffield first thing tomorrow. There's no peace for the wicked.' He gave a toothy grin. 'My name's Fred by the way. What's yours?'

'April.'

'That's a nice name. Where you trying to get to then?'

'Milsham,' said April, taking another bite from her sandwich. All she wanted was to go home. She noticed that Fred was grinning and shaking his head.

'I'm driving down to North London, so I could go through Milsham and drop you off there. He looked at his watch. It's nearly eleven. If we leave now I could have you there by one. I could do with a bit of company on the road.'

April knew he was the sort of driver she should avoid but he seemed so unhappy after losing his wife. It was the only offer she'd had and he would take her home.

'Thanks very much, but I'm alright.'

He stood up looking concerned. 'Please yourself April. If it was my Lorna stuck here I'd be worried stiff. You sure I can't help you?'

She stared down at her plate for several minutes. Finally she nodded, followed him to the door and glancing back as she left, met the eye of the woman at the till. She climbed up into a dirty white van and was assailed by an acrid smell of stale cigarette smoke. Fred climbed in and the engine roared into life.

After Betty's warning, April worried that she had made a mistake. But at least she was on her way home. As they passed the sign for Peterborough, she tried to gather her thoughts until, with a crunching of gears, the van began to slow down and came to a stop in a lay-by. Fred was grinning.

'Sorry April. I've got to have a slash. I'm going into these trees for a minute. You'll have to get out.'

'It's alright. I'll just sit here and wait till you come back.'

'Sorry but you can't. I got to lock the van when I stop and not leave no one inside. Security see. Hop out and stretch your legs. I'll just be a couple of minutes.'

He locked the doors and disappeared into the trees. April looked up and down the road. It was straight and flat. They were the only vehicle in the lay-by. A heavy lorry thundered past heading north, leaving a trail of petrol fumes in its wake. A red sports car whizzed past in the opposite direction before it became quiet again. Then she heard a shout.

'April, are you there? Help me please?'

She tensed. Her instincts told her to stand her ground but the voice called again. She walked to the edge of the trees and stopped.

'What is it?'

'I've dropped my wedding ring. It slipped off my finger down here and I can't see it. I mustn't lose it. Please come and look, you've got sharper eyes than me.'

April followed the sound of his voice, edging cautiously down a slope through a mass of trees and came across him staring at the ground.

'There you are. It's here somewhere. I saw it go.'

She spotted it immediately, stepped forward, bent down and picked it up, handing it over as she straightened up.

She was felled by a hammer blow to the forehead, seeing the blur of the fist too late. She collapsed and passed out. She came round being dragged roughly by her armpits down a slope. Her dress was caught and torn by the bushes and her legs bruised and scratched. Finally she found herself lying at the bottom of a damp stony ditch. She screamed.

'Be quiet and relax.'

April looked around wildly. He was going to rape her. She tried to get up but he pushed her down hard, banging her head on the stones. She felt a stinging pain and her eyes watered. He was fumbling with his trousers. Scrabbling to defend herself, her hand closed over a stick and she raised it as his body came down heavily on top of her. Braced by the floor of the ditch, the stick with a sharp broken end went straight through his chest and into his lung. He gave a strangled cry and rolled sideways, wrenching at it, but it was wedged tightly between his ribs. Finally, exhausted, he lay back and was still.

April passed out again. Drifting back into consciousness she saw he was still lying beside her with his eyes closed. His breathing was uneven with an ominous rasping sound.

She must get away. Her head was throbbing with pain as she edged along the ditch. She didn't get far before passing out again. She dreamt she was inching along the ditch but couldn't get away. *I must get away … get away.*

FIVE

Shirley stood looking out of the bedroom window.
'It's not like April to try and sneak off without telling me.'

'It's not like her to get up early on a Sunday morning either' said Ron sitting up in bed sipping his mug of tea. 'You say she's gone to see this James?'

'That's what she said. Since they broke up last week I haven't been able to get her to talk to me about it.'

'I reckon she's off to sort things out. She can be determined at times.'

'I know, but she never said she was going. She's always talked to me before.'

'Don't worry, love. April's growing up and she'll find her own way. Come back to bed and give us a cuddle.'

'No thanks. I'm going to the bathroom.'

In most respects it was a normal Sunday in the Saunders'

household. Ron spent most of the morning working in the back garden and Shirley busied herself preparing and cooking the dinner. Carol arrived around twelve and stayed until mid-afternoon. She tried to allay her mother's anxiety.

'There's nothing to worry about Mum. April's only gone to see her boyfriend.'

'I hope you're right.' Shirley had saved a dinner for April on a plate that she covered up. 'This will do for her. She'll be hungry when she gets back.'

After dinner, they all sat in the front room, read the paper and listened to the wireless. Eventually Ron fell asleep in the armchair. After Carol had left, Shirley sat knitting with anxious concentration. Sometime later she rose and stood at the window looking up the road.

'Where is she? She should be back by now.'

'What time is it?' asked Ron, emerging from his nap.

'Nearly half past five and she's still not back. I'm getting really worried.'

He rose and put his arms around her.

'Come on love, she won't be long. Let's have tea. I could do with some of that cake you made yesterday.'

'Cake! Is that all you can think about? Suppose something's happened to April?'

Coming down the stairs later on, he found Shirley standing in the hall with her coat and shoes on.

'Where do you think you're going?'

'Up to the High Street to see what time the next Greenline coach gets in. If she's not on it, I'm going to phone the police.'

He was about to remonstrate with her, then realised that it was useless.

'Hang on, I'll come with you.'

'Thanks Ron, I've got this bad feeling. I can't explain it but I've had it all day.'

They waited for the next coach but April wasn't on it. Ron scanned the instructions in the telephone box and dialled 999. April was alright. She'd got held up. It was a fair journey to Stortford. His thoughts were interrupted by an answering voice and he explained the situation. He was assured that it was natural for parents to worry but the usual reason was a delay of some kind. The police would check at the Flemings' house in Cooks Green and someone would be in touch as soon as they had any news.

A policeman called that evening but April hadn't come home. Shirley sat hunched at the kitchen table and wept. Ron was at a loss but tried not to show it. Nothing he said made any difference. Finally he persuaded her to go to bed. Neither of them could sleep but lay dozing and waking in the darkness with the worst kind of fears. From time to time Shirley cried.

At eight o'clock next morning a black police car drew up outside their house. Detective Inspector Alan Lane and Detective Constable Jenny Jones read through their brief notes in the car. Lane was an experienced officer, not long off retirement and who believed in rigorous police work. Jenny Jones was twenty-seven and recently promoted to CID. She'd had to put up with plenty of comments about women trying to do men's work but her ability and cheerful disposition had begun to earn her the respect of her colleagues.

In spite of the serious situation, Lane smiled to himself as he read the police report from Bishops Stortford. They were often sprinkled with pithy descriptions. This one was typical:

The Flemings' house at 4 Manor Cottages in Cooks Green is a small end of terrace cottage with an untidy garden. The husband and wife both do factory work on the industrial estate and they obviously resented our visit. The husband is a sour bully and the wife a timid doormat. They knew nothing about any intended visit from April Saunders. Their son James seemed willing to help and was surprised to learn that she had intended to visit him. He was concerned that she was missing. I believe he was telling the truth. She hadn't visited the house before —

Shirley had been watching the car and, as soon as the police officers came through the gate, she flung open the front door and cried out:

'Have you any news? Have you found her?'

'May we come in madam?' asked Lane.

They sat in the front room and Lane explained about the police visit to Cooks Green and confirmed that they hadn't found April. As he was speaking, Jenny looked round. There was a large clock on the mantelpiece and a polished sideboard with a number of ornaments and family photos in frames, one in a nurse's uniform.

'This must be a very distressing situation and I assure you we will do everything we can to find April,' said Lane. 'First, I need to ask you some questions.'

Patiently he went through a list:

'At what time did April leave yesterday morning? What was she wearing? Did she say where she was going? How did she seem? Was she upset in any way? Did she say when she would be back?'

As the answers came, Jenny wrote them into her notebook. Lane glanced at her from time to time to check she was keeping up.

'Is there anything that would make April want to go away? What are her favourite places that she enjoys visiting or might go to, be alone? I should also like full details of all family members and close friends.' Finally he asked:

'Do you have a recent photograph?'

'I took this a couple of weeks ago,' said Ron. 'It's a good likeness.'

Shirley remembered. He'd used up half a roll of film taking pictures of April in the garden. Carol had been cross.

Lane promised to return the photograph later. Before they left, he asked whether they could see April's room. Shirley led them upstairs and they looked round a neat back bedroom.

'Have you tidied this room since she left?' he asked.

Shirley shook her head.

Jenny looked at a large poster of Elvis on the wall and scanned a notice board covered with revision notes. There were neat piles of papers and books on the study desk. It looked like a room that was being put into good order before saying goodbye.

'Does April keep a diary?' she asked.

'Not that I've ever seen and I clean and tidy this room regularly,' said Shirley.

Before leaving, Lane left his card and asked them to let him know if they remembered something else or received any news.

'If we learn anything, we'll let you know straightaway,' he assured them.

...

Jenny had left school herself barely ten years ago. Walking along the echoing corridor of Milsham Grammar School, she absorbed the familiar smell of the polished floor and the background sounds from the classrooms. Somewhere upstairs a door slammed and for a split second she was back in her class again. The impression passed as quickly as it came and they were soon installed in an interview room.

They began with James Fleming who looked frightened and kept darting glances around the room. He confirmed that he had been seeing April for the last three months until they had broken up a week ago last Saturday.

'Why was that?' asked Lane.

'I decided that we should split up. I've got to concentrate on my A-levels and there wasn't any point in trying to carry on after we'd left school.'

'Was she upset when you told her it was all over?' Jenny asked.

James looked down at his hands on the table before continuing in a barely audible voice.

'Yes she was. She hadn't expected it and didn't say anything so I just walked out,'

'Try to remember precisely what was said. Take us through it and leave nothing out,' said Lane.

James did so, after which he was required to describe his journey home.

'Did you know that she was coming to see you yesterday morning?'

He didn't. She had never been to his home. He gave faltering details of his movements the previous day. He'd gone to his weekend job as usual in the morning and spent the afternoon revising History in his bedroom. After the interview was over, he rose slowly, tense and white-faced.

'This is my fault. You will find her won't you?'

As he stumbled back to his classroom, James remembered coming face to face with April in school on Friday and had been shocked by the change in her appearance. She seemed smaller and had looked so sad. He couldn't face her and had to turn away.

The next interview was with Mandy Daniels. She was pale but remained composed, confirming that she and April were close friends and surprised the officers with the news that April had told her on Saturday that she intended to visit James the following day.

'How was she planning to do that?' Lane asked.

'She said she would take the first Greenline coach to Bishops Stortford on Sunday morning and make her way out to his village.'

'What was your response?'

'I told her she shouldn't bother. If he had cared for her he wouldn't have spoken in the way that he did. He's hurt her badly. I knew it would end this way.'

'Why do you say that?' enquired Jenny.

'April has a wilful nature. When she wants something there's no stopping her.' She paused, twisting her hands in her lap, trying to gather her thoughts. 'She's got a naive innocence and can be quite gullible. I try to look out for her but I can't always.'

'What about James Fleming?'

'He lives in a dream world, wrapped up in some idea of romance, but he looks down on April. She's so open and vulnerable and was bound to get hurt.'

She wiped away tears with her handkerchief before continuing:

'April's a strong person and bright like her sister. Although she's had this crush on James Fleming, she's already recovering and she'll learn from it. There's another thing: she seems very worried about something but won't talk about it.'

'What do you think it could be?'

'I don't know, it's a feeling I have. She seems afraid. Throwing herself at James Fleming was out of character and might be a way of not facing up to what's upsetting her.'

'This may be important. Are you quite sure?' Jenny asked.

'No I'm not. It could be my imagination. When I mentioned it, she insisted there was nothing.'

'Thank you, Mandy. That's all for now.'

She felt tense and was finding it difficult to breathe as she trudged back to her classroom.

Inspector Lane was thoughtful during the drive back to the police station.

'April Saunders seems popular with both her friends.'

'It's a bit more than that, sir,' said Jenny. 'Mandy is obviously very attached to April but I'm not sure whether either of them realises it. James seems to be in love with himself and Mandy can see that. April on the other hand is very much in love, which for a girl of that age can feel like her whole world. In these circumstances, the experience of being rejected can be shattering. The boyfriend might have no idea about her feelings for him and can trample over them in his ignorance.'

Lane nodded. He was familiar with the travails of teenage girls. Thank goodness his two were well past that stage and already married.

'There's something I want you to do when we get back,' he said. 'Check James Fleming's alibi for yesterday morning. He seemed pretty evasive about that.'

Milsham Police Station had been built in the 1930s. Alterations over the last twenty years to cope with an increasing number of occupants had resulted in a warren of narrow corridors. The main CID office doubled as a meeting room with a large notice board and blackboard at one end. At half past ten, Inspector Lane gathered his team together. He was flanked by his sergeant and Jenny Jones. Although still something of a rookie, Jenny was given a key role as the only woman CID officer. The sergeant would organise the search operation.

The news of April's disappearance had reached everyone in the station and Lane had to clap his hands to quell the hubbub.

'Okay. Settle down and listen carefully. We've got a serious situation. A teenage girl from Milsham went missing from the High Street twenty four hours ago. Our job is to find her as quickly as possible. If we don't, then by tomorrow we're going to come under considerable pressure from the whole town, particularly from worried parents. Not to mention what the local newspapers will make of it.'

'Here's what we know. April Saunders, sixteen years old, left home yesterday morning just before eight-thirty to catch the Greenline coach to Bishops Stortford. Once there she intended to make her way out to the hamlet of Cooks Green where her boyfriend James Fleming lives. He didn't know she was coming. We're clear about her intentions because she told her friend the day before and confirmed the same to her mother as she left. She never arrived. The first thing is to check whether she caught that coach. Got that covered, Sergeant?'

'Yes, sir.'

'The Stortford police have been alerted and they're searching at their end. We should be able to establish quickly whether she caught the coach. She was cutting it fine so she could have missed it. If she did, what would she do next?'

'She would catch the train,' said several voices.

'If she did that, any number of people would have seen her walking down Station Road, not to mention the booking clerk or other railway passengers.'

'I've got that covered too, sir.'

'Someone might have offered her a lift,' suggested a young officer.

'That's a possibility. So when you're covering the area, ask around to see if anyone saw that or there were any odd people or unusual vehicles about. We've got to be fast and thorough. People are relying on us and we mustn't let them down. Photos of April are being copied and should be available by now.'

'Suppose she was lying and wasn't intending to go to Stortford at all? Kids can be devious,' suggested an older man.

'Okay, I'll keep that in mind, but let's get on now,' said Lane. 'If you find out anything, contact me, Jenny or Sergeant straight away. We'll meet back here this afternoon at four-thirty.'

Inspector Lane sank down in his cramped office and accepted a welcome cup of coffee. He'd earned it this morning. He needed to think things through. Had he missed anything?

The memory of the Davis case haunted him. He'd been a sergeant in the Edmonton force nearly twenty years ago when eight year old Melanie Davis went missing. In the report after her body had been found, the inspector had been blunt:

'You failed to follow up on a vital piece of evidence in this case. You're a good officer, Lane, so I am only issuing a formal reprimand but you will need to be much more thorough in future. Leave no stone unturned.'

It was on his conscience and his police record. He was determined that nothing like that would happen this time. When people go missing, they usually turn up soon afterwards. He knew from experience that there were three possibilities:

One, she could have gone missing deliberately. Two, she's had an accident somewhere. Three, there's another person involved. He was aware that the chances of her being abducted were statistically less than five percent. Nevertheless he had a bad feeling about this case. When a child or teenage girl goes missing, it is immediately classified by the police as high priority. He must get this one right. It was time to report in. He picked up the telephone. The superintendant listened to his report in silence before responding:

'The news that she's missing will be around the town already. The local press will be onto it before the day's out. Refer them to me.'

'Yes sir. Are you going to give them the story?'

'Not today. If we haven't found her by tomorrow morning, I want you to get her parent's permission to put this in the papers. You know what to do. Handle it personally and, while you're at it, get hold of her diary. There could be something in it.'

'She doesn't keep a diary, sir, according to her mother.'

'Of course she does. Girls of that age all do and they keep it hidden. Find it and see if it gives us anything.'

'Yes sir.'

'I want a full report on my desk at nine tomorrow morning. I'll speak to you again after that.'

SIX

Mandy returned to her classroom ignoring the inquisitive stares. Her head was spinning as she struggled to hold herself together. She couldn't take in any of the lesson and her French grammar lay unread on her desk. At break time she stuffed some books in her case and went to the staff room where news of April's disappearance had led to a sombre atmosphere. Her form teacher, coming to the door, saw an ashen-faced girl verging on tears. She appreciated the situation at once. April and Mandy were inseparable friends and she was in a state of shock.

'What is it, Mandy?'

'I can't stay here. Can I go home? I've got some revision books.'

'Yes of course. Will you be alright? Do you want someone to walk back with you?'

'No thanks, I'll be okay.'

'Will there be anyone there?'

'Yes. Mum's there as my brother Andrew's at home today.'

'That's good. Come back when you feel better and don't worry. I'm sure everything will be alright.'

It had clouded over and begun to rain. Quickening her pace, Mandy arrived home damp and bedraggled, dumped her bulging case in the hall and ran through to the kitchen. Her mother was coming in from the garden with a basket of washing. Seeing Mandy, she put it down.

'What is it love? Are you alright?'

Mandy's response came in a rush:

'April's gone missing…she went to catch the Greenline coach yesterday morning and nobody's seen her since… the police have been up at the school…my teacher said I could come home…I'm so frightened, Mum … I can't stop thinking that something terrible has happened.'

Her mother held her close until the crying stopped.

'Go and get those damp things off, wash your face and come back down. I'll put these sheets on the clothes horse then I'll make us all some hot chocolate. Bring Andrew with you. He's upstairs playing with his cars.'

Mandy did as she was told. Her mother had already tidied her bedroom. Her doll Amy lay on the pillow as usual. Mandy had confided in her for years but not this time. After a wash, she changed into a navy jumper and jeans. Andrew seemed unsurprised by her mid-morning appearance.

They sat together at the kitchen table drinking chocolate and nibbling biscuits.

'Why have you come home?' asked Andrew.

Andrew was thirteen years old. Two years ago he had been knocked down by a lorry and spent several months in hospital. Now he was back home but was brain damaged and struggling to learn everything anew. His therapy class had helped but he still had the mental age of a four year old. Mandy had kept in constant touch with his old gang at school.

'I wasn't feeling well but I'm okay now,' said Mandy with a smile. 'Can I join in your game upstairs?'

'Alright, you can be the robber. I've got the police car.'

'Auntie Sylvia's coming at lunchtime,' said Mandy's mother. 'She's going to see Nan who hasn't been too good lately.'

Sylvia was her mother's sister who lived near Enfield. At lunchtime, the four of them sat around the kitchen table, eating bread and cheese with pickles and fresh lettuce from the garden. Sylvia had received a letter from their brother who was doing well in Australia. He was keen for his two sisters and their families to join him.

'I couldn't leave Mum and there's Andrew to think about,' said Mandy's mother.

'I'm not going to Australia,' said Mandy. 'It's too dangerous with all those poisonous snakes and spiders.' She shuddered.

When Mandy explained about April's disappearance, Sylvia was quick to reassure her.

'I shouldn't worry. Nine times out of ten, the missing person turns up in a day or two.'

'April got on the wrong coach,' said Andrew.

There was a short silence.

'Why do you say that?' asked Mandy.

There was nothing more to come. Andrew continued to eat.

After lunch Mandy sorted out her books, piling them onto the bed. She looked in on Andrew but he seemed to have forgotten about their game. She sat slumped at her desk with her head in her hands. A couple of hours later she went downstairs where her mother was busy ironing.

'I'm going over to April's to see if there's any news.'

'Alright love, see you later.'

...

The front doorbell rang. The sound seemed to fill the house. Shirley flew to answer it and found Mandy on the doorstep.

'What are you doing here? You always come in through the back.'

'I know, I didn't like to somehow. Is there any news?'

'No, dear. Come in. We're in the kitchen.'

Mandy sat cradling a steaming mug of tea. She stared at the check oilcloth cover and milk bottle on the table. Ron sat frowning at a crossword and Shirley stood at the kitchen worktop, busy with bowls and packets.

'I'm making a cake. I bought the things I needed at the *International* this afternoon. Everyone was very nice. Mrs Watts came out to talk to me, offering to help if she could.'

Mandy nodded. Mrs Watts, the next door neighbour, was a cow. She was the road's worst gossip and never had a good word to say about April or her parents. She was obviously trying to extract fresh titbits of news.

'This is April's favourite. It'll be ready for her when she gets back. It'll keep nicely in a tin. She's bound to be hungry when she comes home. She could eat a horse that girl sometimes …'

Her voice trailed away. She stood facing the wall and shuddered, knocking a bag of flour on the floor. Ron rose and put his arms round her.

'Come and sit down, love. You're all in. The tea's still warm in the pot.'

As Shirley sipped her tea, Mandy had a sudden impression of a lost and frightened child.

'I can't stay here all day,' protested Shirley. 'I've got to do something. I feel so helpless. The police told us to leave it to them. They've been up and down the road knocking on doors. Isn't there anything we can do Mandy? I'm scared that something terrible has happened. April's never done anything like this before.'

She stood up, wiped away tears with a damp handkerchief and disappeared upstairs.

She stared into the bathroom mirror at a face that looked tearstained and drawn. She had a wash and brushed her hair before going into the bedroom where she sat huddled on the edge of the bed, rocking to and fro.

'Please, dear God, bring April back safely,' she whispered.

After a while she went back downstairs. Mandy had left.

• • •

Jenny Jones found April's diary under some folders on the top of her wardrobe. With the permission of her parents, she returned with it to the police station. The last entry had been two weeks before her disappearance.

'It says that she knows something is growing inside her and she's got to tell her sister this Sunday,' said Jenny. 'She never did because she left before her sister arrived and never came back.'

'How do you understand that entry?' asked Lane.

'You could take it two ways, sir. Either she's in love or she's pregnant.'

'Good God! Do you think she could be pregnant?'

'I sounded out her parents as tactfully as I could about that possibility. Neither of them thought it was remotely likely. Her father became extremely agitated at the suggestion.'

'That's because she's his little girl and he doesn't want to think about something like that. Believe me, the parents are often the last to know. These kids have had plenty of time to get down to it with her mum and dad being out nearly every Saturday night. I bet that's it. He couldn't resist it, the lustful swine. You do realise what this means? She only had her sixteenth birthday a month ago.'

'I see that sir. If she is pregnant by him, he may be guilty of having had sexual relations with a minor. However, my own feeling is that she's just very much in love.'

'Alright, let's find out. We'll get him down here. I'll give him a going over.'

A police car with two uniformed officers arrived at the school shortly afterwards but James had left. This was not unusual, explained the headmaster, as James had no lessons scheduled for that afternoon so had probably returned home to continue his revision studies. Bishops Stortford police called at his house half an hour later but found no one at home.

The Milsham police team returned to their meeting room at half past four where the sergeant addressed them:

'April Saunders turned left out of her road into the High Street yesterday morning just after eight-thirty. A pensioner at the top of the road was in his front garden at the time and saw her clearly. He knows her by sight it seems.'

'I bet he does, randy old devil.'

'That's enough. We've established that she never caught the eight-thirty Greenline coach. She was cutting it fine and must have missed it. As for the train, no one remembers seeing her walk down to the station. None of the people on the platform saw her nor did the booking clerk. Our colleagues at Bishops Stortford have checked the area around the coach stop and the railway station. They also checked around the town and along the road leading out to Cooks Green with no sightings at all. Finally, we have no news of any suspicious characters or vehicles here at that time of the morning.'

'Good work everyone,' said Lane. 'But we haven't found her, nor do we have the beginning of a trail to follow. I'm open to ideas, but here's one to be going on with: we now have her diary. The last entry is two weeks ago on May 3rd when she writes that she has something important to tell her elder sister on her next visit which was yesterday. However, she left before her sister arrived. The meeting with her boyfriend a week ago only lasted for five minutes before he walked out. Perhaps she told him something and he reacted by saying that they were finished. Now consider this: she might be pregnant.'

A clamour arose across the room. Lane waved them down.

'If she *is* pregnant, that's bad news for the boyfriend who's hoping to go to college in September, particularly as she only turned sixteen last month. I'm going to interview him this evening with a colleague from Stortford. Maybe they met somewhere yesterday. Any further suggestions anyone?'

'Maybe her disappearance has nothing to do with him. She might have gone to some back-street abortionist.'

'If she did that, she must have consulted someone. How about asking her friend or her sister who works in a hospital?'

'April Saunders seems to be a nice girl from a respectable family,' said Lane. 'She's just turned sixteen. If she'd been planning to do something like that, how would she know where to go? Remember that she told her friend and her mother that she was catching the Greenline coach to visit her boyfriend. I'm not closing my mind to the abortion idea but it seems extremely unlikely.'

There were no further suggestions so the meeting was adjourned until the following morning at eight.

...

Mandy hurried down the road. Shirley's desperation had been too much to bear. She needed to do something to find April but she couldn't. The notes and sympathy she was receiving were well meant but had made her feel like a bereaved mother and she couldn't face that awful possibility. Mandy stopped, trying to recall something that Nan had said to her mum after Andrew's accident:

… Grief brings energy. Don't wallow in it. Put it to use. Try and do something practical …

The half remembered advice spoke to her down the years. Rousing herself she set off at a brisk walk, breaking into a run.

Brian Humphries wasn't surprised to see Mandy standing on his doorstep with a determined expression.

They'd known each other for years and he recognised that look. He ushered her into the living room where she came straight out with it.

'I'm going to find April and I need your help.'

'Why me?'

'I need someone I can rely on and I know you care for her as much as I do.'

'Yes, of course.'

Mandy paced up and down the room.

'Brian, I feel so guilty. I threatened James and said things to April that weren't true. She might still be here if I hadn't made up lies about Teresa Marshall.'

She turned towards him, her face a picture of misery.

'April's disappearance isn't your fault Mandy.'

'I wish I could believe that but I feel really bad. I must find her.'

He stepped forward and held her close. She clung to him before breaking away feeling confused. April's disappearance had come as a shock to them both but Brian knew what Mandy was like when she'd made up her mind.

'I'm glad you've come but there's nothing we can do. We'll just be getting in the way of the police.'

'Look, Brian. If the police find her in the next couple of days, that'll be great. But supposing they don't? Even with all their resources they can miss things. Our advantage is that we know April. Tomorrow I'm going to organise my gang from the middle school and this evening you and I can work out a plan. But first I want you to come down to the police station with me.'

'Why? Do you think they'll tell you what they've found out so far?'

'I doubt it but I have an idea I want them to follow up.'

'Shouldn't we bring James in on this?'

'I've no time for James but he might have some useful information. Talk to him tomorrow. If he wants to join us that'll be good but I doubt whether we can count on him.'

Mandy's instincts proved to be right. Tackled in the school corridor the following day, James told Brian about the routes where he and April used to walk but refused to get involved.

'We should leave it to the police. I haven't any time to spare anyway as I'm starting my exams next week.' He started to walk away.

'The police may not find her,' called Brian. 'Your help could be crucial.'

James stopped and turned. He bit his lip. The reaction at home had made things worse. His mother was obviously upset but had said nothing. His father was convinced that he was in trouble with the police:

'I don't know what you've been up to, but you'd better bloody well sort it out. I'm not having them round here again.'

After the clash with his father, he couldn't sleep with worrying about April and his efforts to concentrate on his revision were proving to be impossible.

'I'm sorry, Brian, but I can't get involved. It's a job for the police.'

The desk sergeant was busy with paperwork when he heard a faint cough and turned to see the new girl from the canteen.

'I've been sent to see if you want a mug of tea Sergeant as we haven't seen you today.'

'I haven't had time with sorting out these reports. I'll be glad of a tea and a cheese roll to go with it.'

The girl nodded but didn't move.

'I'm scared Sergeant. I can't help it. The girl that's disappeared is only a year younger than me. There could be some monster out there.

'Now then, don't you go frightening yourself. There's no evidence for anything like that. Off you go and don't forget that cheese roll.'

Fifteen minutes later, he looked up and saw two young people.

'Can I help you?'

'We'd like to speak with Inspector Lane. It's about April Saunders.'

It was a thin earnest looking girl about the same age as the missing girl.

'I see. Do you have some information?'

'Sort of. It's more a line of enquiry really.'

This time it was the boy who'd spoken. He was a big lad, about six feet tall and broad with it. Looked like a rugby player.

'Before we go any further, I need to take your particulars.'

He noted these down.

'I'm sure you appreciate that the inspector is very busy. If you give me the details, I'll see that he gets them as soon as possible.'

'It's just this. We think it's possible that April might have got on the wrong coach by mistake. If she did, then that needs to be followed up, don't you think?'

'Yes of course it does, Mandy. Leave it to me. I'll see the inspector gets your message. We've got your particulars now so we can contact you if we need to. Thanks very much for coming in. If you think of anything else that might help, don't hesitate to contact us again.'

Lane read through the sergeant's report on the day's work. He made a few amendments and sent it to be typed up for the Super. He gulped down a welcome cup of tea and collected the notes that had come in during the day, scanning through them for clues to the puzzle of the girl's disappearance. The last one came from a familiar name: Mandy Daniels and a lad called Brian Humphries, probably also from the school. It was timed about half an hour ago and was just a brief note in the desk sergeant's neat handwriting:

Could April have got on the wrong coach by mistake?

Good try kids, he thought, but he knew already that the Greenline coach came through every two hours on Sundays. After the eight-thirty, the next two had come through on time at ten-thirty and twelve-thirty and she hadn't been on any of them. There weren't any buses or trolleys on Sundays either. He put the note with others in the tray for filing under '*No Action*'.

The meeting with James Fleming at Bishops Stortford Police Station that evening was inconclusive. James apologised for lying about being at work on Sunday morning. He had intended to go there, but was still feeling upset by April's appearance at school on Friday. Although he'd set off for the warehouse as usual, he'd cycled on to the park and stayed there for the rest of the morning trying to sort himself out. He hadn't liked to admit it at the previous interview. He was shocked at the suggestion that April might be pregnant and insisted that it was impossible as they'd never gone that far.

He reiterated that he had known nothing about her intended visit to his home, nor had he met her at any time on Sunday. Lane was inclined to believe him and began to wonder if someone else could be responsible for her pregnancy. Had she been raped?

SEVEN

It had been a week since April had gone missing. Mandy had driven her team on with desperate energy. They had searched throughout Milsham and Bishops Stortford but neither they nor the police had managed to unearth any clues.

After Sunday dinner, Ron, Shirley and Carol sat in the living room drinking tea. Ron leafed through *The News of the World*. There was nothing about the search for April. That story had run its course and, without fresh information, had been dropped. Glancing through the scandals and petty crimes, his eye was caught by a story concerning the strange death of a van driver:

Van driver stabbed
A critically injured man was discovered near the A1 on Tuesday May 19th. Van driver Keith Willard of

London was found stabbed in the chest with a sharp stick in woods near a lay-by south of Peterborough. Mr Willard, 36, was rushed to Peterborough Hospital but died without regaining consciousness. Willard had several convictions for sexual assaults upon women and police are refusing to rule out any connection with his injuries. A police spokesman today claimed that while foul play was suspected, they were examining several lines of enquiry. Anyone passing the southbound lay-by near Peterborough between Sunday the 17th and Tuesday the 19th and who saw any parked vehicles or people in the vicinity should call the police incident room on Peterborough 236.

There had been a first in British police strategy that morning with a re-enactment of April's disappearance. It was the idea of the chief constable, who on a recent visit to the United States had watched such a procedure. A young policewoman in a blonde wig and wearing an identical dress with a similar shoulder bag to April's had set out from the Saunders' house. She had walked briskly up the road and turned into the High Street just after eight thirty. After waiting at the coach stop for about ten minutes, she continued along Station Road to the railway station. It had been well publicised and there was even a television news team filming the historic event, while a curious crowd had turned out to watch. It was a desperate attempt by the police to jog someone's memory and gain a fresh lead.

It had been a terrible week. The local papers had carried the story of April's disappearance on Wednesday and by Thursday it was in the national press. Reporters from London had descended on Milsham, knocking at the Saunders' door as well as their neighbours, looking for background information. They went into the local shops and reporters hung around outside the school to talk to April's classmates. On Friday, one newspaper posed the question: *Was April Pregnant?* Other tabloids, looking for a sensational angle, quoted *local sources* in describing April as *tarty and boy-mad*. The effect on Shirley had been devastating. She was stared at by shoppers and their sympathy seemed to have evaporated. Carol had done the shopping yesterday and had overheard gossip that April had *probably got what she deserved*.

Shirley retreated into herself as the week wore on, going mechanically through the household tasks. She had lost her appetite and spoke hardly at all. Carol called in the doctor who prescribed pills to help her sleep.

'What she needs is to get right away from Milsham for a while,' he said.

That wasn't going to happen at the present time.

. . .

Mandy and Brian stood watching the re-enactment. Their efforts had led nowhere and they were struggling to decide what to do next. Then Mandy spotted a familiar figure watching proceedings from across the road.

'That's the police woman, Jenny Jones. Come on Brian.'

After Brian was introduced, Mandy explained that they had been trying to find April but without success. Jenny nodded.

'We knew about your search and hoped that you might turn up some evidence to help us. Let's hope this morning brings us something.'

'Did you check on the idea that she might have got on the wrong coach?' asked Mandy.

'What do you mean, the wrong coach?'

'We know that she missed the Greenline. Suppose she hadn't realised that and got on another coach by mistake. It could have taken her anywhere.'

'Did you tell anyone about this idea?'

'Yes. We told the desk Sergeant on Monday.'

Jenny stared at them. It had been a frustrating week. They had received so many fruitless reports and even two bogus murder confessions.

'Come with me. Let's try something.'

They went into the newsagent where Jenny produced her identification for the shopkeeper.

'Apart from the regular coaches and buses, are there any other coaches that use this coach stop?'

'Occasionally. It's sometimes used as a pick-up point for excursions.'

'Was there such a coach picking up from here last Sunday at around eight-thirty in the morning?'

'I'm sorry, I didn't notice, although there were several old people calling in for sweets at about that time. They could have been going on an outing somewhere.'

Back in the street, Jenny promised Mandy and Brian that this possibility would be followed up without delay.

'We'll check the coach companies. It's a worthwhile line of enquiry, so well done.'

She hurried off to speak with Lane who was standing by his car in Station Road.

By late morning the next day, the police had established that there had been a coach that had stopped in Milsham that Sunday morning. At twelve thirty, Lane and Jones were in the office of the manager of the coach company in Tottenham. They learned that the coach had taken an old folks' outing to Lincoln for the day. There had been two pick-up points, the first in Enfield and the second in Milsham. The coach was due at Milsham at eight fifteen that morning.

'Could it have been twenty minutes late?'

'Yes it could, but all our drivers log their pick-up and drop-off times. See for yourself, the driver logged his time at Milsham at eight eighteen.'

Lane studied the driver's time sheet and passed it to Jenny Jones.

'Would the coach have waited if there were any passengers missing?' she asked.

'Yes, that's possible. It's up to the driver. He might wait a few minutes but not too long or the rest of the journey gets behind.'

'Could he have falsified the time?' asked Lane. 'If he had been twenty minutes late, he might not want you to know.'

'That's possible but unlikely. We're very strict about time recording.'

'If he had arrived late, surely he could have made up the time on the journey.'

The manager conceded that might be possible. Lane had one last question.

'Would it be possible for someone to get on the coach who wasn't a member of the excursion, like a teenager for instance?'

'Absolutely not. The driver is required to see the tickets and count the numbers at every stop.'

'I'll need to talk to the driver. Can you give me his particulars and tell me where I can find him?'

The manager rose and scanned a chart on the wall.

'Let's see. Here we are. He's taken a party down to Margate for the day. The coach is due back here around eight o'clock tonight.'

'We'll talk to him then. In the meantime, I'd like a list of all the passengers on that coach last Sunday, including their addresses.'

The manager frowned.

'I know what this is about. It's that girl who went missing in Milsham. I read about it in the paper. Surely you don't think she could have got on one of our coaches?'

'We have to examine every possibility, sir. When can we have that list?'

'It'll take about twenty minutes to dig out the information and get it typed up. There's a pub a few doors down the road. Why don't you get a bit of lunch while you're waiting.'

Back in the car thirty minutes later, Lane scanned the list. There had been twenty-eight passengers including five couples who had been picked up in Milsham. He decided to begin with them and phoned the details through to his sergeant. They were to be contacted immediately.

Two constables, a man and woman, had been given several addresses to check in Milsham. Their first call elicited a terrified response from an old lady who insisted that she knew nothing.

'You can't come in. My husband's got a bad chest, and he's infectious.' She shut the door.

The second call produced no response. The couple were obviously out. The third call was entirely different. An elderly man answered the door. The officer was only half way through his explanation when the man shuffled off down the hall.

'Come on in and shut the door.'

He led them into a small, overheated sitting room. There was a budgerigar chirping in a cage. Betty, who had been knitting, looked up anxiously.

'Have you found April yet?'

'I told you we should have gone to the police,' said George.

'How dare you!' retorted Betty. 'You've been preventing me from going all week, saying we should keep out of it.'

'Mrs Jackson, can you confirm whether you saw April Saunders on your coach?'

'Saw her? I sat next to her. She's such a nice girl.'

Betty and George cowered in the interview room at the police station dreading the arrival of Inspector Lane. Suddenly the door swept open and Lane and Jenny Jones appeared and seated themselves opposite the old couple. They quickly established how April had mistakenly got on the wrong coach, which had arrived just after eight-thirty five. She had got off at Wansford Services and was hoping to get a lift back to Bishops Stortford or Milsham. That was the last they saw of her.

'Why didn't you tell us this before?' asked Jenny.

Betty, who had been close to tears, now wept openly.

'I wanted to come, but George wouldn't let me. He said I'd made her get on the coach, so I'd get into trouble. As the days went on, it got harder. He said we'd be guilty of withholding information. I'm ever so sorry.'

They remained while their statement was prepared and signed, then they were given a ride home.

Lane wasted no time. Poring over a map, he saw that Wansford came under the jurisdiction of the Peterborough police. He contacted the police station there and explained the situation. They agreed to start checking all incidents and hospital reports over the last week throughout their area. Photographs of April were despatched immediately and Lane confirmed that he and Jenny Jones would be there at ten the following morning. He telephoned the superintendent who was out of his office and left a message.

The following morning, Lane and Jones arrived at Peterborough Police Headquarters. They were ushered into an office where the local inspector waved them into chairs and ordered coffee.

'We haven't found anything yet. My people are checking all the reports since May 17th and are just over half way. I've sent two officers out to Wansford Services with the girl's photograph. If they turn up anything, they'll ring in. We should have everything covered this morning. Let's hope we find something. It's a bad business.'

Enquiries at Wansford Services drew a blank. The staff claimed that they couldn't remember anything, nor did they recognise the photograph of April. If they had recalled something, they had decided between themselves to forget it. Lane and Jones stayed in Peterborough and scanned all the reports but they showed nothing that merited any further investigation.

Driving back that afternoon they were quiet, each with their own thoughts. Lane knew he'd been given the clue about the wrong coach a week ago and hadn't followed it up. If he had done so, the staff at Wansford Services would have been interviewed before there had been any publicity. They would not have been able to agree a story. Yet again he'd ignored a crucial bit of evidence. It was bound to come to light.

PART 2
LOST IN TIME

EIGHT

When April came round, she couldn't understand why she was lying on a bed of damp decaying leaves in a ditch with daylight filtering through the trees from an overcast sky. As flashes of memory came back, she remembered with horror being attacked by Fred and banging her head. Slowly, her head spinning, she tried to extricate herself from a dense holly bush that scratched and scraped her arms and legs. There was already dried blood on one arm and her legs felt sore. She turned slowly to look along the ditch and felt relieved there was no sign of Fred. He must have gone. She needed to climb back up the slope to reach the road and prayed that he wouldn't be there. Trembling, she moved slowly holding on to branches to steady herself. The trees and bushes were thicker than she remembered but she could hear the traffic's roar at the top and that spurred her on. She edged forward on her hands and knees but had to stop from time to time to hang onto a bush to avoid slipping back. She moved slowly upwards in spite of the nausea and a throbbing headache. She passed out a couple of times and woke up in bewilderment before emerging exhausted onto the road verge and collapsed as a passing car screeched to a stop.

Sarah Kendrick was a doctor in general practice in Cambridge. She turned off her car engine and ran to the slumped figure of a girl in a badly torn dress, covered in mud and dried blood. She looked as if she had been assaulted, possibly raped and was unconscious. She looked up and down the road but there were no other stationary vehicles. Fetching her medical bag and travel blanket, she gave the girl a quick examination. There was a bruise to the forehead and a bad cut with much matted blood on the back of her head. She cleaned up the head wound and put a dressing on it. The girl was clearly barely conscious and obviously dehydrated but she took a little water. Finally, Sarah gave her an injection and wrapping her up in the blanket, eased her gently onto the back seat of the car, holding her in place with the seat belts. She called the police to report the incident and marked the spot on the side of the road for them with a newspaper weighted down with stones.

'I'm taking her straight to A and E at Addenbrookes Hospital.' Sarah informed the police. 'Please notify them that I should be there in about forty-five minutes.'

She drove quickly, watching for police patrol cars. She was lucky, the road wasn't busy and she was soon threading her way through the city to the hospital.

On arrival, April was taken into a cubicle. She had awoken from the effects of the injection and lay beneath a sheet. She closed her eyes because of a strong overhead light. Her head ached, but she managed to turn it from side to side and saw that she was flanked by a doctor and a nurse.

The doctor who had an Indian face asked for her name.

'April Saunders. Will I be alright?'

'I'm sure you will April. Just relax now as we have to do a few tests and get you cleaned up.'

'What day is it?'

'It's Wednesday. Can you remember when you were injured?'

'I think it was Sunday.'

She'd been lying in that ditch for days. Mum and Dad must be going frantic.

After checking her temperature and pulse, a doctor examined her head wound, shone a light in her eyes and asked whether she had any other pains. He issued instructions to the nurse, who left and was replaced by another nurse who brought two tablets and a beaker of water.

'Try to take these. They will help with your headache.'

The nurses now removed her soiled clothing, gently cleaned up her cuts and scratches and put her into a hospital robe.

'Where am I?'

'You're in hospital in Cambridge. Don't worry, you're safe here.'

The reassurance brought April's fears to the surface and she cried out:

'I'm pregnant and I'm really scared. I don't know what to do.'

The nurses looked at each other with concern.

'How long has it been April?'

'I'm not sure. A couple of months I think. He did it. I didn't want him to but he wouldn't leave me alone.'

'The doctor will be here in a moment. You can tell her all about it.'

'No I can't. No one will believe me.'

Moments later a woman doctor appeared and smiled.

'You have to go down to X-Ray now. I will talk to you when you come back.'

Later, the doctor asked her what had happened in the ditch and whether she had been raped. April replied that she hadn't as Fred had rolled away from her when he had been pierced with the stick. When asked about her pregnancy fears, April couldn't speak about it but agreed to an examination. Afterwards she was astounded to learn that she was still *virgo intacta*. She couldn't take it in.

'Are you sure?' she asked.

'Yes. I'm quite sure. You're not pregnant. Now, we're going to admit you for a while so I have arranged for you to be taken up to a ward.'

'I need to tell my mum and dad where I am. They must be so worried.'

'You can give those details to the nurse in the ward. She will see that your parents are notified.'

April was settled into a bed and connected to a saline drip into her arm. A nurse in a dark blue uniform, who introduced herself as the ward sister came to reassure her that there was nothing to worry about. She took down details of April's parents and explained that the police would call on them without delay. She also asked whether there were any other relatives in Milsham in case her family weren't at home. April didn't have any, so she gave details of her school and Mandy's full name and address.

The sister returned to her desk and scanned through the details. April claimed to be sixteen although she looked older. There were no telephone numbers but the police could manage perfectly well. Poor kid, she was still in shock and needed to see her parents.

Kevin tiptoed past the nursing station. It was nearly midnight and the nurse on duty was absorbed in a magazine. He crept past her into the silent ward. Making his way to April's bedside, he stood in the dim light for several minutes gazing at her, then retreated to the staff exit, collected his jacket and cycled home to his tiny flat. His friend in A and E had told him that April had been very upset on her arrival and claimed that she was pregnant, although an examination had shown that she was still a virgin. He made himself a sandwich and a mug of coffee and lapsed into thought.

Kevin Wheeler had been a nurse at the hospital for more than five years. He was dedicated to his job and popular with the patients. His main preoccupation, which he kept to himself, was a particular religious outlook. The following day he thought again about the truth that been revealed. April Saunders had arrived from another place. All the nurses were talking about it. Her importance had come as a shining revelation. Here was a young virgin with an unborn child who had come into this world. He recalled her sleeping peacefully, so full of grace. He must pass the information on to the elders. They would probably disregard it as they had with his previous contributions, but he had seen the light and had to share it. That evening he switched on his computer and typed in an address.

The following morning after taking her medication, April was feeling better and sitting up in bed. A nurse had taken her to the bathroom and she had eaten some cornflakes for breakfast. She looked around with interest. The ward had pale green walls and was light and airy with eight beds all occupied by women. One was reading a book, another was listening to something with headphones but the rest were just lying there. They all looked middle aged or old. There were big windows at one end that looked out over open countryside. They were obviously high up as no sounds came in from the outside world. She had never been in a hospital before and was surprised to see how modern it was, with electronic machines everywhere. Perhaps it was a private hospital where you had to pay. She felt worried that her parents wouldn't be able to afford it and hoped that they would come soon to take her home. She declined the offer of headphones and something to read as she was feeling sleepy. She sank back into her pillows and closed her eyes.

Fred was looming over her with a horrible lecherous expression on his face. She couldn't get away. He came down swiftly on top of her blocking out the light. She started in panic ...

She woke suddenly and saw that the sister was standing by her bed with a man in a smart suit. He was wearing glasses with small rectangular frames.

'Good morning April. How are you feeling this morning?' He introduced himself as Mr Thornhill.

'I'm much better thank you. I think I'm ready to go home.'

'I understand, but you've had a nasty bang on the head and we'd like you to stay a little longer so that we can keep an eye on you. The good news is that your X-Ray examination showed no break in the skull. You're obviously hard-headed,' he said with a smile. 'Is there anything you would like to ask me?'

'Are my parents coming today, sir?'

'I'm afraid I don't know. Do you have any news about that Sister?'

'The local police have been notified and we're awaiting the outcome.'

'That's good,' said Mr Thornhill. 'I'm sure you'll soon be together again.'

Shortly afterwards, a nurse came to say that April had visitors. They were not allowed into the ward during doctor's rounds, so she would take her to a meeting room. April felt relieved. It must be Mum and Dad. She hoped that they wouldn't be too angry with her. She was led down a corridor and ushered into a small room which had a table, a few chairs and a small sink in the corner. It wasn't her parents but a man and woman who introduced themselves as police officers, a detective inspector and a sergeant. They explained that they had come to interview her about the assault on Sunday. Going through her story step by step, they were anxious to learn everything she could remember. She did her best but when it came to describing what had happened, she cried at the memory of the experience. The nurse produced a box of tissues and a glass of water and gave them to her. They waited patiently for her to compose herself.

'I'm sorry to put you through this, April, but we need as much information as possible if we're to catch this man. I assure you that we take this very seriously,' said the inspector. 'One thing I don't understand is your reference to Wansford Services. There isn't such a place on the A1 these days. Are you sure that it wasn't further north? There's a service junction near Grantham. Do you think that could have been the one?'

'I'm sorry but I don't know the A1. I've never been up this way before.'

When they had finished their questions, April asked them whether they had any news of her parents.

'I was going to speak to you about that' the inspector replied. 'I think you must have still been pretty woozy yesterday as the information you gave wasn't right.'

'What do you mean? What wasn't right?'

He withdrew a typed report from his case. 'It says here that the Milsham police visited the home address you gave but it was obviously wrong because your parents don't live there. Your friend doesn't seem to exist anywhere in Milsham either and the school you mentioned closed down in the 1970s.'

April sipped her water and tried to steady herself as she held out an unsteady hand.

'May I see the report please?'

It was handed over and she saw that the details were all correct.

'Are you sure it was the Milsham police?' She was grasping at straws. It said Milsham at the top of the page. 'This can't be right. It says my school closed down in the 1970s. That's wrong for a start as it's 1959.'

There was a silence. April looked from one face to another. At last the nurse took April's hand in hers.

'We're not living in 1959, April. That was forty years ago. This is 1999.'

It couldn't be true. They were all watching at her. She must be in a dream. She jumped up and screamed:

'NO. NO. NO. This isn't real.'

She had to get away. She pulled the door open and ran down the corridor, dodging between startled hospital staff. Hearing a commotion behind her, she increased her speed until she reached the main corridor. She looked along and had a shock. It was silent and completely empty. All the colours and sounds had drained away, leaving an endless white passage stretching on for miles with darkness at the far end. There was a tiny lone figure . . . Her legs buckled and as she fell, two arms encircled her from behind and held her against the wall.

'It's alright April' whispered the policewoman. 'The doctors will take care of you.'

April was helped into a wheelchair. She steeled herself to open her eyes to look at the everlasting corridor. But this time it looked normal with nurses, doctors and other staff walking up and down. She was wheeled back to the ward and soon afterwards a curtain was pulled around her bed. The sister soon appeared with a young doctor.

'I hear you've been trying to break the 100 metre record down the corridor,' he said with a grin. 'What you need is rest. I'm going to give you something to help you sleep. When you wake up you'll feel much better.'

She tried to talk but she couldn't. She felt herself shaking.

'I don't *want* an injection. I want to get out of here. I want . . .'

April opened her eyes letting them get used to the light. Bit by bit she took in her surroundings and saw that she was no longer in the ward but in a room by herself. Apart from the bed, there was a small round table with some comfortable looking chairs and a television. There were two doors, one of which was open and clearly led to a bathroom. A clock on the wall showed it was nearly four o'clock.

'Hi. You're back with us again.' It was a nurse with a black face and a wide smile. 'My name's Shani and I'll be looking after you while you're here.'

'What am I doing here? I was in a ward with other people before I fell asleep.'

Shani smiled. 'This is a private room.'

April lay back. Her body felt heavy. That doctor must have given her something strong to knock her out like that.

'What is this place?'

'It's Addenbrookes Hospital in Cambridge of course. Didn't you know?'

'I'm not sure I know anything anymore. Is it a mental institution?'

'Of course not,' Shani laughed. 'What about a cup of tea?'

She switched on an electric kettle which was on a long white sideboard. She opened one of the doors and extracted a carton of milk from a fridge. Seeing April watching, she smiled.

'All mod cons here,' she said as she brought over two steaming mugs of tea and placed them onto a table that swivelled over the bed.

April studied her face. She'd never spoken to a black person before.

'Where do you come from?'

'Me? I live here in the staff accommodation.'

'What about before that? Before you became a nurse?'

'I grew up in Finsbury Park in North London,' said Shani. 'My parents came over from Jamaica in the seventies.'

The seventies. There it was again. April felt tense.

'Please tell me truthfully?' asked April. 'What year is it?'

'It's 1999 of course! Now if you're feeling better, I've got some grapes, a newspaper and some magazines.'

'Thanks, I'll just have the grapes.'

She ate them one by one and thought what had been said. It couldn't really be 1999. People don't travel forty years into the future. Everyone's pretending we're in the future and they're all in on it. Perhaps it's some kind of test. If it is, then it's a horrible thing to do. The problem is that there's nobody to trust here. She needed to get away but she had to bide her time as she hadn't got any clothes or money. She would ask for some clothes tomorrow and see how they reacted if she went for a walk down the corridor. They had grabbed her last time so she would have to be careful. She decided to slip out during the night to spy out the land. That evening, she managed to distract Shani after she'd been given her overnight medication. She hid the pills in the bed and just drank the glass of water.

It was almost three thirty in the morning when she crept out of her room and along a passage between silent wards and descended some stairs. She was back in the main passageway of the hospital and remembered with dread the experience of the silent everlasting corridor. It must have been something to do with the pills she had been given. This time, there were faint whirring sounds in the distance and a slight smell of disinfectant. There will be cleaners about. She would have to be careful not to be seen. On the wall facing her were signs giving directions to various departments, clinics and wards. To the right she saw more light in the distance and, as she approached it, the corridor opened into a broad space with a newsagent and a cafe, both closed behind metal grills. There was a large seating area and she ducked down behind it when she heard footsteps. Someone walked straight past and it was quiet again. She waited for a couple of minutes then stood up and looked around. There was a short wide corridor leading away to the left which led to entrance doors – the way out. She tried them but they were locked. Back in the sitting area she realised that there must be other exits and some of them might be open. There was a stack of newspapers wrapped in clear plastic by the newsagent. They had obviously been brought in late last night. Kneeling down she looked at the topmost paper. It was *The Daily Express* with a big colour picture on the front and the date at the top that read: Friday May 22nd 1999.

She was in 1999 after all. How could such a thing have happened? April remained still with her face rested on her arms, over the newspapers. She had tried to convince herself that it wasn't true but now the enormity of it overwhelmed her, churning her stomach into tense cramps.

'Allo. What you doin ere?'

Two women, obviously cleaners, had come up and stood watching her.

'Shouldn't you be in bed somewhere?'

'I'm alright, I couldn't sleep,' said April.

'Please yerself then. G'night.'

For a long time she knelt there, rigid with shock and unwilling to believe the horrifying nightmare. Eventually she rose and trudged back towards her ward. At the foot of the stairs were two large vending machines. One dispensed drinks and the other one a selection of snacks and chocolate bars. April had heard of these machines but had never seen one. You put your money in and selected what you wanted. Why hadn't she thought of money before? That couldn't be faked.

Back in bed, she was trembling and couldn't organise her thoughts. She tried not to panic but, drowned in her despair, she realised that everything she knew and had grown up with would be gone. Including her family, her home and her friends. Even Milsham would be different. People of her generation would be strangers in their fifties and sixties and young people of her age wouldn't be interested in her except as a relic from the past. If she had met a girl from forty years ago she would have come from 1919. There would be so many things she wouldn't know. April was afraid she would be a freak show and a very lonely one. After a long time, she slipped into a troubled sleep.

NINE

Sarah Kendrick was keen to find out what had become of April. She was probably surrounded by her family and friends by now. Nevertheless, as she had to be at the hospital this morning, she decided to pay her a visit and found her way to April's room with her daughter Emily. Emily was 19 and on a gap year before going to university to read Medicine in October. She was slim with curly brown hair which framed a lightly freckled face and brown eyes. When she smiled, her whole face smiled. She handed over a large bunch of flowers to Shani.

'They're lovely,' exclaimed Shani.

'Not really, they're only Tesco's,' said Emily.

Sarah was asking April how she was feeling.

'I'm much better. I want to thank you,' said April. 'I was in a bad way when you found me. I don't remember much about it, but I'd been lying in that wood since last Sunday.'

'I'm glad I arrived when I did' said Sarah. 'You're looking like a different girl now. I expect you will be going home soon.'

In spite of her desperate situation, April felt reassured. Sarah had a kind face with a ready smile and an air of quiet authority. Perhaps that came with being a doctor.

'I'd like to go home but I can't,' said April and began to tell her story, hesitatingly at first then, with a cry of anguish, how she had accepted a lift with Fred. April stopped speaking and looked down at her hands.

'I'm so frightened. I don't belong here.'

Sarah leaned forward and took April's hand.

'Of course you belong here. Everything is going to be alright. You've had a head injury and your confusion is understandable. Don't worry, I'll speak with the doctors.'

'I'm not confused, just stranded.'

'Do you need some clothes and stuff?' asked Emily.

April nodded. She had come into this world with nothing.

'Okay, I'll be back later.'

Before they left, April asked them why she had been moved to a private room. They didn't know.

Emily was as good as her word and returned later with two large stripy bags full of clothes that she laid out on the bed,

'Where did all these come from?' asked April. 'There's more here than I've got at home.'

'They're some of my things. You're a similar size to me. Is there anything you'd like to try on?'

April found a green top and some slim white trousers. Once dressed, she looked in the mirror at her reflection.

'Thanks so much. I don't know how I'll be able to repay you.'

'That's not necessary. You've got smaller feet than me.'

They managed with some thick white sports socks and a well laced up pair of trainers. April walked up and down and found them comfortable. In spite of the weight of fear that enveloped her, she began to feel more confident.

After lunch, April had two more visitors. One was a grave Chinese-looking man who introduced himself as Dr Wu. The other man wore a pinstripe suit and carried a briefcase. Shani was sent out and the three sat around the table. The suit nodded to April and smiled.

'My name is Roger Venn and I'm from the Home Office. I have read the report about you and I am here to see whether I can help. I'm bound to tell you that your story about arriving from 1959 won't be believed, as time travel is obviously impossible. However I have been looking at the records for 1959 and should like to check a few details with you.'

April nodded and he began by asking questions about her family, her school and Milsham in general, making careful notes of her answers. She had the distinct impression that the credibility of her story was being meticulously checked. When he had finished, he brought out a folder from his briefcase.

'These are the police reports and newspaper articles about the disappearance of an April Saunders on Sunday May 17th 1959.'

He read out a summary of the final police report. April was alarmed.

'Did the van driver really die from the stick wound?'

'I'm afraid so, but you needn't worry. No one will blame you.'

'Did he lie to me about his wife and daughter?'

'Yes, it was all lies. He was only after you.'

April was stunned. How could she have been so gullible? She was aware that both men were studying her intently. Roger Venn spoke again:

'At the time the van driver was found, the police and ambulance personnel didn't see anyone else. When you emerged from the trees in front of Dr Kendrick on Wednesday, you were, as far as we can tell, about fifty to sixty metres north of where the driver was found.'

'What can you remember after the man was stabbed?' asked Dr Wu, speaking for the first time.

April repeated her story. She had passed out. Then she woke up, caught in a holly bush, feeling in pain, dizzy and very cold.

'Can you recall anything between those two moments? Did you dream?'

April struggled to remember. 'I might have done. I just wanted to get away.'

Suddenly, Venn looked angry.

'I have accepted that you are April Saunders for the sake of this meeting, but now you will tell me who you really are so we can end this charade.'

'I *am* April Saunders and last Sunday I was living at home in Milsham and it *was* 1959 and that's the truth. Until last night, I thought you lot were the ones with the charade, only pretending it was 1999.'

'What made you change your mind?' asked Dr Wu.

'It was the newspapers.'

Venn frowned as he sorted through his papers.

'Very well, let's continue. Do you want to hear about your family? I'm afraid that the news is not good.'

April felt herself tensing up. She closed her eyes. Eventually she nodded.

'Your mother passed away ten years ago after a fatal illness. Your sister Carol was killed in an air crash over Africa in 1979. She was unmarried and had no children.'

A long spell of silence stretched out, broken only by the faint ticking of the wall clock, as April sat looking down into her lap, struggling to take in the terrible news.

'Why was she flying over Africa?'

'She was a nurse and doing good work out there, helping injured people in terrible war conditions. You can be very proud of her.'

'What about my dad? Is he dead as well?'

'No, he isn't. He's in a nursing home and suffering from Alzheimer's disease. Do you know what that is?'

April didn't. Venn explained that her father was unable to recognise anyone. He didn't know his own nurse, or even his name. He certainly wouldn't recognise his daughter.

'What about my friend Mandy Daniels? Do you know what became of her?'

'She was not listed in the 1959 school records, nor were her parents living in Milsham at that time. As far as we are concerned, she didn't exist.'

His face hardened again.

'Now young lady, I want to impress upon you that all this lying will lead you into serious trouble, or even imprisonment.'

April leapt up, knocking her chair over, ran into the bathroom and slammed the door. She had nothing left to hold on to. She was alone in this alien world. She thought of her mother and cried for a long time. When she returned, the men had gone. Shani was back and looking worried.

'I've just been told that no one believes my story and that my family are dead. I'm not sure if I can take any more of this or whether I want to go on. Perhaps it would be better if I died too.'

'I'm so sorry, April' said Shani. 'That's terrible news.'

She unlocked a wall cupboard and took out a small bottle, extracted two pills and gave them to April with a glass of water.

'More pills? What are these for? To send me back to sleep again?'

'They're just to help you. You're tensed up because you've had a shock. These drugs are mild and help your body to relax, which in turn helps the other parts of you to cope.'

'I'm sorry. I've had so many things go wrong in my life during these last two weeks. I don't know what to do.'

She took the pills.

Later that evening, after April had examined the money from Shani's purse, she was shown how to use the TV remote and started to watch various programmes. They were all in colour and there were so many channels, some of them really weird. There were tons of advertisements too, most of which she didn't understand.

'Watch out that you don't become a telly addict,' said Shani, 'or you'll finish up as a couch potato.'

April hadn't heard about a couch potato but the meaning was clear enough.

'It's my education. If I'm here to stay, I'll have to learn about all this.'

The next day was Saturday. Shani was off duty and her replacement was a doleful Irish nurse who explained that there were fewer staff over the weekend and she had to look after several patients. She brought a newspaper at breakfast time and April settled down to read it. She glanced through the sports section. The England cricket team were not expected to do well. Some continuity there she thought. There was a light knock on the door and Emily appeared with a boy of about the same age. He was tall with rimless glasses and short cropped hair.

'This is Jake. He thinks he's my boyfriend.'

He stepped forward and shook hands. April warmed to him at once.

'You don't need to believe that cover story,' he said. 'I'm really Emily's bodyguard. Any bad guys turn up and POW! I zap them with my laser finger. You'll be safe with me kid.' He grinned. 'Let's get out of here.'

'Where are we going?'

'Down to the concourse for a machiatto and danish' said Emily.

'I don't know if I'm allowed to leave.'

'Of course you are,' said Jake. 'Leave a note for your minder if you like. If she gives us any trouble, I'll waste her.' He pointed a forefinger at the door just as it opened and the nurse stood staring at the cheerful trio. She shrugged and was gone.

'Oh dear,' said April. 'What will happen now?'

'Big trouble,' said Jake. 'You've contravened a rule about patients not enjoying themselves.'

'What's a machiatto and danish,' April wanted to know as they set off down the corridor.

'They're just words for coffee and cake' said Emily. 'Practically everything these days has a fancy name and they're all after your money.'

April hadn't got any money. How was she going to survive in this world?

After a short walk they emerged into a large brightly lit area that bustled with life. There were shops all around selling clothes, food, flowers and gifts. There was also a small supermarket. A cheerful buzz of voices came from the bustle of patients, hospital staff and visitors. In the middle were tables and chairs with people eating, drinking and chatting. April found it difficult to believe they were still in a hospital. They sat down and Jake set off to join a queue at the coffee shop. A man at the next table in pyjamas and dressing gown was reading a newspaper. A woman went past with a suspended drip bag on a metal frame with wheels. April spotted a girl with pink hair and small metal rings in her ears and on her face. She turned to Emily who didn't seem to have noticed anything unusual.

'This is a great place. I can't wait to tell my sister.'

Then she remembered. Carol was dead. She felt herself shrink in the chair. Emily squeezed her hand.

'Yes, it's full of life, like the outside world. Patients who are well enough can come down here. Mum reckons it helps them towards recovery.'

April felt her hands were sweaty as she struggled with her fear.

'Tell me about Jake. He seems to be fun.'

Emily laughed. 'Jake Burnstone is just a big kid. He likes to fool around, so I keep an eye on him to make sure he stays out of trouble. He's much brighter than most of us. He came up to Cambridge at 16 to read Computer Science and graduated with a double first last year after only two years. He's staying on to do a doctorate. He seems to understand everything about the future of computers, mobiles and the internet.'

April was about to ask what all these things were, but Jake had returned and she settled back to enjoy the coffee break with her new friends. She told them about her visitors the day before.

'What did that character Venn want yesterday?' asked Jake.

'He wanted to check my story and he said time travel is impossible.'

'I bet he hasn't had much practice. Sometimes I can believe as many as six impossible things before breakfast.'

'Come on, don't start quoting *Alice in Wonderland* again,' said Emily.

'It's *Through the Looking Glass* actually; required reading in the maths department.' He winked at April.

'Take no notice,' said Emily. 'He's just crazy. Now, I have some great news. Tomorrow you're leaving this place and coming to stay with us! If that's alright with you of course?'

TEN

Sarah hadn't made up her mind about April's fantastic story but she recognised that here was a lost girl who needed support. After liaising with social services, she collected her from the Addenbrookes reception hall on Sunday morning. The sun lit up the hospital complex as the car nosed through the grounds. April stared at the tall buildings. It was like a town and there were so many strange-looking cars.

'People don't usually leave hospital at the weekend, but they had no reason to keep you any longer and probably needed your room,' explained Sarah as they emerged on to a tree-lined road. Before long, the car had turned right into a quiet avenue and soon swung into the front drive of the Kendrick house. As Sarah opened the front door, a ginger cat appeared from nowhere and shot into the hall ahead of them.

'You have a cat.' Said April who loved them.

'That's one of them' said Sarah. April was about to ask how many there were when Emily appeared on the stairs.

'Come on up. I'll take you to your room. Then I'll show you around.'

April was impressed with the Kendrick's large double-fronted house with its spacious rooms and conservatory. It had been built in the 1920s and there were a number of mature trees which concealed much of it from the road. She had never seen such a large kitchen, with everything so sleek and built-in. Upstairs there were four bedrooms and two bathrooms. Her bedroom was at the back with a view of a large lawn surrounded by trees, shrubs and flowerbeds.

'Have you always lived in this house?' asked April.

'No, we used to live closer to the city centre,' said Sarah with a smile. Richard and I could walk to work in those days but Emily's new school was out this way so we came here about seven years ago.'

At dinner that evening, April was glad to see Jake was present and she was able to meet Emily's father Dr Richard Kendrick, a physics professor at the university. He was tall with dark greying hair and a small trimmed beard. He greeted April warmly with a firm handshake.

'I've been hearing all about you this week, April, so it's good to meet you in person. I hope you'll be comfortable here.'

April thanked him for his hospitality and expressed her gratitude to the whole family for taking her in. After dinner, they all moved to the living room and Richard was interested to hear about April's visitors at the hospital.

'Who is Dr Wu?' he asked Sarah who was carefully removing a black and white cat from the armchair.

'Who Wu, Wu Who' said Jake. 'I bet he was an owlish character.'

'He's a psychologist,' said Sarah, ignoring him. 'He would have been watching to see if April was alright, as well as looking for signs of a delusional young woman who believes that she is April Saunders.'

April felt alarmed. She wanted to shout: *That's me you're talking about,* but kept quiet and tried to concentrate on the conversation.

'That sounds about right' said Richard. 'I happen to know a bit about Venn. He is the head of the Home Office Disappeared Unit for East Anglia. They must think April's of considerable interest to send in such a senior man.' He paused to stir his coffee. 'Mr Venn would have been looking at you from a different standpoint, April. Did he give you an interrogation?'

'Yes, he wanted to know everything about my family, my friends and my school. There were also lots of questions about Milsham. I'm sure he didn't believe anything I told him and I can understand that.'

Richard nodded. 'He will have assumed that your account is faked and that you're just pretending to be someone who disappeared forty years ago. He will also be determined to break your story. As he hasn't succeeded so far, you probably haven't seen the last of him.'

'Dad, if Mr Venn's concerned with current disappearances, why would he bother with someone who went missing forty years ago?' asked Emily.

'He would if she claims to have come back. A potential returnee is top priority.'

'What does this 'disappeared' mean?' asked April. 'Dr Wu questioned me about it, but I didn't understand what he was talking about.'

Richard looked at April in surprise.

'Are you sure you can't remember the start of the disappearances?' She couldn't.

Everyone looked at Richard who was stirring his coffee again.

'In the 1950s people began to disappear, apparently into thin air. It started in the East and spread steadily into Europe before becoming a world phenomenon. I was young at the time but I can remember the buzz of publicity and speculation. The first occurrences here received plenty of media coverage. I can still recall the case of Mrs Walters in Doncaster in 1958. She had gone to fetch something from a drawer in her front room. When she didn't come back, her husband looked for her and she wasn't there. She wasn't anywhere in the house, the garden or the road either. She was never found. After that, the numbers of people disappearing increased steadily until the mid sixties, when the rate of those vanishing in this way remained constant. It hasn't altered to this day.'

Richard scratched the side of his nose, stood up and stepped over to the fireplace.

'During the early sixties, with the number of disappearances rising each year, there was widespread alarm. The first people claiming to be returnees began to come forward. People realised that the government was powerless and fantastic rumours and theories were everywhere, leading in some cases to outbreaks of disorder. Parliament granted the Home Office new powers to investigate disappearances and check the veracity of anyone claiming to be a returnee. They were also made responsible for providing support services to those who lost family in this way. Similar legislation was being passed in other countries at the time, as governments needed to maintain public order and morale. The Home Office Disappeared Unit has grown over the years to become a large organisation and now has six regional interrogation centres around the country. What goes on in these places is not open to public scrutiny. The Home Office support services for the bereaved are very good but there is increasing concern about their treatment of people claiming to be returnees.'

April stared down at the carpet, trying to hold herself together. There was just one scare after another in this strange world. She wanted to run away.

'Haven't people always disappeared?' she asked.

'Yes, of course they have but this is quite different. Now people vanish in the blink of an eye, leaving no trace of any kind. It can happen at any time, anywhere. Today, the rate of disappearances is almost five times greater than before it all began.'

'What's causing it?'

'That's the big question April, Nobody knows, although there are plenty of theories. As far as we know, no one has ever come back. Of course, some people have faked it for one reason or another and pretended to be returnees but their claims are soon shown to be false.'

'Why should people pretend to have come back?'

'For fame and money I should imagine. There are always people who feel lonely or inadequate. They crave the publicity their claim brings and hope that they can make their fortune as a celebrity. Then there are those who go away and hide for a while before 'returning' with all sorts of weird and wonderful tales to tell, usually about aliens. Yet again, there are sad people who genuinely believe that they are returnees and have researched their subject carefully, sometimes for years.'

Richard had returned to his chair. He offered the coffee pot around before pouring himself a second cup with a little milk. He smiled at April.

'A really convincing story would probably bring worldwide publicity and considerable earnings from media appearances. The criminal fraternity are on to this and are constantly preparing gullible people but none of those who burst upon the scene claiming to be returnees ever last. Their bubble is soon burst and they lapse back into obscurity again.'

April thought of her family and what they must have gone through.

'When people disappear it must be very upsetting for their families.'

'Of course it is,' said Sarah. 'Over time, society has adapted to the situation. When someone vanishes, a Home Office team moves in with support measures to ease people through their loss.'

Emily had been listening intently. She frowned, pushing her cup away.

'What exactly does Mr Venn want with April?'

'He wants to know whether she might be a genuine returnee,' said Richard. 'At this stage, they're just making enquiries but if they come to believe that she might be a returnee, they'll be back and will want to conduct a number of tests.'

April felt herself go cold.

'What sort of tests?'

'I don't know but I can guess that they will include a thorough interrogation designed to break a false story. There may well be use of a lie detector and hypnosis.'

Emily reddened. 'We have no idea what goes on in those wretched Home Office interrogation centres. April's not going to be taken away by any of Venn's thugs if I have anything to do with it.'

The room fell silent with just the small sound of a cup being quietly returned to its saucer. April's eyes were still on Richard. There was a catch in her voice as she asked:

'Do people come back after having these tests?'

'Yes they do. If their claim has been sufficiently prominent, there may be a short press statement confessing the falsity of their original story. As you might expect, these heavy handed procedures and confessions have led to human rights protests and conspiracy theories that it's all too much like *1984*.'

This was getting worse. April had read Orwell's terrifying book.

'Do you think people believe that they're wrong when they confess?'

'They seem to. I've never heard of anyone retracting such a confession. By the way, did they provide you with a new hairbrush in that private bathroom at the hospital?'

'Yes they did. Is that important?'

'I'm sure it is. Your nurse will have been briefed on how to collect samples of your hair from that. If a DNA test shows a close link to your father, it will probably convince them to come back for you.'

'I don't understand about this test but it's ridiculous. I'm just an ordinary person' cried April. 'I don't know why I'm here. Travelling forty years into the future is impossible.'

'Funnily enough, April, there is nothing in the laws of physics to prevent time travel into the future. It's just that in practical terms it's technically unworkable because of the phenomenal amount of energy that would be required. As I see it, there are three possibilities. The first is that you believe you are April. Second, you are just pretending to be April. Third, you really are April and that means you have travelled through time. If that turns out to be true then that raises a number of difficult questions for our physics.'

They were quiet, absorbing the different possibilities. April tensed.

'Which one do you think is true?' she whispered.

'I would go for the first possibility,' said Richard. 'I don't believe that you're trying to deceive us or that you've travelled through time.'

April felt out of her depth. She was aware that Jake had been watching her and periodically frowning at Richard's conclusions. He gave her an encouraging smile and turned to Richard.

'You're dismissing the idea of time travel, Richard, because it's beyond our present understanding. But the disappearances don't fit in with our physics either. I'm sure April is who she says she is and she's not here as a result of a time slip. I believe that April, like the Mrs Walters you referred to and the thousands of others who have disappeared over the years, passed into a parallel universe. Mrs Walters went into her front room to get something from a drawer, but when she looked round, things were subtly different and so was her reality.'

April looked at a picture over the fireplace that showed a woman pouring milk from a jug. There was something solid about the figure: a quality that she felt was slipping away from her life. She brought herself back to what Jake was saying.

He was holding up two coffee spoons, one inside the other.

'We must be intersecting with another universe almost like our own and people pass through into it. It's a one way door though, or it has been until now.' He winked at April.

'You and your parallel universe theories' said Richard with a chuckle. 'That's what comes of reading too much science fiction, although I confess that at your age I found ideas like that attractive. Theoretically, as you well know, for that theory to stand up there has to be an infinite number of universes.'

'That's quite enough physics for now,' said Sarah, who could see that April was becoming upset. She explained briefly what a DNA test was.

'Don't they have to get permission to undertake such a test?' asked Emily.

'Not these days. In this case they are taking advantage of both parties as it's important to them. If there is a close match between you and your father, April, you'll hear pretty soon, probably by the end of the week. If there isn't a match, they will probably leave you alone for the time being.'

'Perhaps you should visit your father,' suggested Jake. 'You only have Venn's word that he's got Alzheimer's.'

'That's a good point' said Sarah. 'You should never accept what others tell you as they might make things up for their own purposes. Always try and verify facts for yourself.'

'I don't know where he is' said April.

'Leave that to me. I'll soon find him' said Jake.

ELEVEN

April woke up. She was back in her own familiar bedroom. Just then, the door opened and her mother came in.

'Mum, I'm home' cried April.

But her mother didn't respond. She walked over to the window and looked out then gave a last look round before leaving and closing the door. April swung out of bed and pulled on her dressing gown and slippers. She stepped out into the hall and called, but there was no answer. Mum must be downstairs. She hurried down and opened the kitchen door. Mum wasn't there but Fluff was sitting on the table.

'Get down Fluff' she said to the cat but Fluff didn't move. Then she remembered. Fluff shouldn't be here. She died more than a year ago.

'Everything's going to be alright April,' said Fluff. She jumped off the table and left through the cat flap in the back *door, her bushy tail disappearing last. April turned round. Someone was knocking at the kitchen door.*

'Come in' she called, but the knocking went on.

She opened her eyes just as Emily peered round the door.

'Hi. Did I wake you up?'

That morning Emily and April went shopping in Cambridge. April was overawed by the mass of traffic and crowds of people. She liked the pedestrian areas best and wanted to look at everything in the shops. There was one window full of colour television screens showing a news item about the queen. She had become an old lady. Emily led them through a number of fashion stores, picking out clothes for her. After a couple of hours, April felt overwhelmed so they retreated to an open air table near the market for a drink.

April sipped her coffee and listened to an overweight woman talking to her companion at the next table:

'The way I see it, I'm entitled to an extra day off each month.'
'Yeah.'
'After all, I've been there much longer than she has.'
'Tha's right.'

'Penny for them?' said Emily. 'You were far away.'

'I was thinking that the world has changed but people seem much the same.'

'I'm not surprised.'

'I'm so grateful for your help,' said April. 'I can't think what would have happened to me if I hadn't met you.'

'Don't worry about it. We were all keen for you to come and stay. Mum could never resist helping waifs and strays. That's why we've got four cats around the place. There's Ginger, Felix who's black and white, Tiger the tabby and Desmond who's long haired and an attractive kind of coffee brown and white.

He hasn't settled in yet and keeps wandering off. They're all castrated males from the rescue centre. Dad put his foot down after two, then again after three.' She laughed. 'I think Mum's got the message at last so we're probably going to settle for four cats. That is, until she hears about another stranded kitty. Watch out for Ginger, though, as he bites.'

'I suppose I'm another stray.'

'Absolutely! But we'll soon get you organised. Drink up, it's time to shop. You need shoes.'

They crowded onto a bus with their shopping bags and unloaded them back at the house, after which they enjoyed a light lunch on the patio.

April moved around her bedroom putting away her new clothes. She sat on the bed and tried to wrestle with the question: why am I here? Will I ever be able to return home? She was scared that she might never be able to adjust to this strange world. The thought that Mr Venn's men could take her away frightened her, but she had no choice but to take each day as it came.

The following morning, she went with Emily to the hairdresser in the city centre. Both girls had their hair done, with April's straight blonde locks cut and bobbed around the ears. It looked great, but she couldn't ignore the nagging feeling of concern when she studied her appearance.

'I didn't recognise myself when I looked in the mirror for the first time in the hospital,' said April. She smiled. 'Now I have no idea who this face belongs to.'

At the same time, the memory of that unfamiliar face worried her. She tried to put it out of her mind.

That afternoon, Emily had an appointment in London so April was left in the house by herself. Everything had been so hectic that she welcomed the chance of some solitude. Emily had provided her with a stack of 'essential' books and magazines to accompany her flow of advice on clothes, customs, music and behaviour. She lay on her bed reading to try and catch up with the last forty years. So much had changed. People dressed and even spoke differently. And they all knew so much more than she did. The more she reflected on her situation, the more vulnerable she felt, wondering whether she could ever fit in. She had no real identity, no family or school. April had never thought how important these things were until they had gone. She had no roots or way of earning a living. The typing she'd learned in school wasn't any use as typewriters had disappeared like the dinosaurs. She needed to talk to Emily. April had stopped trying to understand how she had got here. Even Richard didn't seem to understand it.

In spite of the prosperity and abundance of 1999 and the generosity of the Kendricks, April longed to return home. She had tried reading the magazines Emily had provided but the loneliness gnawed away at her self confidence. It was like being on a desert island where there were no ships to rescue her because there were no ships. She shuddered and looked out onto the garden. There was a squirrel lolloping along by the trees and for a moment she was back in Milsham Park as a little girl holding her mother's hand.

Her attention was drawn back by the sound of a door closing downstairs and a voice calling her name. It was Jake. She ran down to greet him and had to stop herself flinging her arms around his neck. Her knight had arrived in the dark forest to rescue her from dragons. She shrugged off the image and saw that he was clutching a carrier bag. He had been to a sandwich shop and bought lunch. They carried everything out to the table on the patio and ate.

'I'm so glad you came. I'm still struggling to understand what's happened to me,' said April.

'So am I' said Jake, frowning with concentration. 'Think of your life as a book where you live on one page at a time. You can't see ahead or know how many pages there are but the book is always there.'

'It sounds like a diary.'

'Yes it's a bit like that. Our life experience writes in one page at a time. If we were able to look ahead, all the succeeding pages would be blank.'

'It sounds weird. Did you think this up?'

He grinned. 'Yeah, I suppose I did and I'm not sure if it helps. Look, I've brought you a present.' He reached into his carrier bag and passed her a book. It was an attractive hardback with a blue and silver geometrical design on the cover. Opening it, April saw that it was a notebook with ruled pages.

'It's for you to keep as a diary. I remembered you said that you kept a diary before, so I thought you might like it.'

'Thank you, Jake. It's beautiful and so thoughtful of you.'

He squeezed the hand she proffered across the table.

'I'm glad you like it but be careful what you write as it is inevitable that someone will read through it at some time.'

'Emily didn't mention you were coming today. Did she know?'

'No she didn't. I'm not sure whether I should be saying this but there's something about Emily I need to tell you.'

He pushed a piece of bread around his plate. April sat still, wondering what was coming. He looked down and gave an intake of breath and gathered himself together.

'Emily is a lovely person and can be a good friend for you but try not to put all your trust in her.'

'Why not? Is there something I need to know?'

'Yes there is.'

It felt like the ground beneath her was beginning to open up, just as she had begun to feel secure.

'Jake, you have to tell me.'

'I'm not sure if I should, but I reckon you're entitled to know. Seven years ago, when Emily was twelve, her younger sister Becky was knocked down and killed by a car. The sisters were out walking and had an argument. Emily insisted that Becky hold her hand as they crossed the busy road. Becky refused, ran into the road and straight under a car. Emily saw it happen. After the initial shock, she became unstable and has been in therapy ever since. That's where she is today, visiting her shrink. She copes well these days but can't escape from her feelings of guilt.'

'This is terrible. But sisters often argue. Surely it was just an accident.'

'Was it? Emily blames herself. She had become exasperated and told her sister to piss off. She was a bossy elder sister and Becky had reacted and ran away. Emily is convinced that if she hadn't got so angry, Becky would still be alive today. Since that time, Emily has had a hole in her life and she doesn't know how to fill it. She has shut her pain away in a locked room so she can continue to function, but she still finds it difficult to make close friends. The burden of loss runs through the family and is still too painful to be spoken about. Although Becky has gone, the memory of her is still here. Sarah also felt guilty at the time as she had sent the fractious sisters out together.'

He took her hand again.

'I'm telling you this, so you're clear about Emily's situation and why you are so special to the family. If Becky had lived, she would have been sixteen now. I see Sarah's love for her youngest daughter finding its expression in caring for you. Of course, she is well aware of that and you need have no fear that she won't treat you as yourself. You must have found the generosity of the family a bit surprising. You are a gift that they could never have imagined. Promise me that you won't mention any of this.'

April jumped up and turned away.

'I wish you hadn't told me. How do you think it makes me feel? It's bad enough struggling to hold on here without being told that everyone is seeing me as Emily's younger sister.'

She covered her face with her hands. He had no right to put this onto her. She would have to be careful what she said from now on, particularly with Emily.

'I'm sorry, I know you already have a lot to worry about but I thought you ought to know. I never meant to upset you and seem to have put my foot in it again.'

In spite of her resentment, April felt touched by his concern.

'It's alright really. It's such a shock. Emily did warn me you were crazy.'

'I'm not crazy. I've just been mixed up for the last fifteen years.'

'That's better. I like it when you say silly things.'

'It can't be helped. You can find mixed-up people everywhere. You should see the characters in my department.'

'Do many of them suffer from being all mixed-up?'

'Not really, they seem to enjoy it.'

They carried the plates and glasses back to the kitchen and washed and dried them together in silence. As Jake turned away from the cupboard, April was standing close behind him. They came together in a close embrace and April felt the throbbing of her heart.

'Better be getting back,' said Jake with an awkward grin. They walked out to the hall and he was gone.

April could still feel his arms around her. She had wanted him to kiss her.

Felix had come down and was sitting on the bottom stair blinking at her through sleepy eyes. She stroked him and went out into the sunny back garden as she needed to think about what Jake had said. The gardener had mowed the lawn the previous day and she took in the aroma of fresh cut grass as she walked across into the shade of the trees. Feeling a sudden chill, she turned to look back and froze.

The house had become a crumbling ruin. Everything was grey. In the silence there was darkness by the side of the house but it wasn't darkness, it was an empty void; there was nothing there. She turned away shaking with fear and closed her eyes. Her chest felt tight and her heart was pounding. Her legs gave way and she slumped to a kneeling position against the coarse bark of a tree.

She stayed there for a long time before hearing the song of a chaffinch. She opened her eyes and, looking round, was relieved to find everything was back to normal. The colours, the sounds and the smells of the afternoon were as before. Sitting in the kitchen afterwards feeling drained, she tried to think about the terrifying experience. It was like the occasion in the hospital corridor but this time it was far worse and the blackness was much nearer. It must be caused by that bang on her head. She knew she should tell Sarah but that might mean returning to hospital where Mr Venn's men could come and take her away.

She needed to stay with her new family so she said nothing and as the days went by she tried to make herself useful by helping Sarah in the kitchen. It was full of strange inventions like the microwave oven. Sarah explained how it worked but April couldn't see how a few waves could cook things so quickly. The freezer was easy to understand as it was like a fridge only much colder. She loved the ceramic hob that glowed red when you turned it on. She offered to do the washing up but had forgotten about the dishwasher.

Emily had also introduced her to modern technology. Her mobile phone ran on a tiny battery and she could use it anywhere. The real mystery was her laptop and the internet. Emily explained how it worked with satellites but it still seemed like magic. Her bedroom had a big poster of someone called David Bowie on the wall. April was puzzled as he was wearing thick makeup.

Early next morning she opened her new diary, staring at the blank pages. There was so much to write about. Where to begin?

May 27th
I'm frightened and feel so lost here. I'm lucky to have been taken in by a wonderful family, but I'm homesick. Most of all I miss Mum. I'd give anything to go back and be with her, helping with the Sunday dinner again or just going up to the shops arm in arm. The feeling of loss is so painful. It's almost a physical thing. I don't

know what the future holds for me here and I have some serious things to worry about. I can't see how I'll ever get over this feeling of losing all those things that I took for granted. I know I shall have to adapt but right now I don't want to think about it. I want to go home.

. . .

Roger Venn followed the young aide down a long corridor in the Home Office. He was finally ushered into a large room and crossed the faded carpet towards a long table where seven people were already seated in the ornate but bare room. This was a private meeting without a secretary or recording equipment. Sir Harold Anderson who was chairing the meeting, rose and came forward to shake hands and introduce him to the other members. Roger sat down at the end of the table, feeling uncomfortable as he was scrutinised by the committee.

'We've all read your report, Roger,' said Sir Harold. 'It's an interesting case but she must be faking it?'

'If she is sir, it's an impressive effort. She seems wholly genuine and is word perfect on Milsham in 1959, being aware of things you wouldn't have expected her to know.'

'She's obviously got a friend or family member who was a teenager living there at that time. She's been carefully prepared and has absorbed it all as if it were her own experience,' insisted a woman in a navy blue suit.

'Naturally this was my own assessment at first,' conceded Roger, 'but there are a number of things that don't add up. First, she has been beaten up and assaulted. Second, her story is inaccurate in that she seems to be totally unaware of the disappearances, even though they were the most prominent news story throughout 1959. If she had been properly briefed, such an error would be inconceivable. However, her account of the van driver is entirely accurate. One revelation is her claim that she left her bag in the van which contained a book of poetry. She even named the poet. I've checked that and it's true, although no mention of it appeared in any published police report.'

A ripple of astonishment went around the table.

'Clearly we're dealing with a well constructed plan' said navy suit again. 'Someone has gone to a lot of trouble to set this up. It could be a team with access to police files.'

'What's this business about her friend from 1959 not appearing in the records? Is that another inconsistency?' barked a red-faced man.

'No it isn't,' answered Sir Harold. 'Roger was just using a well known technique for destabilising a false story.'

'That's right, sir' agreed Roger. 'Mandy Daniels was still living there at the time, although her family emigrated to Australia in 1965.'

'As you can see from the report,' said Roger, 'in 1959 April was on her way to visit her boyfriend James Fleming when she disappeared. We haven't tracked down Mr Fleming yet but I'm confident we shall do so very soon.'

'When are you getting the DNA test results?' Sir Harold asked.

'They should be through by the end of the week, on Thursday or Friday at the latest.'

Sir Harold nodded. 'That will be a crucial part of the puzzle. If there is no match we can disregard the whole thing. If she moves to exploit her story, a statement to the media should cut her off at the knees. Can you take care of that, Gerald?' He received a nod of assent. 'If there is a DNA match we have to act quickly.'

'There's no rush surely,' said a bald-headed man. 'She doesn't know about the test, so we can make plans in our own time.'

'There may not be much time,' said Roger. 'There are dozens of people already who know about her claims. I'm surprised that the local press hasn't already got onto it.'

'I take your point, Roger' said Sir Harold. 'You've done an excellent job to date but if the DNA result is positive, we shall meet here again next Monday at midday. She will be defined as a potential returnee and Operation Prodigal Son will be implemented straight away. We will move her out to Callingford House in Norfolk for tests. I shall need the usual watertight legal cover. Can you prepare that, Donald?' A tall man with silver hair nodded. 'For the time being, this remains your responsibility, Roger. Make the necessary arrangements to keep her under constant surveillance.'

Roger retraced his steps along the corridor. What had he let himself in for? If anything went wrong he'd be blamed. This wasn't why he had joined the Civil Service. He was proud of the fact that he had risen through the hierarchy without having had an Oxbridge education. He had earned promotion through his ability to grasp a mass of details and organise the appropriate course of action. He was proud of the achievements of his support teams across East Anglia.

It hadn't been easy growing up in a family that was constantly feuding. It was a painful experience for a sensitive child and he had retreated into his own world and avoided painful confrontations ever since. Now he was feeling distinctly uncomfortable. One way or another, he must rid himself of this wretched girl.

Back at his desk after the meeting, Sir Harold sat with concern etched on his face. The committee would have to go through the legal procedures but they were designed to deal with false claims. This case was entirely different. Although he had never seen one before, there was no doubt in his mind that this girl was a genuine returnee and she should disappear without trace as soon as possible.

When the disappearances first began there had been widespread fear and public disorder in some countries. Measures were needed to maintain order and public morale. Anything that jeopardised that needed to be dealt with promptly. There had been a few genuine returnees over the years but they had nothing useful to say and no one had ever found out about them as they had been eliminated quickly to maintain the official line that no one ever came back. He had a special telephone number, although he had never had occasion to use it. All he had to do was to give the order. No one would ever know. He stared at her picture. She looked such an innocent young thing but he had to do his duty. He sighed, unlocked his drawer, found the number and picked up the phone.

TWELVE

Emily and Jake cooked a vegetarian stir fry meal for the family on Wednesday evening. The main news around the dinner table was a visit at Sarah's surgery from the police. They had requested permission to place an officer outside the house. It was a short term measure to protect April's security.

'I think we're expected to agree' she said.

'No more than two weeks' said Richard. 'We don't want them around our necks any longer than is necessary.' He smiled at April. 'I shouldn't worry, I'm sure there's nothing to be concerned about.'

She stared at the floor. What were they protecting her from?

'I also had a call from *The Cambridge Evening News,*' said Sarah. 'They've found out about April and want to come here and interview her, take a few pictures, that sort of thing. I said I'd let them know.' They all discussed it and agreed that as April's doctor, Sarah would call them back and explain that April needed more time and she would contact them in due course. April smiled with relief. She could do without another interrogation.

'April, I've found out where your father is,' said Jake. 'He's in a nursing home in Enfield. Em and I could drive you down there tomorrow. I could do with a break and we could visit Milsham on the way.'

'I'd like to see Milsham' said April, 'but I'm not ready to see my dad.'

'If you are going back to your home town,' warned Sarah, 'you must be prepared to find the experience distressing. There have been considerable changes during the last forty years and much of Milsham may be unrecognisable. It's quite early for you to be doing this. Are you sure you're ready for what is bound to be a something of a shock?'

'I've got to try and live in the present,' said April. 'There's a part of me that believes that my home will be there just as I remember it and that I can go back. I know that seeing Milsham as it is today will be difficult, but in the long run I hope it will help me to adjust to living here now.'

The next morning, the three set off in Emily's car. She had decided to avoid the motorway and drove down the A10. The overnight rain had stopped and the air was still heavy with moisture as the woody smells of the countryside flooded in through the open windows. April sat in the front next to Emily so she would have a good view of the passing green fields. In spite of her confident words the previous evening, she was feeling tense and needed a distraction. She swivelled round to look at Jake.

'Jake. Tell me about yourself and your family?'

'I come from a long line of misfits and ne'er do wells,' said Jake. 'My father is president of the Flat Earth Society and my mother campaigns tirelessly for the return of eighteenth century English. She had her head turned by reading too much Jane Austen as a girl.'

'Jake, stop teasing April or you can walk the rest of the way,' said Emily.

After that, April learned that Jake's family history dated from 1938 when his great grandparents escaped to England from Nazi Germany with a one year old toddler and settled in London's East End. Fearing more anti-Semitism there, they promptly changed their name from Bernstein to Burnstone. Their son grew up and went on to make a fortune in property, the music industry and a string of Italian restaurants. His son, Jake's father, is a senior lecturer in Mathematics at Cardiff University and his mother is a History teacher.

'Mum and dad were teenage lovers. Dad was only nineteen when I was born in 1981.'

'Are your grandparents still alive?' April asked.

'Yes they are. They live in Switzerland but they also have an apartment in London.'

'How about you, April?' asked Emily. 'Tell us about your friends.'

'My two closest friends are Mandy and Brian. I miss them so much. Mr. Venn told me that Mandy didn't exist. I don't understand why.'

'I bet he was lying,' said Emily. 'I wouldn't trust that man.'

'Right enough,' said Jake. 'We can test that. If you give me the details of your friends and their families, I will look them up on the 1961 census records. If Mandy is there, that will prove Venn was lying.'

'If you could trace them that would be super' said April.

'We've passed Hoddesdon and Broxbourne so we're nearly there' said Emily. She signalled left and drove down a long leafy road. 'I'll find somewhere to park, then we can have a look around.'

They walked together down Milsham High Street where men hung around in gloomy shop doorways and stared at them. April looked from side to side. Sometimes she paused and frowned at one of the buildings before they moved on. Finally she stopped and stared down at the pavement.

'This street has been ruined. All the shops have gone, even the newsagent on the corner where I used to badger mum for sweets when I was little. They've all gone. These betting places, scruffy hairdressers and foreign food shops are horrible. It's like the run-down areas of North London I remember. They've reorganised the roads to cope with all the extra cars, but the trolleybus wires have gone. Mandy and I would often catch the trolley down to Edmonton on Saturday mornings to go window shopping. We never had much money to spend.'

They walked on until April stopped at a corner.

'This is my road. I lived down there on the left hand side. Now it's full of cars.'

'Do you want to go and see your old home?' asked Emily.

April looked along the road at the familiar shape of her house behind the line of cars. It was no longer the childhood home that welcomed and enfolded her within its walls. That was forty years in the past. It looked much the same, but it wouldn't know her any more.

'No I don't want to see it. I was living here only two weeks ago. I grew up here. The shops, the local people and everything in the High Street were all part of my life. This is like being in a nightmare. Please can we go?'

'Of course' said Jake. 'Let's get a bite to eat.'

• • •

They sat around a wooden table in the garden of a country pub with three enormous ploughman's lunches. April toyed with her food but had no appetite. Her distress was palpable as she pushed her plate away and bent forward burying her face in her arms and cried. The others were at a loss to know what to say.

'Things will get better over time, I promise you,' said Emily. 'You were brave to come here so soon, as you knew it would be very different.'

'I'm sorry I suggested it. I didn't realise how upsetting it would be for you' said Jake. April sat up and brushed the tears from her face.

'It's alright. I hoped that seeing Milsham would be reassuring, but I never dreamt that it would have changed so much here. It's far worse than it used to be. Even the people have changed. It was a thriving, busy little town. Now it's horrible. How could that have happened?'

'The decline of so many High Streets stems from the changing patterns of work, transport and shopping habits.' said Emily. 'We saw signs for a big supermarket on our way in. That would have seen off most of your little shops as they wouldn't have been able to compete.'

'It's worse in the United States,' said Jake. 'Some town centres have been reduced to empty ghost towns. Huge new shopping malls around the perimeter have sucked all the life out of them.'

'There were some places around here that were special, like the woods and the river walks,' said April. 'I don't want to go near them. I'd like to keep those memories intact.' She managed a sad smile. 'Thanks for bringing me. I'm sorry I've been such poor company.'

'I don't want to hear that kind of talk or I'll insist on my rock'n roll CD being played all the way back,' said Jake.

'Oh no. Anything but that,' cried Emily with mock horror.

'Do you want to go and see your dad this afternoon?' asked Emily.

April shook her head. 'No. This visit has been more than enough.'

'Never mind, we could come down and see him another day?'

'No. I don't want to see him.'

They fell silent again and concentrated on their meal until Jake's phone rang. He prodded a couple of keys and scanned the incoming text, whistling in surprise.

'What was that?' asked Emily.

'Just a message about something I've been working on.'

Before they left, Emily disappeared to the toilet. April saw that Jake was looking at her.

'What is it?'

'I dunno. I feel bad about bringing you here.'

He reached across the table and gave her hand a squeeze, holding onto it as their eyes met. She felt her tension dissolving as her heart beat faster. At that moment she knew that was what she needed. Being constantly organised and told what to do all the time was helpful, but she felt a need for love. She smiled at him and withdrew her hand.

...

After dinner that evening, Sarah beckoned to April who followed her into the study. It was a small book lined room that faced west so the evening sunlight streamed in from across the lawn. The door was closed and they sat together on two easy chairs by the window. A small clock ticked quietly. Sarah looked serious.

'Jake received a text message today showing that the result of your DNA test was negative. He thought it best that I speak to you about it. It means that your dad is not your biological father.'

April stared at her.

'That's not true. Of course he's my father. The test must be wrong. They've got things mixed up.'

'We can't deny that possibility but it's extremely unlikely. I'm sure they would have been thorough. I'm afraid that the result is a near certainty.'

'What have I done to deserve this?' cried April. 'The last three weeks have been a terrible ordeal with one thing after another. I'm trying hard to adjust to life here but every time I gain a bit of confidence something comes along to undermine it. Soon there will be nothing left of my world to hold on to. You were right about going back to Milsham. It was frightening.' She burst into noisy tears. 'I want my mum.'

Sarah rose and hugged her. She was still a little girl inside. She held her close until the crying subsided then produced a box of tissues.

'Do you feel able to talk about this?' April nodded. 'I see that you were born in the middle of the Second World War. As your birth date was in April 1943, your original conception would have been during the summer of the previous year. Was your father at home during that period do you know?'

'Mum and Dad couldn't be together all the time as he was working in the munitions factory in Edmonton. When the bombing started, Mum had gone to live with her sister out near Buckingham. My uncle worked there on a farm. It was much safer for her and Carol out there. I suppose Dad wasn't able to get up very often as he was working six days a week and the trains weren't that reliable.'

'I'm sure you can see what I'm getting at,' said Sarah. 'Your mother, a young woman missing her husband, would have been starved of the love and care that she needed. In those circumstances, it would not be surprising if she succumbed to the attentions of someone else. Such things happened during the war more often than is admitted.'

April sat quietly, feeling at a loss.

'Mum was born in wartime, just like me, except that it was the First World War. Her dad, my granddad, was killed out there so she never knew him and neither did I. Mum said that the battlefield became covered in poppies the following summer, one for the soul of every soldier that was killed. Do people still wear poppies in November?'

'Yes they do.'

April stared down at the regular pattern in the rug. At last she looked up.

'Thanks for telling me and for being so nice. What's going to happen now?'

'Hopefully the Home Office people will conclude that you've been faking it and will leave you alone. On the other hand, they may draw the same conclusion that we have been discussing so we had better prepare for that.'

May 28th
I'm horrified by the changes in Milsham. I can't believe it has changed so much. I felt like a stranger who has descended into hell. It's something else that's been taken away. I'll never be able to go back – Emily says that some places, like Cambridge, became much nicer over the years while others have gone downhill. Why did that have to be my home? Poor old Milsham.

The next day was Friday and April and Emily stayed at home. During the morning they played badminton on the lawn before sitting on the patio with cold drinks. They were surprised by the appearance of a uniformed policeman who had strolled round after hearing their voices. He explained that he was the first one of a rota of officers who would be guarding the house. Emily showed him around, after which he took up his position by the front door. The girls thought he was rather handsome.

After lunch they sat in the living room and April told Emily about her concerns for her future.

'Everything has changed. I'm not equipped to do anything. I should be taking my O-levels this summer but without them

I haven't any qualifications at all. Worst of all, I don't officially exist.'

'Don't worry,' said Emily. 'You're just starting to adjust to life here. You need to absorb the whole culture until you feel part of it, then you will find the confidence to be yourself. For the time being I'll continue to bring you up to date.'

'I'm really grateful but that's another problem. How am I ever going to repay you? You have given me everything and all I can do is take from you. I should like to be able to pay my way or at least make some contribution. Put yourself in my place and see how you would feel?'

'I can't imagine being in your place but I know what you're getting at. We both have enough self respect to resent having to live on others for too long. Let's put our heads together to see whether there might be a way…'

The discussion went on all afternoon, at the end of which they had formed a plan. Over dinner that evening Emily outlined it to the family:

'We're all agreed that April is having a difficult time adjusting to the loss of her family, friends and school. She is making great efforts to adapt and is now coming through that first phase and feels ready to become more involved with life here.'

She looked across at April and continued. 'She wants to try and stand on her own feet and is anxious not to be a burden on this family.'

'You're not a burden,' said Sarah. 'We like having you here and you can stay as long as you like.'

'Absolutely,' said Richard. 'It's important not to try and run before you can walk, April. I know things have been difficult, that was bound to be the case, but you're doing very well. We can talk about what comes next but it's one step at a time.'

'Dad, April is potentially famous. People everywhere will be fascinated by her story. There is a potential for her to earn a great deal from the media.'

'You can't be serious, Emily!' exploded Sarah. 'This isn't one of your pet projects. This is April's life and she's had enough to cope with without the stresses of becoming a celebrity. You know how the media work. They puff you up for a while and then they tear you down. They're only interested in their sales.'

Richard looked at April with a serious expression. 'Trying to sell your story to the media would be opening Pandora's Box. Your life wouldn't be your own any more. You would have no way of knowing where it would end and the outcome could be dangerous. The Disappeared Unit have already got us under surveillance. If they see you trying to capitalise on your situation, they could step in and take you away. We mustn't risk that.'

'Everything you're saying is right,' said Emily, 'but becoming famous will give April some protection from these people. They wouldn't dare pick her up if she's become a household name.'

Sarah rounded on her. 'We can't have this, Emily. I know what you're like when you get the bit between your teeth. We're here to protect and care for April, not exploit her.'

Richard interceded to head off a conflict. 'Emily, your idea that April would be immune from the forces of the state is naive. Even if it were true for a while, they would bide their time as all fame is transitory. When she had slipped back into obscurity, they would pounce and would be bound to give her a hard time. You aren't taking this risk, Emily. It's going to be borne entirely by April. She isn't ready for such an undertaking. I'm surprised you can't see that.'

'Of course there are risks, Dad. April is going to get into the papers whatever we do as they see her as a big news story. We're not equipped to protect her. The tabloids could descend at any time, that's why her exposure to the media needs professional help and guidance. I propose that we ask Marcus Clarke. He may not be universally liked, but he is a respected and successful publicist who has a reputation of supporting his clients. If he takes April on, the media will have to go through him. That will take the pressure off her and ensure that her story is told in a responsible way. April could earn thousands, even tens of thousands of pounds. It would give her some real security.'

The meal was over and they all helped in clearing the table and taking everything out to the kitchen. When the coffee was ready, they were seated in the living room and the debate continued.

'You've obviously thought this through' said Richard. 'I can see the merit in the idea but it's far too soon for April. I don't share your view that the tabloids are about to descend on us. I'm sure if April keeps her head down she can build up her confidence and familiarise herself with this world. If her story is as big as you say, it will still be big in six or twelve months' time.'

'April's not ready to face the stresses of dealing with the media or the sudden fame that could result from the publicity,' warned Sarah. 'Marcus Clarke may be good at what he does but he's in it for the money and will want to maximise the publicity. I don't believe that doing this will keep her safe nor do I feel that she needs anything like this at this time. I have been thinking about your interrupted education, April. We could begin by dealing with that.'

'You're both being overly cautious,' said Emily. 'The plan is that we'll do this together. I'll stick to April like glue. Nobody's going to exploit her. When she feels that she has done enough publicity then we'll stop, whatever Marcus Clarke says. The sooner she is in the public eye the better for the protection it will give her.'

'April hasn't got a national insurance number or even a birth certificate,' said Richard. 'Without these things she isn't employable.'

'She does have a birth certificate from 1943,' said Jake. 'Everything can be derived from that.'

'I wondered how long it would be before we heard from you.' Sarah said.

'Emily rang me at the lab this afternoon to tell me about it,' said Jake. 'I think it's a great idea. I'm all for it and I can help by providing security.'

'The one person we haven't heard from,' said Richard, 'is the one who will have to go through with it. How do you feel about this, April?'

April looked at everyone in turn, wrestling with her uncertainty. The plan agreed with Emily that afternoon had seemed so exciting at the time. Now it seemed dangerous and more than she could manage. She knew she couldn't face it.

'I don't think I'm ready to do this.'

'Don't worry, April' said Emily. 'No one is going to persuade you to do anything you don't feel confident about.'

'It's a wise decision,' said Richard. 'You need to keep your head down for the time being, then hopefully the Home Office will leave you alone. There's time enough to get out into life.'

Later that evening Emily had to face her mother in the study.

'I didn't like to say too much in front of April,' said Sarah, 'but this plan of yours is the opposite of what she needs. She must keep a low profile to avoid the attentions of the Home Office. This is our first priority. I have been speaking to Dad about what we can do to equip her to cope in future. We even discussed the possibility of her renouncing her story to get the Home Office off her back. As her doctor, I could, with her permission, say that she lost her memory because of the accident but is beginning to realise that she isn't April Saunders. Handled carefully, that should satisfy them as they don't like people claiming to be returnees. I'm angry with you for cooking this up without discussing it with me. April isn't your plaything or a social experiment. I don't think either you or Jake can fully appreciate what she is going through at the moment. She isn't able to look after herself. She needs our care and support not your wild schemes for publicity.'

Emily stood looking out into the garden. When she turned, her eyes were full of tears.

'I'm sorry, Mum, but if April wasn't under threat from Venn and his Home Office thugs I would be with you wholeheartedly. But the only way I can see to meet that danger is to get April out into the open. People will rally round her. I know they will. Then the Home Office wouldn't dare touch her. As it happens, she doesn't seem to be ready so we go on as we are.'

The following morning, Sarah and Emily went shopping in the city. They had invited April but she declined. She was worried about the discussion of the previous evening and felt the need to be alone. Before Richard left for work, he had been firm with her about not wandering off. The policeman was there to protect her. April found that hard to believe. She wasn't four years old. It was too lovely a morning to be cooped up. A walk up the avenue wouldn't do any harm. There was never anyone about as far as she could see and she felt the need to do something on her own even if it was only going for a short walk. After Richard had left, she waited until the policeman had walked round to check the back of the house. Then she slipped through the front door and out on the road where she was soon hidden from the house by the trees.

Connaught Avenue was an attractive tree-lined road. April walked slowly, taking in the sights and sounds. Everything was quiet apart from the low rumble of passing traffic along the main road. She saw that the detached houses were all different and several were larger than the Kendricks'. Most were hidden by screens of trees, shrubs or high walls, although they all had open gateways so she was able to see each one as she passed. One impressive residence had bright flowerbeds and an attractive lawn with a sundial in the centre. Another was completely paved over. She supposed that would be for cars. They must have a lot of them. The Kendricks' had three and that was probably normal here. A car started up nearby, edging slowly backwards into the road. She noticed there were a number of cars parked along the road but she had only seen one woman walking a small dog on the other side who hadn't given her a glance.

After about ten minutes she turned and looked back. There were two people standing on the pavement near the Kendricks' house. They seemed to be watching her. She felt unsure and started to walk back. A car door slammed and a man and a woman came up behind her. Two more were crossing the road to intercept her. In minutes she was surrounded by demanding reporters with cameras.

'How are you feeling April? How are you finding 1999?'

'What do you miss most about 1959? What are your future plans?'

'What's it like staying with the Kendricks? Have you traced your family yet?'

They plied her with questions, but she wouldn't answer and held her hand up to her face to ward off the cameras.

'Let me go. I want to go back.'

They wouldn't give way. She was hemmed in so she turned her back on them and screamed as loudly as she could. She soon heard running feet.

'It's the police. Let's go.'

They scattered like rooks after a gunshot, fleeing to their cars.

'Are you all right?' asked the policeman from the house.

'Yes I'm okay. They wouldn't let me come back.'

After that incident, everyone agreed that April should never go out on her own again. April and Emily had been going to the pool for an early swim each morning. Now they had to consider whether that would be possible any more. The newshounds wanted a story and would be unlikely to be put off by Emily's presence. The conversation lapsed into silence.

'Perhaps we should contact Marcus Clarke after all,' said April.

May 30th
What's the matter with me? Richard told me not to go out, but after I sneaked past the policeman into the road, I was surrounded by reporters asking loads of questions. Does this mean I won't be able to go out again? Emily wants me to go with Marcus Clarke but Sarah and Richard don't want me to – it's a scary prospect but I can't see any other way out of this mess —

. . .

Kevin read his incoming email with quivering excitement. His contribution had been recognised at last and he had been given a responsible task. A great historical event was about to unfold and he would be at the centre of it. He read it through again.

Thank you for your message. Representatives will be arriving next week. In the meantime keep her under observation and report any developments immediately. Delete this message after reading and do not print it. Security is paramount.

He could hardly believe it. Elders from the Church of the Second Coming must be on their way to Cambridge all the way from Kansas City. His elation was tempered by the realisation that he was in no position to keep April under observation. He had already agreed to work through this weekend and, now she had left the hospital, he had no idea where she had gone.

On Saturday two London members of the church arrived in Cambridge. They met Kevin on Saturday night and plied him with questions. There were more facts that they wanted to know and Kevin was instructed to make the necessary enquiries as discreetly as he could. By Sunday night they had built up a coherent picture. They knew where she was staying and early on Monday morning a car had taken up a position in Connaught Avenue with a clear view of the Kendrick house entrance. They had also been joined by another couple in a second car.

On Monday morning Emily drove to the railway station with April and they boarded a train to London. They didn't notice an ordinary-looking couple who caught the same train.

THIRTEEN

Both girls felt nervous about the forthcoming appointment with Marcus Clarke that morning. April looked out of the window as the train whined steadily towards London. She tried to smile at Emily. What had she let herself in for? Sarah had been reassuring and explained that if she was worried she could call a halt at any time. She shouldn't allow herself to be intimidated by others or seduced by promises of fame and money. It was her life and she should keep that in mind.

'I'm glad that Emily is with you April, but remember that me and Richard are here for you as well. Contact us any time if you want to talk.'

The steady rhythm of the train lengthened as it slowed and came to a stop at Bishops Stortford. This was where James had caught the train to school every day. April realised with surprise that she had hardly thought about him during the last couple of hectic weeks.

'Wake up' said Emily. 'You looked preoccupied for a moment there.'

'I was remembering James. He used to live near here.'

'Did you like him?'

'Very much and I know he cared for me but he was so wrapped up in his own world there wasn't much room for anyone else. He found it difficult to talk about his feelings and got himself worked up and said horrible things to me when he finished our relationship. I still feel wounded and angry and wonder whether he even understood how he felt.'

'It sounds like he still had some growing up to do. It's not uncommon with boys.'

'How are things with you and Jake? You're alright aren't you?'

'Sure, we're fine. I'm very fond of that crazy guy and we have great sex.'

The train resumed its journey as April thought about this strange new world. Things seemed much the same as in her time but they couldn't be with all the talk about sex everywhere. She found it difficult to cope with. She smiled at Emily.

'When I was fourteen, a boy asked me to go to the pictures with him. I said that I would and he collected me from home. We went to the cinema and after the film he walked me home and said goodnight. In all that time he never touched me. He didn't even hold my hand. I wanted him to hold my hand but he never did. I bet it's not like that these days.'

'Don't be so sure,' said Emily. 'There are still lots of shy boys at that age. Now, I have something for you. It's a pepper spray. Keep it to hand and if someone threatens you, just squirt it in their face and they will be disabled long enough for you to get away. Don't tell anyone that you have it because it's not exactly legal. I'll show you how to use it later.'

She brought out a small cylinder and April popped it into her bag.

'Do you think I might be threatened?'

'Not particularly but, if you become well known, you might meet people who'll make a nuisance of themselves. Keep it for emergencies only.'

April stared at the changes to Liverpool Street Station. She was used to the great dark and dusty concourse with a roof blackened by the soot of the last hundred years. Now it was bright and clean with a colourful assembly of cafes and shops. As they crossed the concourse there was a discernible aroma of coffee and cooked food. They descended into the underground for a short ride to Finsbury Square. A brisk walk soon brought them to Marcus Clarke's office.

Marcus had spent his whole life in journalism, rising through jobs in the local press to a successful career in Fleet Street. After a spell in television he went freelance and had built an impressive reputation as a publicist. His clients included politicians, celebrities and anyone getting negative notices in the press and wealthy enough to purchase his help. He was a tall man in his late forties with greying hair. He exuded charm and confidence as he ushered the girls into his spacious office and supplied them with drinks.

He had originally promised Emily ten minutes in his busy schedule but, after receiving her long and detailed email, he was intrigued and, sensing a potentially lucrative opportunity, had allocated them an hour. That email had been sent from Jake's computer and had been routed through Russia, New Zealand and Brazil before reaching Marcus. Jake was taking his security role seriously.

The interview lasted almost two hours. Marcus had prepared his questions and began by verifying every detail of April's story. He jotted down notes as they spoke and passed them to his secretary so that she could check their accuracy. During the second part of the interview he sought to assess what April was prepared to do and to judge whether she would be able to stand up to the pressures of national publicity. Finally he explained his terms. There would be no fee as April was without means. He would gamble on her success and take a percentage of her media earnings and she would be required to sign a contract to that effect. All this depended on whether he decided to take her on as a client. He was fully aware that there was no time to lose as the tabloids were already on her trail so he would decide as soon as his enquiries were complete. He asked April to telephone him that afternoon between three and four.

'Make the most of this time' said Emily as they strolled down Oxford Street with their shopping bags. 'If you should become well known you won't be able to walk around like this without being recognised.'

April hated that idea. She wanted to be free of such pressures so she could make something of her life. She looked at Emily.

'Sometimes I don't even recognise myself.'

Looking at her reflection in a shop window a few minutes earlier, she had been shocked to see a complete stranger. She felt a tightening in her chest, but the sensation passed and she had dismissed it. April enjoyed exploring the shops in the afternoon sunshine and was glad to see *Marks and Spencer's* and *Selfridges*. There had been *Woolworths* and *Boots* in Cambridge. They were all familiar and reassuring landmarks.

April knew she was out of her depth. Was she doing the right thing? There was still time to say no to Marcus Clarke if he should offer her a contract. What would happen if she decided to withdraw after signing it? Was she allowing Emily's enthusiasm to influence her? Richard and Sarah had strong reservations. She couldn't decide what to do.

'It's time to give Marcus a call,' said Emily, oblivious to April's worries. She punched out his number on her phone and waited to be put through to him.

'He wants to speak to you' she said and passed the phone to April.

Marcus confirmed to April that he would be prepared to handle her publicity and could put the wheels in motion straight away. When he enquired whether she wanted to go ahead, she faltered and asked if she could sleep on it and let him know the following day. He said that was a sensible idea and confirmed that he would await her call.

That evening back in Cambridge, April voiced her reservations to the family. Emily remained quiet as she was aware of what she was getting into and wondered if she had taken on too much. Once they climbed onto this rollercoaster they wouldn't be able to get off.

After everyone had had their say, it was finally agreed that it was April's decision and she should sleep on it and decide the next morning.

June 2nd

I can't decide what to do. I don't want to say yes to Marcus Clarke and hate the idea of becoming famous. Sarah and Richard are concerned as they think it could be dangerous. Yet Emily is dead set on it. I feel pulled in two directions… Marcus Clarke might protect me as Emily believes but if that isn't true Mr Venn will have me taken away – why is all this happening to me?

April couldn't sleep that night and after tossing and turning for a long time, she rose and went down to the kitchen to make herself a drink. She sat at the kitchen table with a mug of tea. The house was quiet but the turmoil of her thoughts and fears continued to haunt her.

'What am I going to do?' she said aloud.

Everything's going to be alright April.

She looked round but there was no one there. Where had that voice come from? She was obviously overtired and trying to reassure herself. She went back to bed.

The next morning in spite of her reservations, there seemed to be no alternative to going ahead with Marcus Clarke, so after breakfast she telephoned him. He wasted no time and asked for her to come to his office the following day. He would arrange secure accommodation for her and Emily for three days. There would be much to do.

April's briefing began at Marcus Clarke's office on that Wednesday morning. After lunch she went with Marcus and Emily to a room in a London hotel where she was interviewed by two journalists with a photographer. The resulting article would appear in a leading Sunday newspaper a few days later. It would be heavily promoted beforehand to maximise sales. This was vital publicity for the big television interview going out on the following Wednesday.

Marcus' assessment was that the TV interview would start the ball rolling and lucrative offers would follow. April claimed to be from the past – a returnee. The Home Office would pull out everything to stop her talking. They didn't like returnees, well sod them. If there were returnees, people had a right to know. April was a lovely, genuine girl. He was sure that the public would take her to their hearts.

The first day also included the first taped recording for April's book. The ghost writer had come to the office after lunch and interviewed her for three hours. There were to be two or three more interviews, he explained, after which he should have sufficient material to write it. A complete draft would be ready in about a week and a half. Once read and corrected it could be on the bookshelves two weeks after that.

'I've already secured a good royalty advance for the book and I'm confident that we shall be able to sell the international rights. It should be a good earner for you April,' said Marcus.

'It's not really by me. I haven't written anything.'

'You're going to be famous. You haven't got time to write your own story. That's why it's being written for you' Emily explained.

Before the TV interview the television company had contacted the Home Office to see what their position was and whether they could provide any more information on April. They were surprised to receive a 'confidential' view that April was a fake.

'It seems that the man she claims to be her father isn't related to her and she has avoided visiting him even though he is nearby. She's been well prepared but there are serious flaws in her story of the 1950s. Her claim that the disappearances hadn't started in 1959 isn't true. They began in the UK in 1958 and there was a considerable amount of publicity at that time. Whether you proceed with this interview is up to you. Just be careful not to be taken for a ride. That could ruin your reputation.'

The television people understood that the Home Office had their own agenda and, after a consultation with Marcus, it was decided that the interview would go ahead as planned next Monday. The final session with the ghost writer was on Saturday morning after which the girls would leave for a rest. Emily had booked them into a select country house hotel in Buckinghamshire with extensive spa facilities. They could relax and be pampered for twenty-four hours before returning to London on Monday morning for the TV session.

...

Pendleton Manor, once a grand country house, was now a luxury hotel set in 160 acres of parkland. It had 38 luxury en suite guest rooms and two restaurants, one of which had won several awards. April had never stayed in a hotel and was impressed with the grandeur of it. She walked around their spacious twin room and looked out onto extensive lawns and a lake in the distance. She felt like a child in a huge toyshop. There was so much to look at. The gleaming bathroom had a Jacuzzi and Emily had to explain what it was.

'How can we afford to stay here?' asked April. 'It must cost a fortune.'

'It does but I'm not bothered as you're paying. I'm putting it on your bill,' said Emily with a grin. 'Don't worry. If Marcus is even half right about your potential earnings, you're going to be a very rich girl so the cost of staying here will be small change for you. As it happens, I've negotiated a discount.'

This turned out to be a photo call with the two girls standing either side of the hotel manager. If April turned out to be world famous, this photograph would form part of a news story: that April Saunders had chosen Pendleton Manor as the ideal place for rest and relaxation.

'That's not true. You booked it.'

'Shh. You mustn't let facts get in the way of a good story.'

The hotel brochure in their room described all the hotel services in lavish detail. The spa facilities designed to 'restore body and soul' included a heated indoor swimming pool, a gym, steam room, sauna, whirlpool bath, infra-red therapy, beauty treatment rooms and a hairdressing salon.

After an excellent Sunday lunch, April stretched out on a comfortable recliner in the sun lounge while Emily had gone to have a hot stone treatment, whatever that was. April felt that she could get used to this. She relaxed and closed her eyes.

'Excuse me, miss. There's a gentleman to see you in the hall.'

'Are you sure it's me you want?' Emily had told no one about their visit.

'Yes. He asked to see you, Miss Saunders.'

She followed the woman down to the front hall where a man stood near the door. He was a burly middle aged fellow in a suit. April didn't like the look of him. Seeing her he stepped forward and introduced himself as a police officer, showing her his card.

'I'm sorry to disturb you Miss Saunders, but I regret that there may have been a mistake in the information you have been given by the Home Office about your mother. It seems that she may be alive and well after all. This is an unofficial visit as my department are concerned that you could have been inadvertently misled so we need to check with you. My inspector has some photos and documents which we would like you to examine. It will only take a few minutes.' He gestured to a large black car just outside the front door.

April could hardly believe it. Mum could still be alive! She hesitated by the door as the policeman gave a nod and a smile. She followed him slowly onto the drive and stepped into the back seat of the car. There was another policeman in the back and the man who had spoken to her climbed into the front passenger seat and the car sped swiftly down the long drive away from the hotel.

'What's happening? Where are we going? I thought you had some things to show me.'

The man beside her held up his hand.

'Don't worry, Miss Saunders. The material is at our office. It's only about ten minutes away. You can look through it and then we'll bring you back to the hotel.'

The car continued through the countryside and April grew more and more apprehensive with each twist and turn. Eventually they slowed down in a narrow lane and bumped up a dirt track until they reached a wide open space at the site of an enormous rubbish tip. To their left there was a large yellow bulldozer and a cabin. Standing in front of it was a powerful looking thickset man who strode towards them. April felt hot, her mouth was dry and she shook with fear. The driver got out and approached the man who was peering into the car. Seeing April's terrified face, he reacted angrily.

'You're a bunch of bloody murderers. I'm having nothing to do with this.'

'You'll do as you're told or you'll finish up in the tip yourself.'

At this, the bulldozer driver reacted with a punch that would have felled an elephant. The policeman collapsed senseless. The other policeman from the front of the car leapt out and drew a gun. The bulldozer man edged slowly backwards towards his cabin followed by the policeman. The big man sprang into his cabin, locked the door and reached for his phone The gunman kicked the door down and forced his way in. There was a loud commotion before a gunshot sounded and all was quiet.

April seized her chance. She brought out her pepper spray and squirted it into the face of the man beside her. As he recoiled, she slipped out of the car and ran down the track, cutting to her left and scrambling downhill through trees and bushes. She heard the crack of a shot and a bullet smacked through the foliage above her. Reaching a lane she saw a cottage to her left. Ignoring it she turned right and pushed through a hedge on the far side and into a pasture field. She ran along the roadside hedge doubled up to avoid being seen. The field rose up to an area of woodland at the top. If she could get up there she could hide. She couldn't risk being seen running across an open field so continued along the hedge and pushed through another hedge into the next field. Now she chanced the climb. Stumbling up the hill, she kept tight into the hedge until she reached the top. Stepping carefully over a rusty wire fence, she entered the safety of the wood and looked back across the open fields to the lane. There were no signs of pursuit.

April stumbled through the cool dappled light of the wood until she finally stopped and sat on an old mossy tree trunk to recover her breath. The copse was silent as she bent forward and closed her eyes, resting her head in her hands. Why were the police trying to kill her? She remembered the great pit and shuddered. Exhausted by her flight, she drifted into sleep. Eventually, she looked up and rubbed her eyes. She had no idea where she was. A twig snapped underfoot. April was instantly awake and spun round. Two middle aged men stood together barely ten feet away. They were watching her and didn't look dangerous, but she tensed ready to run.

'Hello. You startled me.'

They came forward cautiously

'We saw you running and looking round. We thought someone must be after you but there hasn't been anyone coming while you were asleep.'

'I've been asleep?'

'Yes, about ten minutes I'd say.'

'This wood is private and there are big notices up on the road. They keep people out.' said the other man.

'But not you two it seems.'

'No. We ignore them. We like coming here sometimes for a picnic. You should see this wood in the spring. The whole floor is covered in bluebells. It's a beautiful sight.'

April reflected that half an hour ago a bunch of thugs were set to kill her. Now she was hearing about bluebells from a couple who seemed more wary of her than the other way round. She felt herself relax and smiled.

'Is anyone looking for you?' asked one of the men, looking around.

'No one is after me any more' said April, sensing his nervousness. 'I had some man trouble and had to get away. Can you help me? I need to get in touch with my friend who'll come and pick me up. Have you got a phone?'

One of the men produced a mobile phone and passed it to her.

'I don't know the number. She's at the Pendleton Manor Hotel. I need a directory.'

The man took the phone back and after a couple of minutes tapping away at the keys, he handed the phone back to April.

'It's ringing.'

She was soon put through to Emily. April parried all Emily's frantic questions then after consulting with her companions, it was arranged that they would all meet at the *Yummy Burger* restaurant in Aylesbury High Street in an hour.

'Bring all my things and make sure you aren't followed when you leave,' said April. 'We need to get straight back to London.'

April and her companions emerged from the wood on to a country lane where the shady verge was dotted with pink Campion flowers. She felt nervous and strained to listen for oncoming cars, while watching out for signs of her would be murderers. She was tense, ready to dive back into the safety of the wood to hide and started suddenly at a loud chattering of magpies. One of her new friends beamed.

'Just wait till you see the field by the car. It's quite a sight.'

They finally arrived and stood together looking through a gate at a field that was red with thousands of poppies.

'We were here three weeks ago and there were just a few then but look at them now.'

April didn't want to look any more. She remembered her grandfather who'd been killed in the First World War. It was a field of the blood of all the dead soldiers. She climbed into the back of the car and ducked down out of sight.

'Don't worry. We'll be in Aylesbury in about fifteen minutes. You'll soon be able to rejoin your friend.'

In spite of their friendly manner and reassurances, April felt tense. What if these men were part of the police team? She'd meekly got into a car with strangers again. Whom could she trust?

She felt relieved as they entered Aylesbury High Street and parked opposite the *Yummy Burger* restaurant. April chose a table near the kitchen door at the back with a clear view of the road.

When Emily arrived later, all three were tucking into cokes with cheeseburgers and chips. The afternoon's terrible adventure had given April a ravenous appetite. With heartfelt thanks, a hug and big kiss for each of her two saviours, she left with Emily for London.

'Trust you to bunk off to a burger restaurant with a couple of gays when my back's turned' said Emily.' What on earth's been going on and why all the cloak and dagger stuff about not being followed?'

April recounted the whole story. Emily became quiet and tried to concentrate on her driving, glancing nervously in the rear view mirror.

'They couldn't have been police. Who were they and why should they want to kill you?'

'I've no idea but they were well organised. They knew exactly where I was and the moment when I was on my own. Thinking about it, I bet the woman who took me down to the front door was one of them. They already had a bulldozer driver waiting at the dump. If he hadn't refused to drive, I would be in the rubbish tip now.'

'You would have disappeared and no one would have known what had happened,' said Emily thoughtfully. 'Someone wants you out of the way for good. You'd better stick close to me from now on. There are some very dangerous people about. Maybe we should report it to the police.'

'They said they were the police.'

Back at the safe house, Emily stared out of the window frowning with determination and trying to collect her thoughts. They went over the incident again and again to try and understand who was behind it. Eventually they gave up and decided to say nothing to anyone. April would go ahead with the forthcoming television interview.

June 7th
Can things get any worse than being kidnapped, shot and buried in a rubbish tip? It's the worst nightmare come true and I want to talk to Sarah and Richard about it but I can't because I have to prepare for the television interview in the morning – my life is no longer my own and I'm sure things are going to get

worse. I want to run away but I don't know how. Emily has changed – she's no longer breezy and confident. She's badly rattled and obviously regretting this whole publicity thing. The situation is sapping my confidence – I must try to be strong –

FOURTEEN

James rose from his desk. He had heard the crunch of gravel as a car drove onto his front drive. He watched from the window as two men got out and approached his front door. He moved into the hall and opened it as they arrived.

'Can I help you?'

'Are you James Fleming?' He was.

'We are from the Home Office, sir, and would like to ask you a few questions.'

James studied the two men both in suits and trying to look official and intimidating.

'What's this about? Has someone disappeared?'

The heavier of the two men fixed him with what James supposed was his best aggressive stare.

'It's about April Saunders, sir. May we come in? It will only take a few minutes.'

James led them into the sitting room and waved them into armchairs. He had been expecting a visit and was glad he was alone in the house.

'Have you read the news about April Saunders and her claim to have returned from the past?'

'Yes I have seen that.'

'Of course you have, Mr Fleming. You were at school together and were seeing each other on a regular basis during your final term. Is that not so?'

'You have been doing your homework and you're right. We had been going together but we broke up and a week later she disappeared. That had nothing to do with me.'

The man rose and gave him a photograph.

'This is the young woman who claims she is April Saunders. Look at it carefully and tell me if it is her. Take your time.'

He tensed as he looked at the picture. He walked to the window and studied it with his back to the men. It was a familiar face with that slight tilt of her head that he remembered so well. He closed his eyes as painful memories flooded back with an unexpected intensity. They had only been kids but ...the words of the poet John Clare came to him:

I never saw so sweet a face as that I stood before.
My heart has left its dwelling-place and can return no more.

His relationship with April was forty years ago and he thought he was over it but now he realised that his feelings for her had always been there, buried deep inside and this picture had brought them to the surface. He felt again his need for her and the guilt at his weakness in running away.

He had never told her how much she had meant to him. He had lied and never apologised. After she disappeared, the opportunity to put things right had gone. He pulled himself together and studied the picture again. After taking a deep breath, he turned and handed it back.

'No. It isn't her.'

'Are you sure? It's been a long time.'

'I'm sure. It's not her. It's someone else.'

'Thank you, Mr Fleming. That will be all for now. She is being interviewed on the television next Wednesday. Make sure you watch that. We may need to speak to you again afterwards.'

...

Sir Harold Anderson was informed at his club on Monday evening of the bungled assassination attempt. He could barely contain his fury and insisted that he wanted nothing further to do with the matter. His committee would follow the legal procedures as planned and that was all. He was assured that there would be no further attempts on her life. Nevertheless he felt concerned. There would be an enquiry and the disaster might be traced back to him. He should never have made that telephone call.

Half an hour later, sitting alone and deep in thought, he was approached by a fellow club member.

'You seem a bit grim tonight, Harry. Look like you could do with a stiff brandy.'

'I could do with being left alone. Bugger off.'

FIFTEEN

Before the television interview, Marcus had coached April on how to behave in front of the cameras. Keep still and try to stay relaxed. Don't move your arms about. If a question is awkward or unexpected take your time to get the answer right. Smile from time to time and be truthful as you can be sure that they will have done their homework. He also warned about possible pitfalls and leading questions and how to deal with them.

In spite of his advice April was feeling anxious as she sat on the edge of her chair, hands tight together in her lap facing the television interviewer. They chatted for a few minutes beforehand. The interview was to be divided into three parts. The first would be about April's life in 1959. The second part would cover her impressions of life in the present day and finally they would look at what April hoped to do in the future.

The interview began smoothly. April found answering questions about the 1950s easy as she relaxed and felt her tensions subside.

'Before we come to the present day, tell us what you can remember about the disappearances in 1959 that had begun the year before.'

'I remember nothing of them.'

'Look, April, that's not really credible. I have a number of newspapers here from that time and it's all over the front pages. Everyone must have been talking about it.'

April paused and looked straight at the interviewer.

'I was there three weeks ago. There was nothing anywhere about it. I read nothing, heard nothing on the radio nor was anyone speaking about it.'

'Hmm. Let's move on to the present day.'

April was asked about her impressions of current fashions, food, shopping and the high standard of living. She confirmed that she was impressed with all these things.

'You must be delighted to have had the opportunity to experience the prosperity and the wide range of choices today.'

'Yes, there are lots of choices everywhere – in the shops, supermarkets and even television channels but I am used to a time when I wasn't bombarded with so much choice. I find it stressful.'

'What's stressful about having plenty of things to choose from?'

'It just is so for me. The first time I went into a giant supermarket, I couldn't wait to get out again.'

'But surely you must prefer it to the drabness of the 1950s?'

'No I don't. I'm still a stranger here. Every day I wish I could return to my own time. It's a time that I don't recognise from your description. Life in Britain was transformed during the fifties. We were all much better off at the end of the decade. I do remember that fact in the papers and being talked about.' She smiled.

Marcus felt the tension in his shoulders relax. April was handling the questions well.

'I see. So what do you miss most about 1959?'

'I'm missing my family, my friends and my home. I've lost them all.'

'Yes of course. So what things do you like best about the present day?'

'First of all, my new friends who have helped me so much. After that I suppose there's shopping and pizzas.'

'Are there some things you don't like about the present?'

April paused. Marcus had warned her about this approach. *Don't go negative* he had advised her.

'As I said earlier, I'd feel happier if there was less of everything.'

'What would you like to do in the future?'

'I should like to live a simple, wholesome life.'

'What do you mean by that?'

April paused again. 'I'm sure the viewers will understand.'

The interviewer was taken aback. It was time to play her ace.

'You haven't really come from 1959 have you, April?'

'What do you mean?'

'I understand that April Saunders' father is still alive and yet you have avoided meeting him, although he's living nearby. He's not really your father is he?'

'No, he isn't my father. I can't say more. There are some things that I can't speak about at this time.'

'There's another thing. You had a boyfriend at school didn't you?'

'Yes. We broke up about four weeks ago.'

You may be interested to know that he has seen a photo of you taken recently and was definite in his opinion that you are not April Saunders.'

In spite of herself, April laughed.

'He must be nearly sixty now. His memory obviously isn't that reliable. Even so, it might be fun to meet up with him again.'

Thanks Marcus, she thought. He'd prepared her for that one too.

Again the interviewer was wrong footed. They were nearly out of time and she had no more questions. There was one last opportunity to tempt April into saying something controversial.

'Is there anything else that you would like to say?'

April's mind was racing. What was there to say? She composed herself and spoke quietly:

'The World is too much with us; late and soon / Getting and spending we lay waste our powers / little we see in Nature that is ours / We have given our hearts away, a sordid boon!'

'Thank you, April.'

The interview was over. April gave a sigh of relief. As she walked away, Marcus grabbed her by the arms.

'Let go, you're hurting me.'

'I'm sorry but you can't go quoting *Wordsworth* on

prime time television. God knows what people will make of it. Why on earth did you do it?'

'I don't know. I had to think of something quickly. I've been studying that poem for O-level. Perhaps it's just a reaction, but I thought that James might be watching and I didn't want him to remember me as some bimbo who was only there to admire his eloquence.'

She wasn't wrong. Watching the interview, James felt as if something was pressing down on his face. He had let her down all those years ago. Perhaps now he could do something to make amends. He decided to write to her.

June 10th.

– survived the nerve racking television interview – Marcus and Emily wanted me to do it but I feel a fraud and I'm worried that the whole pack of cards will collapse around me – I DON'T WANT TO BE FAMOUS. I never did. How did I get myself into this? I feel scared about going away with just Jake and Emily – I want to go back to Cambridge to stay with Richard and Sarah and keep my head down so I can feel safe but I'm afraid it could be too late for that .

...

The newspaper article attracted considerable interest but April's television appearance excited a worldwide audience, stimulating arguments about whether she was or was not a genuine returnee. Marcus Clarke's office was bombarded with requests for further newspaper, magazine, radio and television interviews from all over the world. After consulting April and Emily, he arranged a series of meetings and appearances finishing at lunchtime on Saturday after which the girls would get away for a complete break.

On Saturday afternoon, acting on Home Office instructions, the police swept into Marcus Clarke's office to pick up April; then realising that she wasn't there, demanded to know her whereabouts. Marcus stood firm, insisting that he had no knowledge of where she was and asked them to leave. When threatened with obstructing the police in their duty, he pointed out that the whole event was being filmed on his security cameras. Their heavy-handed tactics would make an interesting news item. They left.

Outside the safe house, the occupant of a small blue car parked along the road, observed the girls return and phoned his church colleagues. Emily and April started packing their things, ready to drive to the West End and link up with Jake at his family flat in Muncaster Square. It was just off Wigmore Street and close to Bond Street tube station.

'If we should ever get separated, we'll meet up at the Burnstone apartment in the square. It's in a newish block,' said Emily.

The following morning, they planned to leave London in Jake's car and go to Wales for a holiday. However, soon after their arrival at the safe house they received an urgent call from Marcus about the police raid at his office, urging them to leave at once. They rushed to gather their things as there was a knock at the front door. It was the police.

There were three uniformed officers on the doorstep – two men and a woman. They produced their identity badges and walked into the house.

'Are you Emily Kendrick?'

'Yes I am. What's all this about?'

'We're here on Home Office instructions to collect April Saunders.'

'On what grounds?'

'I cannot discuss this with you Miss Kendrick.'

He looked past her as the woman police officer was leading April into the room.

'Miss April Saunders?' April nodded. 'I'm sorry miss, but I have instructions to collect you. It's a Home Office matter.'

April's face was pale. She drew back.

'I haven't done anything wrong.'

'No one is accusing you of anything, but you have to come with us.'

'In that case, I'll come with you' said Emily.

'I'm sorry Miss Kendrick, but we have instructions to collect only Miss Saunders.'

'Where are you taking her?'

'I can't tell you that. Come along now Miss Saunders.'

'Wait, you'll need your bag April. I'll get it.'

Emily ran into the kitchen, opened April's shoulder bag and closed it again before returning with it. The WPC took the bag, looked through the contents and passed it over. April was ushered into the waiting police car which sped up the road and out of sight, causing the watcher in the blue car to phone urgently for instructions.

Emily stood by the front door looking up the road. It had happened so quickly. The enormity of it shocked her. She had promised April that they would stay together and had believed the publicity would protect her, but it had produced the opposite effect. Mum and dad had been right. If April had kept her head down, she would still be safely at home in Cambridge. She slammed the front door, stumbled into the living room and slumped into an armchair. She needed to think.

A few minutes later she rang Jake at the flat. She had never known him to be so upset. Next she called Marcus and described what had happened. He remained calm and told her not to worry.

'This was always a possibility Emily. It's not your fault. It was on the cards ever since April arrived with the story that she was from the past. Hopefully, this is where the media can help. I'll put this out as a news story now and I want you to stay there as a TV crew may come to interview you. This is the only way we can get April back quickly.'

He rang off and called in his PA.

'The police have snatched April. I'm drafting the story now. I want you to send it to the TV and Radio Channels in five minutes. Mark it urgent.'

'Ok but what about the press?'

'There's time enough for them later. We could be in for a busy evening.'

'Poor girl, she must be terrified.'

...

April was terrified. She stared at the passing streets as the car moved swiftly through North London.

'Where are we going?'

The policeman in the front passenger seat turned and smiled.

'We're not sure ourselves at the moment. We're awaiting

further instructions. Hopefully it won't be too far. Try not to worry.'

The car came to a halt at traffic lights. April looked out at the people walking on the pavement. There were two girls about her age, bouncing along and laughing. They were carrying large bags and had obviously been shopping. She remembered walking down Oxford Street with Emily and how she had enjoyed that afternoon. Emily had warned her that if she became well known she wouldn't have the same freedom. Now she'd lost her freedom altogether. As the car moved away, she thought about those girls. They were free, they belonged here. This was their world.

'I was going on holiday with my friends tomorrow,' said April. 'Now I'll never see them again.'

'Of course you will. The Home Office only want to talk to you. You'll be back in no time,' said the WPC.

'Not if I'm murdered I won't. I'm frightened. I don't want to die.'

'You're just frightening yourself. No one's going to murder you. You're quite safe.'

'The police tried to murder me last week.'

'Come along young lady. You know that's not true. This is England. The police are here to protect the public not go around killing them.'

The officer in the front, who was obviously senior to the others, turned to April and studied her face.

'Would you like to tell me about it?'

April wasn't listening. She was staring into the putrid rubbish pit that would have been her grave.

'April? I'd like to hear about it.'

She tried to tell him but the memory was too painful. She stammered and shook as the story came out in bits and pieces until she'd finished. The police were quiet. They recognised from experience when someone had been traumatised.

'Have you told anyone else about this?'

'Only Emily. We wanted to do the television interview, so we kept quiet about it. Perhaps we shouldn't have.'

'You should have reported it. This was a serious crime and you should have received medical attention. I can assure you that those people weren't police officers.'

Just then the radio on the dashboard crackled into life and he leaned forward to listen to the incoming message. He turned back to April.

'We've had our instructions. We're delivering you to a police station in Essex and you're to stay there overnight before being collected by Home Office officials in the morning. We should be there in about an hour. When we arrive I want you to make a full statement about this incident. I know it will be an ordeal for you but you need to talk about it. Will you do that?'

April nodded her assent.

At the same time, the London disciples of the *Church of the Second Coming* were reporting to their head people in Kansas City that they had lost touch with April. They were informed that the return of the Saviour was close at hand and April Saunders was believed to be an important messenger. Moreover, the head of the church was already on his way. When his private jet landed, he would expect to hear that they had found her again.

. . .

When the custody sergeant at Chelmsford Police Station received the news of April's imminent arrival he could hardly believe it. They had met before. Forty years ago he'd been one of Mandy Daniels' trusted gang at school. It had started when her brother had his accident. Andrew had been their friend and Mandy kept them up to date with his progress in hospital and encouraged them to visit after he returned home. The link had remained and later, when her friend April blossomed into the prettiest girl in the school, they were queuing up to help Mandy in order to get close to April. She was a goddess beyond the reach of thirteen year old boys.

'G'night Sarge.'

Two constables going off duty headed for the back door. He acknowledged them with a wave of the hand.

He remembered that night at the youth club when the two girls were trying to get April and James Fleming together. Mandy had tied April to a chair, after which she went off to fetch Fleming. He and his mate had been asked to wait behind. He'd never been so close to April before. She'd smiled and thanked him for helping out. He'd been so tongue-tied that he couldn't say anything. When Fleming arrived, they ran out as instructed. He'd never liked Fleming, but no one knew it was all going to go so wrong. He turned out to be a right bastard.

'Is everything all right Sergeant ?'

It was the new inspector.

'Yes sir, just making the most of a bit of peace and quiet before the drunks start coming in.'

'Right, I'll be in my office if you need me. Carry on.'

Bloody patronising sod. God knows how he made

inspector. He sits at his desk playing cards on his computer and expects everyone to fetch and carry for him. He'd been transferred from the Met about three months ago. Bet they were glad to be shot of him. The powers here had his number alright. He'd been mostly confined to nights where he couldn't do any harm.

His thoughts turned back to April. When Fleming had upset her, Mandy suggested that we boys could get our own back, provided that we weren't caught. We didn't need telling. James Fleming is a shit was chalked on the playground wall. Everyone saw it before the caretaker scrubbed it off. He smiled at the memory. The head was furious and called on the culprit to own up but no one moved. Later a bottle of ink was poured all over Fleming's books and papers in his briefcase which he'd left unattended in the library. No one there had seen anything.

When April went missing that was something else. The whole school was in shock. Mandy and Fleming walked out of school that morning in tears after being interviewed by the police. We all got busy after that. Mandy and Brian Humphries had us searching everywhere for April. At one time there were more than twenty kids searching the woods but nothing was found. Eventually they traced April back to a cafe on the A1 but that proved to be a dead end.

Now, after all these years, she was on her way to see him and by some miracle she was still sixteen. She wouldn't recognise him of course. He was fifty-three now and looking forward to early retirement and spending time with some serious fishing.

'Cup of tea, Sarge?'

It was one of the young constables. He accepted it with a nod although at that moment he would have preferred a large scotch. He mused on the instructions he'd received. April was to be kept in overnight and would be collected by Home Office gorillas tomorrow morning. He knew what that meant – a visit to one of their bloody interrogation centres. God knows what they'd do to force her to retract her story. He'd watched her television interview after reading about her in the paper. She'd already received so much publicity; the bastards would have to break her spirit and she might not survive. He was determined that wasn't going to happen if he could help it. He had to get her out tonight.

...

Emily phoned her parents and told them what had happened to April. They were shocked but promised to do what they could.

'If you are interviewed by reporters,' said Sarah, 'make sure you stick to the facts. It doesn't matter if you're upset, they'll expect that. Just don't accuse anyone of anything, even yourself. People following the interview are perfectly capable of making up their own minds.'

Emily needed to do something. She rang Marcus again and told him that she had some more news for him. Perhaps he would like to record it. After he agreed, she told him the whole story of the bungled assassination attempt on April's life the previous weekend. Marcus, who'd heard a few stories in his time, was flabbergasted.

'Emily, I understand that you're upset but you can't just make up fantastic stories to get the police into trouble. Let's just pretend I haven't heard this.'

'It's true, Marcus, every word. I don't think they were police at all. You're a smart man, you know people. Check out the hotel and my sudden departure. Locate that rubbish dump and the bulldozer driver that was shot. This is a story that might mobilise public opinion behind April.'

'Alright. I'll get on to it. If medical college doesn't work out, there could be a job for you here.'

He put down the phone and grinned. This story was getting bigger and bigger. Perhaps they could beat the bastards this time. Rumours of Home Office assassination squads were one thing. Concrete evidence was something else altogether. They would have tidied up at the dump but inevitably they'll be a number of loose ends this time. The frightening thing was that April, their intended victim, was even now falling into Home Office hands. He picked up the phone.

'Get me the editor of *The Daily Telegraph*.'

SIXTEEN

April was led through the back door of the police station and around a corner to a large counter manned by a custody sergeant and a young policeman. They were joined almost immediately by a female police officer.

The senior officer from London explained to the sergeant about April's need to make a statement concerning the assassination attempt on her life. The sergeant raised his eyebrows in surprise and looked at April with concern. He looked nice, she thought, in spite of her predicament. Once April had been formally handed over, the London police left. The sergeant picked up the phone and pretended to inform the inspector.

The police woman, whose name was Beryl, took April's bag and removed the contents, noting down every item and even counting the cash in her purse. This was all placed in a box beneath the counter and April signed the list provided. She was surprised and relieved that the pepper spray wasn't there as it wasn't legal. Emily, quick thinking as always, must have removed it before she left. She was led to an interview room and the sergeant sat with her and the police woman and took April through her statement after which she was offered a hot meal. She declined but the young policeman was despatched anyway and, within ten minutes, a plate of chicken, chips and peas arrived with a mug of strong tea.

'You can stay here and have your dinner while your statement is being typed up,' explained the sergeant. 'Beryl will keep you company.'

Ten minutes later he returned with the typed statement which April read through and signed. The sergeant returned to his desk behind the counter and made a copy of it which he faxed with a short note to the chief inspector in Aylesbury. They would have to follow it up. It wasn't his place to send this without authorisation but if he sent it upstairs to the inspector he knew that nothing would be done. He made another copy for himself and slipped it into his wallet as he might need some insurance. Returning to the interview room, he saw that April had eaten some of the food and had pushed the plate and mug away. She was still looking scared which wasn't surprising after what she'd been through.

He asked Beryl to take the remains of the meal back to the canteen.

'Shouldn't I escort her to her cell first?'

'I'll do that. I want this greasy smell out of this room now.' She gathered up the things and left.

The sergeant moved to sit opposite April and spoke quietly.

'Listen carefully. I'm getting you out of here. As soon as I return, you follow me to the back door and I'll let you out. When you're outside, turn left, then left again and keep going until you reach the railway station. It's about ten minutes walk. There's a train to Liverpool Street every fifteen minutes. Once you're out, keep a low profile. Go straight to the station. Don't run, don't talk to anyone or look people in the face. Your escape could be discovered at any time so there's no time to lose. Also, when you arrive at Liverpool Street leave immediately as police there could have been alerted to look for you. Is all this clear?'

'Yes. Thank you, but why are you doing this for me?'

'Never you mind, April. There's just one thing. If you are picked up, it wasn't me who let you out.'

'No. Of course not.'

Returning to his desk, the sergeant asked the young constable to print out the night time crime figures for the last three months, which placed him at the computer with his back to the entrance corridor. Then he took a ruler from his drawer and slipped around the corner into the passage facing the back door. He reached up and moved the CCTV camera near the ceiling so that it was no longer pointing towards the door. It would now give a view of the wall. The next one gave a view of the door of the interview room and the passage leading down to the cells. He reached up and turned this one without the constable looking round. Next he opened the door of the interrogation room and summoned April. He held a finger to his lips to signal absolute silence and took her around to the back door and opened it. He pressed some money into her hand.

'Now get going and good luck.'

He closed the door and had just realigned the CCTV cameras when Beryl re-appeared.

'Shall I take her down now sarge?'

'I've already done it. She's in number six and seems fine, so I shan't need you for the time being. I'll call you if we get any troublesome women in later on.'

...

April crossed the car park at the back of the police station, went up a short lane and into the road. She turned left and left again at a crossroads and was alarmed to find herself in front of the police station. She hurried on, crossing the road and passing a big church on her right, before coming to a road junction. There was no railway station or any signs for it. She walked around, looking down each road in turn. There was a tall building on one side with a clock that read almost eight forty five. She'd been out for ten minutes already. A man on the other side of the street was staring at her. She needed help and it was arriving in the shape of four teenagers coming towards her. She decided to risk speaking to them.

'Excuse me. Can you tell me the way to the railway station?'

'Whadya wanna go there for' said the biggest boy. 'We're goin to the pub. You come with us.'

'We're goin to get pissed' said the other boy with a grin.

'Aint I seen you before?' A girl with metal studs and rings on her face glared at April.

This was going badly. Any moment now she might remember the TV interview.

'Don't mind them'. It was the other girl who took April aside. 'You're going the right way. Straight down here, over the main road, then you'll see it.'

April thanked her and hurried on, increasing her pace as she went. She must have been out at least fifteen minutes by now. The police could be looking for her already. They might be at the railway station even now. She broke into a run and cannoned straight into a couple emerging from an Indian takeaway. The woman staggered back against the shop window, but the man tumbled over with April on top of him. The bag containing their meal slid into the gutter.

'What the hell?' shouted the woman. 'You should look where you're going.'

April got up and helped the man to his feet. He bent over and retrieved his cartons of curry and rice.

'I'm so sorry,' said April. 'I didn't see you. Are you alright?'

'I seem to be in one piece. No bones broken. The food seems to be okay as well.'

'You would've had to pay up if they'd spilled.'

The woman was determined to have her say. The people in the takeaway and others across the street were all staring.

With a final apology April hurried on, remembering what the sergeant had said and aware she wasn't doing well at being unnoticed. At the main road, she entered the railway station and bought a ticket for Liverpool Street. After climbing two flights of stairs to reach the platform, she saw there was a wait of nine minutes before the next train. There was nowhere to hide. If the police came, that would be it.

After the longest nine minutes she could ever remember the train finally arrived and April sat on the far side of the carriage. As it pulled out, she glanced across at the platform and for a split second, found herself looking at two policemen who were standing at the top of the stairs. They were scanning the train as it left for London.

They'd seen her. They knew where she was going. They had probably reported it already. There'd be police waiting when she arrived at Liverpool Street. She needed to get off the train.

'Does this train stop at any stations before Liverpool Street?' April asked a woman who was studying her mobile phone.

'Only Stratford. They nearly all stop at Stratford.'

April thanked her. She would get off there and find her way to Bond Street underground station that was near Jake's apartment. At Stratford she got off and saw that the Jubilee Line went straight through to Bond Street. She bought a ticket and waited on the platform. It never occurred to her that there could have been police waiting for her at Stratford as well.

The carriage began to fill up as they approached the West End. She studied her fellow passengers. They were a mixed lot and all ages. Two were black, two were reading newspapers and one young woman was engrossed in a book. A youth opposite her had a wire going into his ear and she could hear some faint tinny music coming from it.

There was a scruffy overweight youth at the end of the carriage who reminded her of Fatty Gates. It wasn't nice to make fun of people who were fat but he was an exception as he was so odious and always had been. At primary school he used to come up from behind and pull her plaits which really hurt. In recent years he'd grown big and fat and would swagger around with a couple of cronies making nasty remarks to April and her friends. Mandy had called him a repulsive toad to his face. It wasn't that he hated girls, she thought, but he had no confidence so being horrible was his way of getting a reaction. Horrid though he was, she would give anything to see him again. There wasn't anyone from her world anywhere and the loneliness was a continuous ache. She looked around the carriage again. No one took any notice of anybody else. That hadn't changed. It had always been like that in London.

She alighted at Bond Street station and rode up the escalator, praying that Jake and Emily would be at the apartment. She feared they could have gone back to Cambridge. She glanced across at the people on the down escalator. It was then that she saw Mandy.

...

'Sarge, did you say that girl was in number six?' It was the young constable. 'She ought to have a copy of the list of her possessions. I forgot to give it to her.'

'There's no rush. Beryl will be down in a minute. She'll deal with it.'

Ten minutes later Beryl appeared and took the list down to the cell.

'She's not in number six, Sarge.'

'You sure you checked properly?'

'Yes. I opened it and she wasn't there.'

'Come with me.' He led her down to the cells. April wasn't in number six or in any of the other empty cells which he opened without success.

'She's not here. Where the hell is she?'

'Search me Sarge.'

They returned to the custody counter. It was time to ring the inspector. The news was received with anger at the other end.

'Who is this girl, Sergeant. What was she in for?'

'She's Home Office property sir and top priority apparently. They're coming to collect her in the morning.'

'What! Why wasn't I informed?'

'You were sir. I telephoned you when she arrived.'

'No you bloody didn't! Custody prisoners are your responsibility, Sergeant. If you've lost her, you're in serious trouble.'

'She couldn't have got out through the back door, sir, as it's electronically locked. She must still be in the building. May I suggest that you organise a thorough search. She's bound to be hiding somewhere.'

He put down the phone. That'll keep the idiot busy for a while. Ten minutes later, the Inspector appeared in the custody suite. He looked deflated and nervous.

'There's nothing so far. I'm concerned that she could have got out somehow, through a window perhaps. We should start a search around the town. She could be anywhere.

'She was brought up from London this evening, sir. She doesn't know the town and she hasn't any money. If she has got out, she's probably wondering what to do. He glanced at his watch. She had left twenty-five minutes ago and should be on the train by now. It was time for one last delaying tactic.

'I suggest we try the town centre pubs, sir. It's the one place she might be able to cadge a lift. She's quite pretty.'

'Pretty is she? Someone has let her out. That's the answer. He glared at each of them. Which one of you is responsible for this?'

They all looked at each other in surprise. No one spoke.

'There's no one here that would do such a thing, sir. I can personally vouch for these officers.'

'What about you, Sergeant? Can you vouch for yourself?'

'I'm not sure what you're implying sir but my record in the force for the last thirty years speaks for itself.'

The telephone rang. The sergeant picked it up and listened.

'The search is over sir. She's not here in the station.'

'Perhaps she disappeared,' suggested the young constable.

'Of course she's bloody disappeared,' the inspector screamed, taking his frustration out on him.

'No sir. I mean perhaps she's become one of the disappeared. One moment she was here then suddenly she was gone.'

For a split second, hope flitted across the inspector's face. Then he realised that explanation would get short shrift from the Home Office officials.

The telephone rang again. The sergeant picked it up and passed it to the inspector.

'It's a Mr Venn from the Home Office sir. He wishes to speak to you about April Saunders.'

SEVENTEEN

April was stunned by the sight of Mandy disappearing down the other escalator. She dare not shout out and draw attention to herself. Charging up the moving stairs, she ran down the descending staircase until she was held up by a group of foreigners blocking her way.

'Please let me through' she cried.

They shuffled about to make way for her. She ran to the eastbound platform and sprinted up and down but Mandy wasn't there. A train was pulling in on the westbound side. The doors opened and people flooded onto the platform, through those waiting to get on. There were so many people it was impossible to recognise anyone. Then as the last few passengers were getting into the train, she saw Mandy at the far end, stepping into the carriage. April ran through the crowd. The train doors shut as she arrived and saw Mandy sitting with her back to the platform. She banged on the window with her fists as the train slid away. Mandy turned, but it wasn't her.

She rode back up to the street. What was she thinking of? It couldn't have been Mandy. She felt as if all her anxieties had drained her energy. Crossing Oxford Street, she plodded along Wigmore Street and into Muncaster Square. She found Jake's apartment block and pressed a bell that said Burnstone. Please be at home, Jake. I won't know what to do if you're not here. Then with a surge of relief she heard his voice enquiring who the visitor was.

'It's April.'

'Christ. Are you alone?'

The door buzzed and she took the lift to the sixth floor. Emily was there with outstretched arms. They hugged and went quickly into the flat where she was embraced again by Jake.

'How on earth did you get here?' they both asked at once.

'I escaped. A friendly policeman helped me. I don't know why.'

'Come and sit down and tell us all about it,' said Emily. April recounted her story but left out the bit about Mandy.

Emily explained how Marcus had contacted the television people and the BBC had interviewed her in front of the house. After that she had driven to the flat and she and Jake had eaten a quiet meal together, although neither had much appetite.

'The interview made the ten o'clock news' said Emily. 'Jake recorded it. Would you like to see it?' April said she would, so Emily scrolled through the video recorder and found it.

'I'm outside a house in North London where April Saunders, the girl claiming to be from 1959, was taken away by police this afternoon. With me is her friend Emily Kendrick who was with her at the time. Can you tell us what happened?'

'The police came and said they had orders from the Home Office to take April away. They wouldn't say where they were taking her, nor would they let me go with her. It was all very quick.'

'How did April take it?'

'She was terrified. She's only sixteen and is still struggling to adapt to life in this time. She's lost all her family and friends and now this. It's outrageous.'

'I take it that you believe she really is from 1959 then?'

'Of course she is. The Home Office know it too.'

'Aren't you overreacting? Surely they just want to interview her?'

'They've already done that. This is something else. We're supposed to be a free country. How would you feel if your sixteen year old daughter was snatched and taken away?'

'What do you think?' said Emily. 'I was trying to get public opinion behind you.'

April didn't answer. She had fallen asleep.

'I've been making some calls,' said Jake, emerging from the bedroom. 'Now they've lost April, the police will be going flat out to find her again. It's only a matter of time before they turn up here. We can't afford to wait any longer and need to get going now. My car is packed and ready to go.'

They took the lift to the basement car park. Jake drove slowly onto the square and through the West End. No one noticed a small black Fiat start up and tuck in behind them. Jake headed into west London and onto the M4.

'So we're off to Wales. Are we staying with your parents in Cardiff tonight?' asked Emily.

'No. I've arranged for us to stay over at Harvey's place. We'll go on to Wales in the morning. Harvey and Ruth live in a village near Reading. He's trustworthy so we'll be safe there. He's looking forward to seeing us and meeting April.'

Harvey Weinberg was a psychologist whose books also encompassed philosophy and spiritual teachings. His work was widely respected and his reputation as an original thinker across academic disciplines was recognised worldwide. His family had been close friends with the Burnstones for many years.

'I'm looking forward to meeting them. Thank goodness they could take us in at such short notice' said Emily. She looked over at the back seat with a mixture of affection and anxiety at April who was asleep curled up on the back seat with some cushions under a blanket.

The Fiat that that was following them was unable to identify Jake's car in the darkness of the motorway. It missed seeing him turn off at the Reading junction and continued driving towards Newbury and Swindon, straining to recognise the rear lights of Jake's Escort. Eventually, realising that they had lost him, they pulled into a service station and phoned through the details of their failure. The private jet carrying their leader had just touched down near Birmingham.

After the village of Westcott Green, Jake slowed down and turned through a gateway onto a tree lined drive. It curved round and finished in front of a large Georgian house. Emily whistled in surprise.

'Are all your family friends millionaires?'

'No, of course not but Harvey's father was a director of one of the city's biggest merchant banks. He sold out when there was so much foreign money moving in.'

April had woken up and joined Emily and Jake on the front drive. The front door opened and a rubicund figure stood beaming at them.

'Welcome, welcome, come on in. It's a pleasure to see you all.' Introductions were made and Harvey's wife Ruth, a slim woman with greying hair and glasses, led them upstairs to their bedrooms.

'When you're ready, come down and we'll have a drink before supper.'

They gathered in the drawing room with gin and tonics. April clutched her large cut glass of the fizzing drink with ice cubes and a slice of lemon. It was her first G and T and she found it refreshing. This really was a new world. The large room lit by several lamps reminded her of Pendleton Manor and she winced at the memory of that terrible journey to the rubbish tip. Jake and Harvey were talking about family matters while Ruth chatted to the girls. She had read about April and watched her interview on television.

'I'm delighted to see you all. We're interested to hear how things are going for you April,' she said.

They moved into the dining room where there was homemade soup with hot rolls. Harvey moved around the table with bottles of red and white wine. April was the main topic of conversation and their hosts listened attentively as they heard of the suffering she had endured.

At the end of the meal, Ruth asked Jake and Emily to join her and help with the washing up.

'I think that Harvey might like to have a little talk with April,' she said.

Harvey turned to April and smiled.

'Is that is alright with you?'

'Yes of course.'

He led her across the hall and into a large book lined room. At the far end there was a desk with a computer and a side table with a reading lamp that glowed green through its glass shade. They sat together in two comfortable armchairs.

There was silence between them for a while.

'Is there anything you'd like to ask me, April?'

'Do you believe me? That I've come from forty years ago?'

'Yes I do.'

'I'm frightened and tired of being pursued. I haven't done anything wrong.'

'No, of course you haven't.'

'I'm beginning to think Emily's parents were right. If I'd kept quiet the Home Office might have left me alone.'

'Weren't the newspapers after you?'

'Yes. I suppose I couldn't have avoided them. Emily thought that if I went with Marcus Clarke I'd be immune from being picked up by the police. She was wrong.'

'Not entirely. She was right that publicity could help you. The actions of the Home Office can be affected by public opinion. That is your best hope now. I'm sure that Marcus Clarke won't keep quiet. You're his client after all. I shouldn't be surprised if he's prepared a press statement already. You are not on your own, April. You have allies and good friends in Emily and Jake.'

'I hope so. I could do with all the help I can get.'

'You must face the fact that the Home Office will catch up with you again. From their point of view, you're like an illegal immigrant who shouldn't be here but they can't send you back to where you came from.'

'If they could send me back they wouldn't need to catch me, I'd turn myself in tomorrow.'

They lapsed into silence again. April felt like screaming 'YOU MUST HELP ME.' But when she looked into Harvey's face she saw compassion there and became still, with her hands folded in her lap.

'Can you help me?'

Harvey closed his eyes and was silent for a few minutes.

'When the van driver in 1959 told you he was going to Milsham, didn't you suspect that it wasn't true?'

'Yes. I suppose so.'

'When the man at Pendleton Manor told you that your mother might still be alive, didn't you suspect that that wasn't true?'

'I suppose I wanted to believe it.'

'What about your friend Mandy. When Mr Venn told you that she didn't exist, didn't you suspect that he might be lying?'

'I didn't know what to think at the time, I was so shocked.'

'Do you understand what I'm talking about?'

'Yes I do. I've been a right idiot.'

'Don't put yourself down, April. You have a right to be here and you need to respect and take care of yourself. No one knows why you are here. Try to remember that.'

April told him about Jake's idea that we live our lives like the pages of a book. Harvey nodded with a smile.

'In your world, the disappearances weren't taking place. If you have arrived from the past, I should imagine you may have been living in a different book.'

'What will happen to me?'

Harvey looked at her tenderly but there was sadness in his eyes.

'You are on a journey, which is not of your choosing. There will be more challenges. Some of them may be difficult and frightening.'

'But why?'

'That's just how it is for now. I'm glad that you're questioning my assertions. By asking questions we learn things and get nearer to the truth. Try to be yourself. Try to be brave and don't be afraid of people, whoever they are.'

'What's the end of my journey going to be?'

'No one knows. Perhaps you will return to where you came from. Hold on to what is real.'

After their guests had retired, Harvey and Ruth sat in the drawing room. The encounter had made an impression on both of them.

'Have you come to any conclusions about April? Is she delusional?' asked Ruth.

'If she is, it's an unusual delusion. So much so, that I'm inclined to believe that she might be exactly who she says she is. There is no doubt she believes it.'

'How is such a thing possible?'

'I don't know. She arrived here by accident and needs care and support. Both Jake and the Kendricks recognise this but unfortunately the apparatchiks at the Home Office do not. The problem is that they're bound to catch her again before long.'

'What will they do to her?'

'They will squeeze her dry to extract all the information they can, then they will have to dispose of her.'

'What do you mean? They can't just kill her.'

'I'm afraid they will have to. She is already too well known to be kept alive or released, even if they could force her to retract her story. Once out she could go abroad and reveal everything they had done to her. However, they will need to be careful. Public opinion, the media and politicians will want to know what is happening.'

'Isn't there anything we can do? Hide her here perhaps?'

'It wouldn't work Ruthy. They'd soon find her. However, she seems to be under some divine protection so far and things could start to develop in her favour. She may continue to evade her pursuers. April is an outsider who could turn out to be an unwitting catalyst for change. We shall see.'

He paused and looked into his brandy.

'People are afraid of the disappearances so they don't want to think about the Home Office interrogation centres or what happens in them. They accept the explanation that they are simply places where false returnee claims are tested and shown to be false.'

'You've said in the past that this is a kind of mass psychosis. But where's the evidence that returnees are seen as a threat?'

'They disturb what people want to believe. My concern is with what goes on in these centres and the power they wield through their secrecy. Their activities have grown over the last forty years and it isn't easy to recognise things that move slowly, until one day something erupts and we all wonder how we got here. I feel sure there is a crunch coming.'

He poured himself another brandy.

'The more I delve into things, the more I realise how little we know. It's the answers that get in the way. We get attached to them so our thoughts run along familiar tramlines and prevent further exploration. In April's case, I need to see what is in front of me, although that isn't enough. There is an old Chinese saying: *Beneath the still ice the river runs deep.* I want to understand what is going on below the surface. What is extraordinary is her insistence that there were no disappearances happening in 1959. If she really is from the past, it isn't ours.'

June 14th

…lovely people and such a beautiful house, a bit like the hotel and there's me drinking gin and tonic! – my talk with Harvey was difficult, but he was straight with me, even saying that the police are bound to catch me again – I've been so gullible in the past – I'll remember to question what people say in future and try to be brave – I'm not sure why, but I don't feel so frightened now.

EIGHTEEN

Jake drove back to the motorway, weaving through the villages in the morning mist. April was thinking about what Harvey had said the previous evening. He'd been quite hard in a way but she didn't mind. She would try to challenge what people said in future.

They rejoined the M4 at the Reading junction and headed west. The pursuing Fiat from the night before was waiting near Swindon, hoping to catch sight of Jake's car. However, it was the small blue Peugeot that had driven out of London overnight and positioned itself at the Reading turn off that saw them first. It slid in behind them on the M4 and phoned the information through to the Fiat and to a silver Mercedes that was heading down the M5.

Jake had been busy during the previous week preparing for their holiday. The boot of his car contained three backpacks with their clothes and other personal belongings. There were also several boxes of food for their forthcoming stay. His parents lived in Cardiff and had recently purchased a small stone cottage near Carmarthen as a weekend retreat. It was tucked away up a muddy track, and well screened by trees. This was to be their home for the coming week. It would provide the three of them with complete privacy and a chance to relax and make plans on how to keep April safe in future.

'You had a long talk with Harvey last night. Did you find it helpful?' asked Emily.

'Yes, I think so. He told me not to be afraid and that I shouldn't believe everything I'm told.'

'That sounds like good advice.' said Jake. 'Was there anything else?'

'He said that the police would catch up with me eventually.'

'We'll see about that' said Jake, frowning at the road ahead.

He knew that the police all over the country would be looking for April. Once in the cottage, he would monitor their activities through the computer. It hadn't occurred to him that there might not be an internet connection there.

'Harvey also said that you were right about the publicity Emily and that public opinion may help me.'

'I'm sure it will. We'll have to liaise with Marcus as he doesn't know that you're free.'

'He will by now. Harvey was going to contact him this morning.'

'I checked the records for your friends in Milsham,' said Jake. 'The 1961 census showed both Mandy and Brian at home.'

'That proves Venn was lying about Mandy' said Emily. 'The question is why?'

'I've no idea' said April. 'Thanks very much Jake. It's given me a much needed link with the past.'

For all his thoroughness, Jake had neglected to top up the car with petrol, so they had to stop at a service station on the M4 near Swindon. He soon filled the Escort and went into the shop to pay. Emily started suddenly.

'I forgot to ask him to get me some mints. I'll be right back.'

She stepped out of the car and hurried into the shop. April could see them queuing up. She was feeling shut in and opened the car door to stretch her legs and get some fresh air.

Walking across to the slip road she suddenly felt cold and knew something was wrong. There were no sounds. She found it hard to breathe and forced herself to turn around. The whole area was empty. The cars and petrol pumps had gone and the shop was a grey derelict shell. Grass was growing through cracks in the tarmac. The light hurt her eyes. There was a freezing wind and through the silence she heard a faint scraping sound. Something terrible was coming. She couldn't cry out as she stumbled into the trees. It was growing dark. Her head was hurting and her legs gave way. She sank down and put her arms over her head.

'What are you doing over here?' asked Emily, helping April to her feet. 'You look like you've seen a ghost. You're as white as a sheet.'

She helped the shivering girl into the back seat of the car and got in beside her.

'You had us worried. We couldn't find you anywhere.'

The car eased away and rejoined the motorway, quickly picking up speed.

'I don't know what happened' said April. 'I get really scared sometimes, but I'm alright now.'

The event had worried them and they continued their journey in silence. As they approached the Severn Bridge, they were overtaken by a police car which didn't give them a second glance.

'At least the traffic police don't seem to be looking for us' said Emily. 'If they had been, they would have recognised the car.'

'Oh, I don't know' said Jake. 'There are dozens of cars on the road like this one.'

'Maybe, smarty pants, but there's only one with your number plates,' said Emily.

'Ah yes. Maybe there aren't any Escorts with my number plates at the moment.'

'You've changed the number plates and without telling me. That's illegal.'

'Bravo. Three out of three,' chuckled Jake.

Entering Cardiff, Jake went straight to his parent's house. The leafy suburb had neat hornbeams lined up on both sides of the road like giant green tulips. His parents were out so he drove into the garage and closed the door. Lunch had been set out for them on the pine kitchen table, together with the keys to the cottage and instructions on how to find it. After more discussion about number plates, they were ready to resume their journey.

'You drive this time Em and I'll navigate' said Jake.

'Have you removed those false number plates?' Yes he had.

'If the car had the wrong number plates, wouldn't the police spot that?' asked April as they resumed their journey along the motorway.

'It's possible, but unlikely as we didn't have the wrong plates. There's an identical car in London. I just had his plates copied.'

'That's clever' said April.

'Don't encourage him' muttered Emily.

'What's even cleverer' said Jake. 'There's another Escort just like this one in Cardiff. We're using those plates now, but we'll be okay as that car is owned by a woman.'

'Just you wait Jake Burnstone.' gritted Emily. 'I'll deal with you later. You're infuriating sometimes.'

'I certainly hope so. I've put a lot of time and effort into it.'

'There you are April, I told you he was crazy.'

April didn't reply. She knew this banter was their way of trying to cheer her up. What none of them had noticed when they left the house in Cardiff, was a woman standing behind a tree about thirty yards down the road, observing their departure through a small telescope. As they left, she returned to a silver Mercedes which began to follow them.

...

Joshua had received a revelation ten years ago that the coming of the Lord was at hand. In order to prepare the way, he had founded the *Church of the Second Coming of Christ*. Starting in Kansas City, it had spread throughout the United States and now had its own television spot each week. Although there were members throughout the world, he knew something dramatic was needed to boost its funds and membership further. He was always on the lookout for opportunities to achieve this.

After receiving Kevin's email, he had contacted two trusted members of his church in London and asked them to go to Cambridge to investigate the situation. The first couple, delivering their report a few days later, confirmed the girl's existence and her belief that she had just arrived from 1959. The medical diagnosis that she was a virgin was bound to be accurate so her rumoured pregnancy was extremely unlikely. Teenage girls are inclined to imagine things. After her move to the Kendrick's home, the second church couple moved into Cambridge so that her movements could be monitored in detail. She was also under close observation by the police. Joshua knew that if the British Home Office became convinced she was a returnee, they would lose no time in picking her up. Then she would disappear from public view for good. Kevin's email revealed that he had a fertile imagination, but he had inadvertently put his finger on a heaven sent opportunity for the church.

April's television appearance convinced Joshua that he should act immediately. He had flown with his wife Rachel to a private airfield near Birmingham. He was convinced that April must be brought to Kansas. Her arrival, properly managed, would cause a worldwide sensation and bring in millions of dollars for the church. They would be able to have their own television station and would become truly global.

Their arrival in England had coincided with April's journey to South Wales and the two church teams that were following her. Joshua had picked up a Mercedes hire car and he and Rachel headed down the M5 motorway; finally arriving in Cardiff just in time to see the young people set off again.

· · ·

Jake was watching the road behind them as they drove further into South Wales.

'I hope I'm imagining this, but I suspect that we're being followed.'

'Really? By whom?' asked Emily, looking at her rear view mirror.

'There are two cars. A black one and a dark blue one. They have both been following us since Swindon as far as I can tell. Now they're following us again even though we stopped for lunch.'

'Maybe they stopped for lunch too' suggested Emily.

'Yeah, it's possible, but I think we should run a couple of tests.'

He studied the map. 'There's a turning coming up in about ten minutes. I'd like you to pull off there, and we'll see if our friends follow us.'

Emily pulled off the motorway as instructed and paused on the roundabout at the top. As the black car turned off, she drove quickly around and back down the slip road onto the motorway again. The church couple hadn't seen this and turned left at the roundabout and speeded up to try and find them.

'That's one down and one to go, said Jake with a grin. We'll need a different strategy to lose the other one. Keep your speed up Em. Our turning is in about fifteen minutes.'

On his instructions, Emily pulled onto the hard shoulder just before their turning. Jake jumped out, pretending to look in the boot and saw with a feeling of satisfaction, the other car continued on past the junction. Now they turned off the motorway and Emily drove the supercharged Escort rapidly through the twisting lanes with Jake studying the instructions on his lap. Rounding a bend, they went left onto a narrow road that curved through thick woodland, before slowing onto a dirt track that opened into a field. Their home for the next seven days stood on the far side against a backdrop of trees.

The stone cottage was painted white under a grey slate roof. Inside the thick walls there were stone flagged floors. Downstairs consisted of a small kitchen and a living room with a dining table and chairs and some comfortable easy chairs clustered around a squat woodstove. Upstairs there were two bedrooms and a small bathroom. The cottage had electricity and water, but no gas or telephone.

The girls opened the windows to clear the musty smell and Jake busied himself bringing in supplies from the car. When everything had been put away, Emily put the kettle on and rummaged for some mugs. Jake was musing aloud about the cars that had been following them.

'We've given those people the slip for the time being, but they may not give up. We could find them lurking about if we leave here. We have enough food for a week, so let's see if they can wait that long.'

'Do you think they were the police?' asked April.

'No. I don't think they drive along motorways in such small cars. They could just be your fans April, but we need to be careful as they might not only be after your autograph.'

'How do you think they found us?' asked Emily.

'They've probably been on our tail since London. If that's true then our stay here may be shorter than planned, so we must make contingency plans. Any approaching car can be seen emerging from the trees fifty yards away. That's enough time for April to grab her things, slip out through the back door and into the forest. The cottage will effectively hide her escape from any unwanted visitors. If you do have to go April, climb up through the trees to the top of the hill and follow the path to the right. According to the Ordnance Survey map, there's a small clearing after a couple of hundred yards. Wait there, and when the coast is clear, I'll come and find you. From now on we'll have to watch and listen out for any unexpected arrivals.'

'Suppose they come at night?' asked April.

'If they do, we'll be able to hear them and pick up their car headlights at least 500 yards away so that shouldn't be a problem. Let's get prepared.' He rummaged in his backpack and produced a mobile phone. This is for you, April. There's no signal here but if we get separated we can talk to each other. I've entered my number, together with Em's and her parents' so you won't need to memorise them. It needs charging overnight so I will show you how to use it later.'

Next he brought out a money belt and gave it to April. It had £200 in notes and Emily's debit card inside it.

'As you know, April, payments for your media fees are being paid into a subsidiary part of Emily's bank account. Use the cash for purchases and only use the debit card for drawing out more cash when you need it. You'll need the card pin number to draw out the cash. It's 4071 so remember it.'

'Perhaps I should write it down.'

'No. You must remember it. Where do North Sea fishermen keep their money?'

'I've no idea.'

'In the Dogger Bank, of course. I thought everyone knew that. Remember it and convert the letters DOGA into numbers and there you have it.'

'It's just a mnemonic and typical Burnstone' said Emily with a smile.

'Promise me April that you will wear the money belt at all times. It could save you.'

April looked into his face. He was in earnest.

'Alright Jake, I promise. You're so well organised. What's your lab like?'

'It's a bit like school with desks, computers and a blackboard. I've got my own notice board with lists of stuff, a photo of Em and a sign that says BANG HERE. We're all head bangers there.'

NINETEEN

'Let's prepare dinner,' said Jake.' April's been asking about pasta so tonight I'm going to show her how to make a proper sauce.'

'Are you sure you want me to do this Jake?'

'Yeah. If you're going to be in our gang, you've got to know how to make pasta sauce. Ain't that right, Em?'

'It sure is Big Jake. What am I doing?'

'Nothing much. Just make the salad and dressing, prepare the garlic bread and lay the table. You could begin by pouring out some of that red wine.

Emily poured out three glasses of *Côte du Rhone* and passed one each to April and Jake at the kitchen counter. She stood by the table and watched them from behind. Jake crushed open a garlic and was showing April how to skin and slice the separate cloves. He turned to wink at Emily before turning back and proceeding to peel and chop two large red onions.

She watched Jake and April standing close together, speaking quietly and absorbed in their task. She stomped off to find the salad leaves, slashed them into smaller sections, rinsed and tossed them into a bowl with some halved small tomatoes. She helped herself to some of Jake's chopped onion and mixed that into the salad. After which she sat with a second glass of wine and continued to watch them. When she spoke, her voice had a bitter edge.

'This is all my fault, being chased by all and sundry. Headstrong, Mum used to call me as a girl. I always went my own way and never listened to anyone else.'

Jake was cutting the tops off two Romano peppers. He split one and showed April how to remove the seeds and chop it into small pieces. He put a pan on the stove, poured some olive oil into it and set it on a low heat. Emily began again, an unsteady tension in her voice.

'I thought it would be exciting with April being in the papers and on television. I didn't want to think about the consequences.'

April put the garlic and onion into the saucepan as Jake selected a small red chilli and stripped out the seeds. It was cut up and went into the saucepan with the peppers while he washed his knife and his hands at the sink. Jake turned to Emily as she poured herself a third glass of wine.

'Better go easy on that, Em.'

'Mum and Dad warned me not to go ahead but I knew better. Have you been listening to me? We're in a mess and it's my fault,' she shouted.

She gulped down the rest of her wine, brushed away tears and stomped noisily upstairs.

'Is Emily okay?'

'Of course she is. She's just tired and can't cope with too much wine. I'm going up to talk to her.' He cut the corner off a carton of passata and passed it to April.

'If I'm not back in five minutes, pour this into the pan and stir it in.'

He found Emily sitting on the bed still wiping away tears.

'I'm sorry, Jake, I can't help it. I pretended to myself all along that April was going to be alright but when the police took her away, I had to face up to the fact that I'd put her in real danger. I've exploited her and now there's nothing I can do.'

'You haven't exploited anyone.'

He sat beside her and held her close.

'If I hear any more of this, you'll have to go to your room.'

'I'm already in my room. I'll be alright. You'd better go and see to April before she tips the salad into the saucepan.'

When he returned, Jake took the pan off the heat, put his arms around April, drew her close and kissed her. She kissed him back and they stood together as she began to cry. Everything felt mixed up – the happiness she so desperately needed and her growing anxiety about Emily. She felt certain that she and Jake were going to be together.

When Emily came down a few minutes later she found Jake and April with their arms around each other. April had been crying.

She stood staring at the floor, waiting for her tensions to drain away. When she looked up again she spoke sadly.

'I'm sorry April, I shouldn't have said those things. I get worked up sometimes.'

April stretched out an arm and they came together in a three-way hug.

'All for one and one for all!' said Jake.

'Okay, D'Artagnan, what's the next assignment?'

'Whip out your trusty sword, cut up the garlic bread and don't forget to make that salad dressing. The future of France depends on it.'

After the meal they relaxed while Jake made coffee.

'We forgot to listen out for approaching visitors,' said April.

Jake put the coffee mugs on the table and sat down.

'True enough but I wasn't expecting anyone to find us tonight. We're safe enough for the time being.'

There was a sharp knock at the door. They stared wildly at each other. Jake gestured to April to get out of sight. He opened the door and saw in the light from the room a short figure with grey curly hair. He was holding a chainsaw.

'I'm sorry to bother you but I saw the car earlier and thought I'd better return the saw. Mr Burnstone lent it to me.'

'I see. Thanks for returning it, Mr ..?'

'Jones is the name. I live just across the valley but you can hear a saw a mile away see.'

'Yes, I suppose you can.'

'Mine's broken down. I need a new one but I can't afford it at the moment, what with everything going up. Take the cost of diesel now…'

'Thank you again, Mr Jones, but you'll have to excuse me now.'

As he took the chainsaw and closed the door, Jake caught a glimpse of a collie dog sitting quietly behind their visitor. They all gave a sigh of relief.

Later they sat around the woodstove with the crackle of burning logs and firelight flickering on the walls.

'Tell us something about your life in 1959,' suggested Jake.

'There's not much to tell.'

'What about your sister?' asked Emily. 'You've never said much about her.'

'Carol was three years older than me. She was clever and passed eight O-levels. The school wanted her to stay on but she wouldn't. She applied to train in nursing and left home to live in London. I still miss her, even though she came back as often as she could.'

'Why did she leave do you think?'

'She told me that she wanted to work in London. I was only thirteen at the time. We've remained close.'

She gazed into the flames.

'Tell me, Emily. How can one be pregnant one day and not the day after?'

Emily knew where this question was coming from. April had been convinced that she was pregnant on her arrival in Addenbrookes but it had turned out to be a false alarm.

'There could be two reasons. Either the woman is mistaken, which is not uncommon, or she has had a miscarriage.'

'There is a third possibility,' said Jake. 'If she happens to be a rabbit, she could absorb her young in the womb if she became stressed.'

'That's not helpful,' said Emily. 'But how on earth did you know about that?'

'I kept rabbits when I was a kid. It's amazing what you can learn. Did you know that a woman was sent to prison for giving birth to rabbits in the eighteenth century?'

'I think you'd better stop right there or we'll be rabbiting on all night,' said Emily. 'I'm getting sleepy and am ready for bed.'

They were all feeling tired and decided that they would make their plans the following morning.

Later, snuggled down in bed, Emily wanted to talk.

'I didn't like to mention this in front of April, but do you think those people following us could be dangerous?'

'I don't know. You're not scared are you, Em?'

'Of course I'm scared and so is April. For all we know they could be fanatics with weapons and murderous intentions.'

'Hang on, don't upset yourself. If we do run into trouble, we'll have to face up to them and get April away.'

'That's what I'm worried about. She's badly disturbed Jake. No one should ever have to go through what she's had to endure. Remember what happened at the Swindon services?'

'What do you think did happen exactly?'

'I'm no psychologist but she seems to me to have had a severe panic attack. I can only assume that she sometimes remembers the horrors of the last few weeks and she can't cope. I found her cowering in the bushes. There's something very wrong. I should talk to mum about it. I'm telling you this because, if we do get visitors and she gets away, there'll be no one to pick her up if she has another breakdown.'

Jake lay silently for a while.

'What are we going to do, Em?'

'I don't know but we need to find out who's after her and why. Think back to that attempt to kill her at the rubbish tip. If they'd succeeded, no one would ever have known what had happened. There would have been no television interview. I reckon someone was trying to prevent that happening.'

'Who? Surely not the Home Office? They don't employ assassins.'

'Don't they? They wouldn't see it as murder, simply state security.'

'It doesn't make any sense, Em. April isn't a threat to the state.'

'They might not see it that way. That's why I'm concerned about those trailing us. We're in no position to defend ourselves. If they do move in and grab her, they won't want us around as witnesses afterwards.'

They left it at that and slipped into a troubled sleep. In the early hours, as it was becoming light, Emily was woken by sounds from the bathroom. It was obviously April as Jake was still asleep and breathing quietly beside her. She listened to the singing of the dawn chorus for a while. She nudged Jake.

'Are you awake?'

'I am now. What is it? Did you hear something?'

'No, but there's something I need to know.'

'What's that?'

'How do you feel about April?'

'What do you mean?'

'I've seen how you look at her. You fancy her don't you?'

'You've got it wrong. It's not like that. She needs both of us to take care of her at the moment, that's all.'

'Are you sure? Sometimes you can't take your eyes off her. I might as well not be there.'

'I admit that I feel real affection for her but it's not the same as what's between us. I just have this feeling that I want to protect her.'

'Do you have such feelings for me?'

'Of course I do. The difference is that I love you and only you.'

'Come here then…'

June 15th

I know I shouldn't write things that might upset people, but I can't hide my love for Jake any longer and I'm sure he feels the same about me. What can I say to Emily? She's been so good to me and I value our friendship above everything but I can't help how I feel – I can't tell her and will have to leave it to Jake – so frightened by the experience at the garage, but I dare not show it – these visions are getting worse each time. What with that, the people following us, the police and everything, I am trying not to panic but I'm beginning to feel a bit like The Ancient Mariner:

> *Like one that on a lonesome road, doth walk in fear and dread*
>
> *Because he knows a frightful fiend doth close behind him tread.*

Hopefully I'll feel better in the morning.

TWENTY

Roger Venn was furious. Sir Harold had been scathing about April's escape from custody.

'What were you playing at, Roger? She should not have been left overnight in a police station. They obviously felt sorry for her and let her out. You're in overall charge with the resources of the police throughout the country at your disposal. She's to be picked up and removed to the nearest Home Office secure facility as soon as possible. No more slip ups.'

Roger gritted his teeth. This was a career breaker. He was beginning to hate this teenager. She wasn't going to make a fool of him again, not this time. He'd see to that. He pulled himself together and tried to focus on the problem. He ordered the police to check on a number of possible scenarios. Jake Burnstone was missing and so was his car. He could be driving the two girls as they hadn't been seen either. His parents should be checked in Cardiff.

When Mr and Mrs Burnstone returned home on Sunday evening, two policemen called, enquiring about Jake. They told the officers that they hadn't seen Jake for some time and had no idea where he was. The inspector looked concerned.

'I don't want to worry you but since April Saunders made that television broadcast, there have been a number of people trying to track her down. Our main concern is a dangerous group who are currently pursuing them and who were reported to be in Cardiff early today. For the safety of your son and his friends, you must tell me if you know of their whereabouts as they need police protection.'

Mrs Burnstone hesitated and looked at her husband who gave a reluctant nod. She told the police about the cottage and confirmed that Jake had picked the keys up earlier that day. They worried afterwards whether they had done the right thing but they couldn't warn Jake as there was no mobile phone signal there.

Later that evening a constable at Carmarthen Police Station received a call from Cardiff police asking them to pick up three young people and bring them in for questioning. He jotted down the details.

'I'll get onto it right away,' he assured the caller.

He put the phone down. It being Sunday evening, they were short staffed. The inspector had already gone to chapel and he himself would be leaving for home in the next ten minutes and going on to the *The Drover's Arms* with his wife for an evening with friends. Collecting these kids would be a two hour round trip with the paperwork and all. Better to deal with it in the morning. They'll still be there. *Duw*, there hadn't even been a crime.

. . .

Joshua had seen Jake's car turn off the motorway and head north. He gathered his followers and deployed them to comb the countryside discreetly to avoid being seen. He hoped that the trio had gone to ground nearby. Nearly four hours later his patience was rewarded by a sighting of Jake's car next to a remote cottage. That night they all booked into a Carmarthen hotel and Joshua laid out his plan. The next morning they would approach and encircle the cottage on foot. When they were in position, Joshua and Rachel would drive in and take April away while the others restrained Emily and Jake. They would also disable Jake's car to prevent pursuit. It would take time to set up so they agreed that everyone would be in position and ready to strike at precisely eleven o'clock.

Just before ten o'clock the next morning, Emily heard police sirens in the distance. They all stopped and listened. The police cars were nearby and getting closer. April grabbed her backpack, slipped out of the back door and was soon out of sight climbing up through the trees. Emily and Jake raced around preparing for their visitors. At the last minute Jake saw April's phone and threw it out of the back window. By the time Carmarthen's finest reached the cottage, April was well away heading through the forest to their agreed reunion place.

The police team found two young people, not the three they had expected. Their friend April Saunders was still in London apparently. They searched the cottage and found no one else nor was there any evidence that a third person had been there as the breakfast things were still on the table and it had only been laid for two. They decided to bring the couple in anyway and returned with them to the police station.

One member of Joshua's team had crept close to the cottage just in time to see Emily and Jake being taken away by the police. Where was April?

...

The manager of The Pendleton Manor Hotel drove through the countryside in the early morning. The air was crystal clear and the rich greens of the fields and trees looked beautiful but he wasn't able to enjoy the scenery. His duty manager had informed him on the telephone at home that the police wished to interview him and an appointment had been made for ten thirty. He hoped that it wasn't anything to do with the Saunders girl. Whatever it was, it was not good news. The hotel was a retreat for those who had the means to relax in comfort and enjoy total privacy. On arrival just before eight-thirty he found a senior reporter from *The Daily Telegraph* waiting for him in reception. His instinct was to send him away but good relations with newspapers like the *Telegraph* were important. The last thing the hotel needed was bad publicity. He realised with a sinking feeling that it must have something to do with Saunders girl. He'd heard Marcus Clarke on the radio that morning calling on the Home Office to stop hounding her.

His secretary showed the reporter into his office. It was an elegant room tastefully furnished with antiques. One wall had a number of framed photographs of rich and famous people who had stayed at the hotel. The manager braced himself for an awkward interview, scrutinising the reporter with a feeling of anxiety. The man was businesslike and, after seeking permission, took out a small recorder and placed it on the desk between them.

'I understand that April Saunders and her friend Emily Kendrick booked into here on Saturday afternoon just over a week ago and had planned to stay until Monday morning. Can you confirm that?'

'I'm afraid not. I don't keep the details of the visits of individual guests. Their privacy here is of paramount importance.'

'I appreciate that. But are you aware that April Saunders was lured out of the hotel early on Sunday afternoon, leaving all her belongings behind?'

'No. I have no knowledge of this. What do you mean by lured?'

'I understand that a female member of your staff led her down to reception on the pretext that the police were wishing to see her. She was promptly packed into a car and driven away. It seems that these men weren't police at all, which I believe will be confirmed when the Superintendent from Aylesbury comes to see you this morning.'

'This is most disturbing. I knew nothing about it.'

'So you were unaware that Miss Kendrick was turning the place upside down frantically looking for her friend?'

'No. As I said, I hadn't heard anything.'

The reporter leaned forward and turned off his recorder. He studied the manager's blank expression. The man obviously hadn't a clue what had been going on under his nose.

'It's likely that the story of April's kidnap will be in the paper tomorrow and will be picked up by the rest of the media as it involves both a possible murder and an attempted assassination. This hotel will be featured which will do nothing for its reputation. That must be important to you so I would urge you to cooperate fully and tell me everything you know about this matter.'

The manager could hardly believe his ears. What on earth was this about murder and assassination? The publicity would ruin the reputation of the hotel and bring a swift end to his career.

'Very well. We have no secrets here. I'll do my best to answer your questions and you are free to interview other staff members as you see fit, providing you are discreet and undertake not to pry into the personal details of our guests.'

'That's the right decision. I can assure you that I have no interest in embarrassing your guests or damaging the reputation of this hotel.'

After the interview was complete, the manager was accompanying him through his secretary's office when the reporter paused.

'I understand that you had your photograph taken with April Saunders. I shall need a copy of that.'

At the same time other *Daily Telegraph* reporters were making enquiries at the rubbish tip and the *Yummy Burger* Restaurant. By lunchtime they had their story ready and the editor was seeking a statement from the Home Secretary.

...

April walked along a narrow country road. She had waited at the clearing for over two hours before deciding to move on, afraid that the police might send a search party. She found herself in the ancient forest of Glyncorrwg and had followed a path that led onto this road that was now winding upwards gradually leaving the trees behind. She stepped gingerly over a cattle grid and found herself crossing moorland with rocks jutting up through the heather. Oblivious to April's passing, sheep wandered about cropping the grass. The air was clean and cool and it was quiet apart from a faraway sound like a baby calling. She looked up. There were two birds of prey circling high up in the sky and keening with that strange cry. She wondered if they might be eagles.

The police were looking for her here in Wales. Jake had been right about that. She should try to get back to London, but had no idea how to do it. She wasn't going to thumb a lift and ought to hide from passing traffic as the police could be patrolling these roads. Too late she saw a Land Rover coming. There was no point in trying to hide as the driver had already seen her. The vehicle swept past, the driver acknowledging the walker with a brief nod. The road continued to climb upwards. There were no houses here or any to be seen on the surrounding green hills.

As she trudged along, she remembered Emily saying Jake was crazy and he needed her to keep him in order. It wasn't just a joke, she believed it. April wondered whether Emily was drawn to people she could manipulate. If so, where did that leave her? She skirted round a couple of sheep standing in the road.

There was nothing crazy about Jake. That day in the Kendricks' garden, he had told her about his childhood. A boy years ahead of others in the school branded as a swot and who tried to win acceptance by saying silly things. This was the Jake who had talked to her that morning about Tennyson and could quote passages from *Ulysses* and poor *Tithonus* who had pleaded for eternal life, then changed his mind later to no avail, as *Even the Gods cannot recall their gifts*. So here she was in 1999 and it was no good pleading with Gods or scientists. There was no way back.

As she continued to climb higher, it grew misty and cold. She shivered as she found herself enveloped in fog. She stopped, unhitched her backpack and pulled out a thick jumper. Kitted up and ready to go on, she suddenly remembered the mobile phone. Jake had plugged it in last night and, in their rush, had both forgotten it this morning. How were they going to contact each other now? She was cut off from her friends and from everyone else in this fog. She plodded on, skirting round a couple of sheep and wondered if anything else could go wrong. She remembered how Jake had hugged her in the kitchen in Cambridge, how he had understood her grief after the visit to Milsham and had held her hand. And who had kissed her so tenderly in the cottage last night.

Her thoughts were interrupted by the arrival of a large silver car that had come up silently from behind and stopped just ahead of her. A woman got out and stood smiling as April approached.

'Are you alone up here? You'll get frozen. There aren't any villages for miles. Can we offer you a lift?'

'No thanks. It's alright really. I'm fine.'

'Just as you wish but do have something to warm you up.'

She reached into the car and removing a flask, poured out a steaming mug of hot chocolate and passed it over. It was hot and sweet and tasted very good. April drank it all and thanked her and felt herself relax at once. Now the driver stepped out of the car and April looked at him in amazement. He was tall and heavily built with a beard and bright brown eyes. He introduced himself in a warm resonant voice.

'I am Father Joshua and this is my wife, Rachel. We're over here from the United States on a brief visit.'

April had never met such a man. He had great presence and there was something reassuring about him.

'Are you a priest?'

'Indeed I am, young lady and I'm concerned that you are by yourself in this cold and lonely place. I feel that it is my duty to help you. He gently took her arm and April found herself in back of the Mercedes as it glided away. She sank into the comfortable seat and fell asleep.

A couple of hours later she awoke as the car bumped over a rutted track.

'Take it easy, you've woken our guest,' said Rachel.

'Okay I'll slow down some.'

The car rolled slowly over the dirt road and eventually stopped. They all got out and looked around. It was a beautiful place with a rocky outcrop to their left and an area of rich green grass away to their right beyond which flowed a tumbling river in front of a dense stand of trees.

'This is ideal,' exclaimed Rachel. 'We're going to have a picnic. Come and help me.'

April helped her carry out a large square bag and a cool box from the car boot. A tablecloth was spread on the grass, followed by an assortment of food, including cold roast chicken, French bread, butter, cheeses, chutney, tomatoes and fruit. April began to feel very hungry.

Joshua strode across to the river and knelt beside it, lifting great handfuls of cold water to drink and cover his face. He remained there in silent prayer as Rachel walked around the picnic spread putting down plates, glasses, cutlery and small bottles of water. Finally cushions were placed on three sides and the women sat facing each other and waited quietly. Joshua soon joined them and said prayers. First he blessed the food before them. Next he called on Almighty God to protect his beloved wife Rachel and beseeched the Lord to provide guidance in his ministry. Finally he turned to April and, in a soft and gentle voice, gave special thanks to God for delivering the Blessed April into their loving care and out of the hands of those who would persecute her.

TWENTY-ONE

April couldn't think clearly. Confusing images swirled in her mind as she struggled to make sense of what she had heard. How did he know who she was? She kept her eyes lowered and accepted the food that was being passed round. No one spoke in the quietness of that beautiful place and for a while, she felt safe.

'How do you know who I am?' she asked.

'I have known of your arrival from the beginning' said Joshua. 'The Lord came to me one night and bid me leave my church and journey across the ocean to be on hand to help you. Your arrival here is no surprise. I have been waiting for you.'

'What do you mean? No one knows how I came to be here.'

Joshua stood up and offered a hand to April.

'Come and walk with me.'

They walked across the grass to the river. Joshua seemed thoughtful. Finally he smiled at her and spoke quietly:

'I follow the teaching of the Lord Jesus Christ, who came into this world to deliver men from sin. People need to open their hearts to the love of the creator. The teachings of Jesus are there to help us find the way. Unfortunately over time, many have turned away from God. Nature has sought to maintain a balance by increasing the number of souls. Today there are already far too many people in this world and the trend is for more and more. Everyone knows that this cannot go on.'

They stopped at the edge of the river. Joshua gazed through the trees as if he could see all the sadness of the world.

'People in the rich countries April, have been seduced by the false gods of wealth and sexual debauchery, but they don't bring happiness or personal fulfilment. Now we face great dangers.'

'What dangers?'

'The degradation of the planet arising from overpopulation has already caused many plant and animal species to die out. Today we have the most terrifying warning of all, the disappearances. Everywhere people are being removed at random as a final warning for man to wake up, but people aren't listening and the numbers disappearing are increasing in number, although the authorities everywhere are trying to keep this secret.'

'But no one knows what's causing the disappearances. Why are you so sure that you're right?'

'It's the only answer that makes any sense April. My fear is that the four horsemen of the apocalypse will soon sweep across the entire world bringing war, famine, disease and death. Amid all the dying and destruction, the time will be right for a second coming of a messenger from Almighty God and mankind will at last be ready to accept his word. I have long believed this will happen in the United States, a strong country with a living Christian tradition.'

Joshua stared into the swirling waters of the river.

'The world needs a great torrent to wash away years of ignorance and misunderstandings and bring people once more to the light of Jesus' teaching.'

He turned and looked into April's eyes. She had the impression that he could see right inside her and knew all her hopes and anxieties. They turned and began to walk back to the car. Joshua's ideas seemed to be a bit extreme but he was obviously sincere. She turned to him.

'No one understands about the disappearances and no one knows how I came to be here either.'

They seated themselves around the picnic again and Joshua continued:

'I watched your television broadcast and saw you resist the interviewer's attempt to intimidate you. Your answer that 'he is not my true father' will have caused many to question who you really are. Also your words about the emptiness of our present society have awoken many people around the world to the reality of their own shallow lives. Are you aware of why you are here?'

'I'm just a girl who has slipped through time. I'm not a blessed anybody.'

'Your candour is refreshing,' said Joshua. 'It is clear your journey has some way to go before you begin to understand. Do not be alarmed, April, but there are forces gathering at this moment who are conspiring to take you away and imprison you. Your arrival has disturbed them. The time has come, dear child, for you to leave this place and travel into the west to a place of safety.'

'I know there are people who want to kill me,' said April and told him of the incident at the rubbish tip.

Joshua looked grave. There were tears in his eyes.

'May God forgive them for their wickedness. During that terrible time I can see that you were truly under the Lord's protection.'

'We would like you to remain with us this evening,' said Rachel. 'We are travelling to the city of Worcester and staying at the home of two members of our church. A room can be provided for you, then tomorrow you can decide whether you wish to return with us to the United States.'

'You must not return to Cambridge,' warned Joshua. The Kendricks' house is being watched by police. Also your friends Emily and Jake are in custody. These are good people who have been guided to ease your transition into this world. They have provided you with the love and support you needed but now you must prepare to move on as the forces of repression grow stronger here. This country is no longer safe for you. We can take you to the United States and provide you with a secure place, surrounded by loving friends. It is important that you leave as soon as possible so that your baby may be born without further worry or interference.'

'I'm not pregnant,' exclaimed April in surprise. She looked at Rachel. 'I'm still a virgin, the doctor said so.'

'Perhaps so, but weren't you convinced that you were pregnant before that?' asked Rachel.

April stared at her in disbelief. How could she possibly have known?

'I thought I was but it wasn't true.'

'Don't be so sure. Do you know who the father was?'

'Yes, but I cannot speak about it.'

'Have you been sick, April?'

April admitted that she had. She had awoken early that morning around five o'clock and had been sick. She'd put it down to too much wine and pasta last night. She had also been sick at the hotel after the television interview. Emily had said that it was probably just nerves.

Joshua looked at Rachel. 'I see the hand of the Lord in this. I believe that you may be truly blessed April.'

April scrutinised Joshua's face wondering if she should tell him of her frightening visions. They were getting worse and she was becoming increasingly frightened. She decided to unburden herself and told him of the endless corridor in the hospital, the Kendricks' garden where the sounds and colours drained away and the house was derelict. Finally she spoke of her terror at the petrol station and the encroaching darkness. Her fears had all been bottled up inside. Now as she let them out, she wept uncontrollably.

Joshua was at her side at once. He knelt down and cupped her head in his great hands. She felt the warmth of his palm on her forehead and her fear and panic began to subside.

'These are terrible visions, April,' said Joshua. 'You have seen the coming desolation of the end of days but do not be afraid as these things may not come to pass. A second coming of the Lord Jesus is at hand. Try to be strong and keep your faith in God.'

April stood up and walked away. She stood facing the river. Somehow his explanation didn't feel right and it was too much to take in. She decided to be on her guard.

They resumed their journey and it was clear that Rachel was having difficulty finding her way. As a result, it was getting dark when they drew up outside a suburban house in Worcester. Rachel went in first and spoke with the householders, followed by Joshua with his arm draped protectively around April's shoulders. He looked solemnly at his hosts.

'I am Joshua and this is the Blessed April.'

He smiled fondly down at her. She stepped forward to greet the couple. They were called John and Miriam and seemed overawed. They introduced themselves and Miriam bobbed a small curtsey to April. Rachel quickly took charge and led April upstairs to a bedroom with a double bed and an en suite bathroom. It was obviously their host's own bedroom. Later they sat down to a meal of fresh salmon, salad and new potatoes, followed by fruit compote. Miriam was concerned her guests weren't eating much. April hadn't much appetite after the picnic.

'Those who carry the spirit of the Lord within them do not need as much earthly food.' said Joshua with a nod to April.

'It was a delicious meal' said Rachel, who was helping Miriam to clear the table. The women retired to the kitchen as the others moved to the sitting room. There was a large framed colour photograph of Joshua above the fireplace.

'Have you anything you wish to say to our host?' asked Joshua.

'I'm grateful to you and your wife for taking me in and for an excellent meal,' said April.

'It's a privilege to have you all here.'

Coffee appeared. April sipped hers but it tasted bitter and she pushed her cup away.

Later, as they sat around the comfortable room, John and Miriam sought guidance on the relevance of Jesus' teaching in the present day. Joshua was in his element. There was no theorising, just the need for down to earth faith and constant prayer. He holds them in the palm of his hand thought April, reminding them of why they are here and their duty to the creator. After a while, she had heard enough religious talk and retired to her bedroom to be alone. She needed time to think.

She sat on the bed wondering whether she should go to America. How could that be arranged and what would it be like over there? Would she be safe? Would she ever be able to return? Joshua seemed to be showing her off like a prize lamb. What would he do when he discovered she wasn't pregnant? Did he think she was like the Virgin Mary? If so, he must be barmy. She thought back on her extraordinary day and what Joshua and Rachel had said. They knew a great deal about her. She didn't believe all that talk about being informed by God. He must have had people spying on her. That's how he'd got the information. He hadn't mentioned Harvey Weinberg. That's because his spies didn't know about him. She wished that he'd been honest about that and not so caught up in his predictions of doom. She felt Joshua was essentially a good man, but could she trust him? Leaving for America would be a drastic step.

Staying in England was also a problem as everything was going wrong. When the police caught her next time there would be no escape, just lots of questions. But what would happen after that? Would she have to make a public confession that she'd been lying? That would be awful but better than the rubbish dump. On the other hand, if she continued to run, she might be able to link up with Emily and Jake again.

There was a picture on the bedroom wall of roses in a bowl. It reminded her of a similar one in the hall at home. Her mother was fond of it. The memory of her mother was painful, touching something deep inside her. She'd never come to terms with the fact that her mum was dead and longed to see her again. She thought of her friends and her allies, Marcus and Harvey. She was not alone. At that moment, she knew that she would stay in England. She would tell Joshua and Rachel of her decision in the morning and would face the future and try to be brave.

She was startled out of her thoughts by a tentative knock at the door and the appearance of a nervous Miriam carrying a mug of hot milk on a plate.

'Rachel thought this might help you sleep.'

April thanked her and took the milk. Miriam seemed rooted to the spot and was clearly agitated.

'What's the matter?' asked April.

'Oh Miss, you mustn't drink the milk. It's drugged to make you sleep. Then they're going to drive you to an airfield. They've got a plane ready to fly to America. By the time you wake up you'll be over there.'

'How do you know this?'

'He was making arrangements on his phone in the garden just now. I'd just gone out for a cigarette and he didn't know I was there. Have I done the right thing in telling you?'

April felt something go cold inside.

'Yes, you were right to tell me. Thank you very much.'

'I've been told to lock up the house but I'll leave the front door unlocked for the time being if you want to leave.'

'Thank you. I should like to go in a few minutes.'

April took the milk to the bathroom and poured it away. 'There. You can tell them I drank it.'

'I'd better go now.' Miriam hesitated by the door and went down on one knee. 'Will you bless me?' she asked.

April took a deep breath and thought for a moment. Then she stepped forward and placed her hand on Miriam's head.

'You have my thanks and the blessing of Almighty God for you have listened to the voice of your conscience this night and obeyed His will. Go in peace. Be strong and may the Lord always be with you.'

Miriam crept out and went downstairs. I ought to be on the stage thought April. That wasn't at all bad. So they were planning to kidnap me? They'd been lying all along. She felt disappointed in Joshua. He'd obviously gone bad somewhere along the way. There was no time to lose. She grabbed her backpack, tiptoed down the stairs and crept silently along the hall to where Miriam was waiting by the front door.

'Where are you going?'

Rachel had come into the hall from the kitchen. April turned and looked her in the eye:

'I've decided to leave.'

Rachel walked forward slowly closing the gap between them.

'You can't go now. We agreed to wait until morning.'

'I'm going now,' said April turning towards the front door.

'No you're not.' Rachel sprang forward and grabbed April around the neck from behind, pulling her backwards.

Miriam wrenched a walking stick from the hallstand, ran forward and brought it down with a crack on Rachel's head who slumped to the ground. She ran to the front door, opened it, threw out April's backpack and shouted:

'Go now.'

April slipped through the door and disappeared into the night. Joshua, hearing the commotion came out into the hall. He gave a little cry and knelt down beside Rachel.

'What happened here?'

'I hit her with this because she was trying to stop April leaving,' said Miriam. She stood defiantly with her back to the door brandishing the walking stick.

Incomprehension clouded Joshua's face.

'She couldn't have, April's asleep upstairs.'

'No she's not. She's gone.'

Joshua stared at her. His face hardened.

'You struck Rachel with that stick?'

'Yes. I had to get April away.'

Rachel was groaning and holding her head as Joshua helped her up, just as John came into the hall, wondering where everyone had got to. He was surprised to see his wife, her face set with determination, gripping a walking stick.

'Is everything all right?'

April ran down the dark suburban street. Getting out had been easy. Knowing what to do next was not. A car came round the corner and she dived into a front garden for cover until it had passed. I'm hiding from passing cars she thought. Get a grip. Apart from Joshua, no one knows you are here. She walked briskly on into the city centre. Although it was Sunday night, quite a lot of young revellers were still on the streets. She moved easily among them, heartened by their presence.

Eventually she found the sign she was looking for and made her way to the empty railway station. She scanned the timetables on the wall and saw that the first train to London left at six thirty in the morning. What could she do for the remaining six hours? Staying on the station wasn't a good idea. It was one of the places that Joshua would check. Going to a hotel might also be risky. He could check those too. She'd better try to find somewhere to lie low for the rest of the night. At that moment, she heard a car approaching. It stopped in the road outside. A door slammed and she heard footsteps approaching. She shrank back into the shadows and held her breath.

'Hello April. I thought I'd find you here.'

TWENTY-TWO

April's disappearance was a shock to Joshua. How had she withstood the sleeping drug? He confronted Miriam, challenging her that she had encouraged April to leave. To his surprise she stood firm, no longer a timid mouse but a strong assertive woman determined to hold her ground. What could have brought about such a transformation? He was sure that it could only be the power of faith. Something must have happened during those few minutes she had shared with April when she took up the milk. He had travelled all the way to England to find April and now she had gone. Driving around Worcester in the dark looking for her would be useless and without Rachel's navigation he might not be able to find his way back. He wondered whether there could be some truth in his assertions about this girl. Was it possible that April had been truly sent by God?

He thought back to her arrival from a distant time, her extraordinary television appearance and those terrible visions. This was no ordinary girl. She had both questioned and challenged his faith. None of his followers had ever done that. He saw with a feeling of deep sadness that he was not meant to play a part in her destiny.

He went to his bedroom with Rachel to pray and ask for God's forgiveness. He had tried to interfere with God's chosen instrument on earth and now his greed and ambition were painfully and mercilessly revealed. The Lord was showing him the need for true humility. Much chastened, they gathered their belongings and, after thanking their hosts, departed for the airfield for the return to Kansas City.

...

'Jake! How on earth did you find me?'

April ran into his arms and they hugged and kissed.

'There's no time to waste kid. We gotta split before the fuzz turn up.'

As the silver Mini rolled on through the darkness, April sat watching the road unfold before them in the headlights. She felt secure and happy with Jake, marvelling at the change from the loneliness she had felt at the railway station. Jake loved her. He had said so and she knew that she wanted to be with him. Everything felt different when they were together. It was a kind of contentedness and a certainty that they belonged with each other. She couldn't imagine how she had believed herself to be in love with James Fleming all those weeks ago. That had come out of her fear of being pregnant. But she wasn't pregnant and in spite of all the burdens she carried, she and Jake had found each other. There would be difficulties ahead. She was worried about Emily and couldn't help feeling guilty about betraying her friend. It wouldn't be possible to return to the Kendricks' home but Jake had promised to keep her safe and she believed him. Their love had saved her from the feelings of terror about her pursuers. She didn't know what lay ahead but she was with Jake. He made her feel alive and she had never needed anyone so much.

As they drove north along on the M5 towards Birmingham, Jake explained how the money belt she was wearing contained two miniature tracking devices so, when she went AWOL, he was able to locate her. One was a vague long distance indicator and the other was fairly accurate over a short range.

'They're two bits of kit that I put together and they're not that reliable so I was lucky to find you.'

'I'm the lucky one,' said April. 'I have never been so glad to see anyone in my life. What happened to you and where's Emily? Is she alright?'

'I'm sure she's fine. The police kept us at the station in Carmarthen until a senior officer came over from Cardiff. We stuck to our story that you were in London. We were threatened with being kept there overnight but I insisted on phoning my parents. Shortly after that, the police received a telephone call from my parents' solicitor in London and we were promptly released and returned to the cottage. After the police had gone, I went up and checked the clearing in the wood. It was already early afternoon and I assumed that you were long gone. We packed and set off back to London along the motorway with the police discreetly following us.

Emily managed to drop me off in Cardiff without them noticing. I returned the cottage keys to my parents and hired this car.'

'Emily continued her journey to London without me, hopefully being followed by the cops. She'll have taken her time, making some long stops along the way. By now she should be safely back in my apartment in the West End.'

'Are we going to London?'

'No. We're heading for the Kendricks' weekend cottage in Norfolk. Now what have you been up to?'

'I'm not sure you'll believe it but here goes anyway.' She told him everything.

'That's quite a story,' said Jake at last. 'Those weirdos did well to find you but I don't think they'll trouble you again. The police already knew about them and seemed genuinely concerned for your welfare. They had staked out their plane at the airfield so Joshua would never have got you out of the country. If he had tried, he would have found himself down at the police station assisting them with their enquiries.'

'We'll stop at the next service station for petrol. I fancy a strong coffee to keep me going and, if I'm lucky, a quick blessing.'

'Any more of that and you'll get a quick thump.'

'Emily will meet us tomorrow and that will give us a chance to review the situation. Your Old Testament prophet was right about one thing. This country isn't safe for you at the moment. We need to get you out as soon as possible.'

Later, as the car hummed along the A14, April was feeling washed out. She had been sick again in the toilets at the service station and wondered if she should mention it. She had spoken of her frightening visions to Joshua but his apocalyptic views had only added to her anxieties. She trusted Jake and decided to tell him. He listened in silence until she had finished. He kept his eyes on the road and asked questions about her sensory awareness and what, if anything, she had heard or smelled at the time. He was particularly concerned about the pain she was experiencing in her head.

'Why didn't you tell us about this earlier?'

'I thought it might be something to do with my head injury and I didn't want to go back into hospital. Do you know what's going on, Jake?'

'I think that it's almost certainly a medical problem so you should speak to Sarah as soon as possible.' He stared ahead as the lights picked out the road. 'This is outside my field, although I have an outlandish idea that I must think about.'

'What idea?'

'As I said it's a bit wacky, so let's leave it.'

'No. I don't care how wacky it is, I want to hear it.' She stared across at him. 'I'm sorry, Jake, but you don't know what it's like. It's frightens me and it's getting worse. I feel I'm on the edge of something. If it happens again, I might not survive.'

'Alright, I'll try if you insist. It'll probably sound mad so don't take it to heart. Have you heard of entropy?' She hadn't. 'No, of course you haven't. In one sense it's a way of measuring the stability of systems. This world is a dynamic but fundamentally stable system where scientific laws are consistent. If it weren't stable, any kind of odd thing could happen.'

'You've lost me already,' said April. 'What has this got to do with me?'

'I'm thinking about your personal reality,' said Jake. 'You arrive here and everything appears to be normal but there are moments of instability. Although your position in this world is stable, these visions are like a wobble in your reality and I'm sure they must be terrifying.'

'What do they mean?'

'They mean that you don't belong here. Your temporal roots are still in 1959 and your personal reality hasn't fully integrated into this time so there are breakdowns.'

'Will they get worse?'

'I have no idea. There is a tendency for systems to stabilise, so you might be alright in the long run. However I am concerned that things are getting worse at present, as that indicates that your link here is slipping. You could lose your connection with this world completely.'

'What will happen to me?'

'Again, I don't know. Think of it as a body rejecting something that doesn't belong. You came into this world and may pass out of it again.'

'Jake, you're frightening me. I was hoping for some reassurance.'

'I'm sorry, but you did press me to share my thoughts. I should have kept my big mouth shut. I care for you, April and I'd do anything if I thought it would help, but this is beyond me. As I said before, it's most likely to be a medical problem. We'll talk to Emily about it tomorrow.'

April was quiet for a long time.

'If I disappear, where will I go? Am I going to die?'

'I'm sorry, I just don't know.'

He felt terrible. He couldn't resist showing off and now he'd upset her. The car rolled past Cambridge and into East

Anglia. He looked across in the dim light and saw her face was wet with tears. He was filled with guilt and couldn't find any words. He wanted to stop the car, take her in his arms and promise her that everything was going to be alright. He drove on.

The eastern sky was already lightening when they reached the cottage just before three thirty in the morning. They went straight to bed. After they had made love, Jake held her close as they sank into sleep.

She was kneeling on the edge of a vast pit. She'd been shot and her blood was dripping down into the rubbish far below. She could see the drops. They were spreading out and turning into blood-red poppies. The whole tip was filled with them. She was dying and falling down into the land of the dead.

'No! No, I don't want to die,' she cried out in her sleep.

Jake could see her frightened face in the early morning light. Her eyes were still closed although tears streamed down her face.

'It's alright, my love. It's just a bad dream,' he whispered. He kissed away the salty tears and stroked her face gently until she relaxed and slipped back into sleep.

He awoke around eight with the morning light streaming in around the edges of the curtains. April still lay snuggled up to him. She was lying on his arm. He gently freed it and she stirred but didn't wake.

He watched her sleeping peacefully and remembered the words of Sir Lancelot as he looked upon the Lady of Shallot:

She has a lovely face; God in his mercy lend her grace.

'Please don't die April. I couldn't bear that.' He leant forward and kissed her gently on the forehead.

Later that morning, April came down to find Jake peeling mushrooms for breakfast.

'Where did these come from?'

'I picked them a few minutes ago. They grow in the field alongside the hedge.'

'Are you sure they're edible?'

'All mushrooms are edible, but some of them only once.' He grinned at her look of concern. 'Don't worry, these are ceps and they're delicious.'

...

Emily knew that her journey to London had been tracked by the police. She hoped no one had been able to follow Jake and he'd been able to find April. The security gate clanged shut behind the car as she drove into the private underground car park beneath the apartment block. She was soon up in the Burnstone flat.

Early next morning there was a short text on her mobile from Jake. *Collected the parcel and brought it home.* He had picked up April and they had arrived safely at the cottage. It was welcome news but she felt anxious that they were together. She pushed the painful feelings away and downed a refreshing glass of cold orange juice.

At a quarter to seven she emerged on foot through the service door at the back of the building and walked through a maze of streets to an address in Portland Place where a prearranged taxi was waiting for her. He drove her to Finsbury Square, where she bought a copy of *The Daily Telegraph* and slipped into a cafe for coffee and a bacon sandwich. The *Telegraph* had the Pendleton Hotel story and they were pointing the finger, without saying in so many words, at the activities of the Disappeared Unit within the Home Office. Marcus had fed them the information and they had got their teeth into it. She knew it wouldn't stop there. The rest of the media would be on to it by now.

At eight o'clock she walked into Marcus Clarke's office and collected some letters addressed to April and the manuscript of her ghost written book. It was a short journey from there to Liverpool Street Station where she took a train to Norwich.

At the same time the unmarked police car outside the Burnstone apartment block was still waiting for Emily to emerge. The shift changed at eight and a 'no-show' report was sent back.

After breakfast, Jake and April drove to Norwich Station to collect Emily. On their return, they stopped at a supermarket to collect supplies. As April was likely to be recognised, she stayed in the car as the others did the shopping. Back at the cottage, Emily listened with amazement to April's story.

'You were lucky that woman helped you. If the Americans had kidnapped you, they wouldn't have been able to get you out of the country but you would have finished up in police custody.'

Back at the cottage, prompted by Jake, April told Emily about her frightening visions and the accompanying physical symptoms. Emily was horrified and found it difficult to hide her alarm.

'I wish you'd told us this before. If I had known I would never have proposed all that publicity.'

She immediately sent a text to Sarah. An hour later, she received a call from Edinburgh and took it in the garden. Sarah was at a conference and wouldn't be back in Cambridge until the following day. She asked about April's symptoms, the pain in her head and the scraping sound. She also asked whether she had been sick. She had. Sarah said that she would come out to the cottage as soon as possible but it would be the following afternoon. In the meantime April should not be left alone, even for a minute.

April opened a letter Emily had collected from Marcus's office and was surprised to see it was from James. She took it into the garden and sat on the bench seat to read it:

> My Dear April,
> I have been in turmoil since seeing you on television. The shock was physical, like a blow to the solar plexus. There you were, composed, dignified and strong. You seemed subtly changed physically but I could feel the essence of you so powerfully that I gasped. I was transported back forty years to the wonderful feeling of being with you and was almost immediately hit with crippling anguish and remorse at my betrayal of you. How could I have hurt you so? It's no excuse but I was immature and inexperienced and couldn't handle the overpowering feelings of my first love. I was terrified of losing control of my life and selfishly pursued my desire for personal advance over you. I made a terrible mistake. I want you to know how sorry I am and how much I regret my behaviour.
>
> I must tell you that I am truly concerned for your safety. I lied to the Home Office about your identity

in order to protect you. I feel strongly that going public is a big mistake. There are people who will not have your interests at heart. I so much want to protect you and urge you to get in touch with me if you would like my help.

I cannot imagine how desperate you must feel, trapped in another time and separated from the places and people that gave you meaning and belonging. I am at least someone you know and perhaps contact with me could give you some sense of connectedness even though I am now a generation or two older than you.

Of course a lot has happened to me over the last forty years (less than forty days for you). For ten years after I left you so cruelly I was alone but since then have found happiness in marriage and children. I taught for many years but, as my success as a novelist grew, I gave up teaching for full-time writing. Please get in touch. I am sure you would love my family and I know my wife and children would embrace you.

My warmest wishes,

James.

In spite of everything, April was touched by his love and concern for her welfare. A sign of true love was when you cared more for your partner than for yourself. She tried to recall a sonnet by Shakespeare about that but her memory wasn't working very well. She returned to the cottage and penned a brief reply:

Dear James,

It feels strange to receive your letter. Although it's forty years ago for you, I still feel raw when I remember how you rejected me. After my initial distress and bewilderment I felt a burning anger towards you. Now with your letter there is some relief that perhaps I am not as worthless as you made me feel. There is sadness at what we have lost but I am sure that in time I shall be able to be more objective and your letter will help me come to terms with the trauma of our parting. Thank you for writing so honestly. I cannot think about these things as there is so much happening. Sometimes, especially alone at night, the unspeakable terror of my situation, trapped in another time almost chokes me. What dominates is the constant threat from those forces intent on my destruction. The people who have befriended me are more valuable than words. Without them I would perish. Thank you for your offer of friendship and protection. I may need it.

April

Returning to the cottage after a walk into the village to post April's letter, they sat around the kitchen table going through the manuscript of April's book, scribbling in masses of alterations. They finished around four and decided they would give it to Sarah the next day so she could return it to the publisher. After a walk around the garden they brewed up a pot of tea and Jake unveiled his plan.

TWENTY-THREE

Roger Venn picked at the unappetising salad lunch on his desk. They were blaming him for the police's failure to pick up April Saunders. No one knew where she was. Even worse, her two friends had gone to ground. Emily Kendrick was obviously no longer at the flat, even though the car was still in the underground garage. She'd walked out and the police didn't know when she had left or where she'd gone. Apparently she had dropped off Jake Burnstone somewhere on the way to London and no one seemed to know where he was either. It was a shambles and he was being held responsible. The kids had been clever, he had to give them that, but they couldn't hide for long. He sat back and closed his eyes. He needed to think. After a while he returned to the reports on his desk. The American church couple had left Birmingham with a flight plan that returned them to the Mid-West, so that was the end of them. They'd left empty handed. He wondered why they had given up so easily after coming so far to find April.

The telephone rang. It was one of Sir Harold's assistants and his message was uncompromising:

'… frankly Venn your inability to get this girl picked up is unacceptable. Sir Harold is deeply disappointed. You won't get the job done by sitting at a desk in London and leaving provincial police forces to decide what to do. You need to grip the situation and get out there yourself. You have twenty four hours to resolve this or we'll have to find someone else to do it. I don't need to tell you that could result in another posting for you, probably to the Outer Hebrides.'

Roger bristled with anger. Sir Harold was no longer prepared to speak to him. He'd obviously given this fellow carte blanche to rough him up. He threw his half eaten salad across the room, followed by almost everything else on his desk.

He would kill that wretched girl with his bare hands if necessary. He raged up and down the office before finally sinking back into his chair. After a visit to the washroom, he tried to steady his thoughts and focus on the problem. He mused on the young couple's visit to Wales. They insisted that they'd left April in London, but why? They were April's friends. It didn't make sense. He was inclined to think that she'd been at the cottage all the time and had managed to give the local plods the slip. Another thing troubled him. If Jake and Emily were planning to have a week's holiday at the cottage, why did they take off as soon as they were released? It was a long way to go just for a day or two.

He drummed his fingers on the desk. They must be together, but where? They hadn't returned to Cambridge. He'd made sure the surveillance there was watertight. If they were in London somewhere, it would be difficult to find them, particularly if they didn't make phone calls or use their credit cards. Perhaps the Kendricks' have a weekend cottage. It might be somewhere in East Anglia and would be hard to locate but there are ways of finding these things out. He picked up the telephone.

...

Sir Walter Cunningham-Smith, the Member of Parliament for North Buckinghamshire, believed passionately that people should be allowed to get on with their lives without interference from socialists, bureaucrats or foreigners. The revelations that he'd read in *The Daily Telegraph* over breakfast that morning about a dastardly crime in his constituency had come as a shock. No one had the decency to inform him about it at the time. Crimes like the kidnapping of and attempted murder of this poor girl didn't happen in Buckinghamshire. These villains were obviously outsiders. His calls to the Chief Constable and the Home Office had elicited no more information. The announcement from his office of a press conference at mid-day in the House of Commons on this matter had attracted a large number of reporters. Sir Walter could always be relied on for some good copy and this was a matter of topical interest. He surveyed the serried ranks of newspaper, radio and television reporters with satisfaction then wasted no time in launching into his statement:

'Learnt of this appalling incident this morning ... one of Britain's most exclusive hotels ... innocent gal trying to relax after a busy week, snatched by a gang of ruthless villains ...

intended to murder her and bury her body in a rubbish tip … an outrage … bulldozer driver refused to cooperate and shot… saved her life and probably paid for it with his own … No trace of him… Bad smell about this. Very bad indeed.'

Sir Walter's angry demeanour now changed to a look of deep concern.

'Who were these men, posing as police officers?'

'How did they know this gal was staying at the hotel? No one had been told.'

'Who sent these murderers? And gave them their orders?'

'I have asked for a clear statement from the Home Secretary this morning as to what is going on.'

'Furthermore, I understand that this poor child is still being pursued by the police on the orders of the Home Office. This has got to stop. I expect the Home Secretary to issue a clear statement to that effect.'

Sir Walter paused and surveyed the room.

'It's within living memory for some of us that thousands of people gave their lives in a war against fascism so that this country would remain free. In spite of that, today the Home Office have a network of secret interrogation centres that are not open to public scrutiny. For some time they have behaved as if they are above the law. If some part of the Home Office is behind this crime, then it's time to act now. It was Thomas Jefferson who said that: *The price of freedom is eternal vigilance.* He was quite right. I fear that we may have taken our eye off the ball for too long.'

Sir Walter took a number of questions, but wouldn't be drawn further about his suspicions concerning Home Office complicity. He had sowed some seeds. It was up to the media now.

The journalists trooped out. Sir Walter hadn't let them down.

...

'April needs to get out of this country as soon as possible,' said Jake. 'We've been lucky so far but we can't go on hiding. The bloodhounds will soon be back on our trail. Sooner or later the tractor boys are likely to turn up here.'

'Who are the tractor boys?' asked April.

'That's just a term for the local police. They're generally held to be a bit slow' said Emily. She turned to Jake. 'How do you propose to get April out of Britain and where is she to go?'

'Switzerland. Granddad can fly in and pick her up. I've already spoken to him and he's tickled pink at the idea. I think he enjoys a challenge.'

'But April hasn't got a passport?'

'That can be taken care of. Leave it to Uncle Jake.'

'That sounds illegal. Don't forget it's my job to keep you out of trouble. In any event, Mum's coming to see April tomorrow. We can talk to her and decide what to do after that. How do you feel about going abroad, April?'

They looked across the room but April wasn't there. She'd gone out to the back garden to be by herself. She needed to think. It wasn't safe for her here and she couldn't expect Jake and Emily to keep putting themselves out for her. They would be in trouble with the police themselves before long. She stood at the bottom of the garden near the big oak tree by the back fence.

'What am I going to do?' she said aloud.

Everything's going to be alright April.

She looked around but there was no one there. She looked behind the tree but there was no one there either.

'Are you okay?' called Emily hurrying down the garden.

'Yes. I'm fine. I just needed some air. Funny thing though; just before you came I heard a woman's voice. It sounded like my mother. Perhaps I'm going round the bend.'

'Of course you're not. What did the voice say?'

'She was telling me that everything's going to be alright.'

'I'm sure it is. Come on back to the house. It's my turn to cook this evening and you're helping.'

After dinner they played scrabble. They were laughing about a rude word that Emily had spelled when, out of the blue, April spoke:

'I'm ready to leave. I don't belong here. You said it yourself Jake and you were right.'

'No he wasn't,' retorted Emily. 'He had no right to say such a thing. You do belong here and we're going to see that you're safe.'

'I don't think you can. It feels like my time is running out and I'm slipping away. Perhaps all the stresses of the last month have been too much. I'm grateful for everything you've done for me. If I should go, I'd like you to remember that. No one could have had better friends.'

That night the two girls shared the double bed. April wasn't herself and couldn't be left alone. She confessed that she'd slept with Jake the previous night. Emily said that she understood and it was alright but it wasn't. Everything was going wrong and Jake had obviously become infatuated with her. She felt herself seething inside.

One way or another, April would have to go.

• • •

The next morning it was raining. Sir Harold Anderson was woken at his club by a call at quarter past six in the morning. The Home Secretary wanted to see him at eight o'clock. He presented himself on time and was shown in.

'Thanks for turning out so early Harold. I spoke to the Prime Minister last night about this Saunders girl business. There's been a lot of media speculation about the Pendleton Hotel fiasco. I expect you've heard about it.'

'Yes, indeed I have. It's a terrible business.'

'Quite. The problem is that people are trying to blame it on the Home Office. Frankly I'm just as much in the dark as you are. The Prime Minister is going to have to answer questions about this in the house this afternoon and I have given him my word that this girl is not being sought by police.'

'You do know that she's a returnee.'

'Do I? Why hasn't she aged? She's a deluded girl, that's all. Although she's probably got a persecution complex by now. I want the police hunt stopped immediately and that's an order.'

'Very well, Home Secretary. I'll see that's done straight away.'

'Thank you, Harold. How are the family these days?'

• • •

Jake drove up the lane in the early morning drizzle as far as the next cottage. He left the car there and jogged back feeling sad and confused. Why had he frightened April? Faced with her distress, he had retreated into the comfortable world of ideas, when what she needed were words of comfort and reassurance.

A woman passing with her dog gave him a furtive glance.

He'd been so intent on showing off he'd forgotten about the burden she was carrying. He'd let her down. When she was explaining what he'd said yesterday, Emily had given him such a venomous look. He'd apologised but the damage had been done. She was starting to believe that she didn't belong here, undoing everything that Richard, Sarah and Harvey had told her. What makes us kick people when they're down, he wondered? Especially those we love?

'You're a waste of space, Burnstone,' he said aloud as he approached the cottage.

At the same time he couldn't shut out the experience of making love to April. He wanted it to happen again.

When the girls appeared, Jake already had the kettle on and was preparing breakfast.

'Have you been out?' asked Emily, noticing his damp jeans.

'Yep, I've been up to Roke cottage.'

'Were they there?'

'No. They only come at odd weekends these days.'

The owners, Robin and Heike, lived in Norwich. They had bought the small cottage last year as a weekend retreat. The problem was that Heike was a real *hausfrau*. She found the cottage too primitive and never wanted to leave the sleek modern kitchen in their city flat.

Later that morning, Jake noticed a car driving slowly up the lane.

'That'll be the tractor lads.'

'It can't be,' said Emily. 'They would have stopped here.'

'If my guess is right, they'll soon be calling at Roke cottage. I switched the house names this morning and left the Mini up there.' He grinned.

'A good move but I don't believe the local police are as dim as you think,' said Emily. 'They may call to ask if we know anything. Let's clear the breakfast things, sort out the upstairs and hide April's backpack. She can wait at the bottom of the garden. I'll deal with them if they call. She pulled on an apron and poured flour on the kitchen table. She swished it around and smeared it onto her apron. 'Heike' was ready to face all comers.

The car drew up and two uniformed officers came to the door.

'Miss Kendrick, I wonder if we might come in.'

'Kendrick? Nein. Ich bin Heike.'

'It's alright, Miss Kendrick. It seems that children have been swapping some of the house names around.'

Emily stepped back as they entered the little kitchen.

'We've come to speak to Miss April Saunders. Will you ask her to come here please?'

Emily stiffened. Her voice was cold.

'She's in the back garden. You can take her away now.'

Jake started in disbelief at this betrayal. He stepped forward to block the back door.

'What's the hell's the matter with you, Em?'

'You know what the matter is. After everything I've done for her she stabs me in the back.' Her voice rose to a furious scream – 'I want her out of here NOW.'

Seeing the fury on Jake's face, a policeman moved between them.

'Calm down you two and listen to me. We haven't come to collect April but to inform her in person that the Home Office are no longer seeking her.'

In the ensuing silence Emily slumped to the floor with her hands over her face.

. . .

Hiding behind the oak tree at the end of the garden, April waits and watches the back of the cottage with its pebbly walls and brown tiled roof. She sees a car draw up and two policemen get out and go inside. The fields beyond the little house glow bright green in the morning sunlight. Along their edges, the lines of Scots pines are contorted into dramatic patterns by winter winds. In this flat Norfolk landscape, coastal gales sweep inland before their force is weakened by the trees. The light blue sky is fading to a delicate pink at the horizon. In spite of her past fears, April feels happy and hopeful that all will be well.

But as she watches the fields beyond the cottage, she experiences a sharp stab of horror. Beneath the line of trees, a shadow is slowly rising and beginning to advance across the field towards the road and the cottage. As it increases in speed, she hears a rasping sound in her head and it begins to ache. Now the darkness is expanding and moving rapidly towards her. For a moment the cottage stands out against the total blackness before it too disappears. Her head burns with pain as the noise rises to a thunderous roar. Darkness rushes down the garden swallowing everything before it. There is no longer any ground or sky. April stumbles over the back fence and runs desperately across the field until her legs give way and she collapses, crying out for her mother before oblivion finally claims her.

A rider cantering along the field boundary sees someone running at full speed before falling down. He spurs his horse on until he reaches the figure collapsed in a crouching position. He dismounts and approaches her.

'Are you alright?'

There is no response. He reaches down and touches her arm. She rolls over. It is a white-faced girl who is unconscious. Staring round, he realises she must have come from the cottage on the lane. He runs towards it vaults over the fence, dashes up the garden and hammers on the back door.

'Is anyone there?'

The door bursts open. Three men stare at him as a young woman in an apron pushes herself to the front and, on hearing his breathless news, races down the garden and into the field, followed by the men. They catch up with her, kneeling with her ear on April's chest. Emily looks up in desperation.

'She's alive, but only just …'

PART 3

FINDING APRIL

TWENTY-FOUR

The London rock concert in May 1959 was a sell-out. Among the fans were three lads from Sheffield.

Alec Gorman was just seventeen. He'd enjoyed the Concert. Bill had managed to get tickets and Des had borrowed his dad's car. The three drove down to London together. It was a long way but a straight run down the A1 and had been a great adventure until they'd stopped for a piss on the way back the next day. Des had been dying to go and had driven across the road into a lay-by on the southbound side. There were woods there so they all got out and went into the trees.

Bill saw her first. He spotted something at the bottom of the slope and climbed down to investigate. He shouted to the others who came to stare at the figure of a girl in the ditch. She was obviously unconscious and lying with her back to them. Her legs were cut and badly scratched and there was dried blood on the back of her head and the skirt of her dress.

'She must have been here for days' said Alec.

He knelt down and felt her wrist for a pulse.

'She's very cold but she's still alive. We'd better contact the police and ambulance people straight away.'

They clambered back up the slope to decide what to do.

'I'm having nothin to do with the police,' said Des, who had recently had a run in with the local constabulary. 'She's bin raped and the police will be lookin for someone to blame. That'll be us. I know how they work. If she's dead, we'll be charged with murder and you know what that means.'

The others looked scared.

'That won't happen,' said Alec. 'If we report it now, they'll know we didn't do it. They'll thank us for telling them.'

'Doan you believe it,' said Des. 'They'll say we picked her up on the way down, raped her, then stopped this mornin to see if she was still here. They'll pin this on us for sure.'

'What we gonna do?' asked Bill.

'I'm not leaving her,' said Alec. 'You two go if you want to. I'll stay and flag down the first lorry driver. He'll know what to do.' He started to look up and down the road.

'If you do that the police might think it was me and Des who beat her up cause we're runnin' away,' moaned Bill.

They stared at each other as they tried to decide.

'What are we going to do?' said Alec.

'We'll leave a message at the next garage,' said Des.

'Yeah, les do that 'said Bill.

'No. She's still alive,' said Alec. 'If we leave a message, she might not be found until it's too late. We've got to help her now.'

'Okay. Let's bring her up and I'll drive to the nearest hospital. Then we'll leg it.'

This was agreed so they edged down to the ditch, lifted the girl and carried her slowly up the steep slope.

Alec sat with her lying across the back seat, covered with a rug from the car boot. Her head rested in his lap and he held on to prevent her slipping on to the floor.

'Drive carefully. We don't want her thrown about,' he warned.

They set off, continuing their journey north. They had passed Peterborough which had the nearest hospital but Des wasn't prepared to go back.

'Lucky you had that rug in the back,' said Bill. 'She'd got really cold in that ditch.'

'Stamford's coming up. We can drop her here,' suggested Alec.

Des drove on without answering for a while.

'Stamford's just a little place. I bet they haven't got a hospital. We'll go on to Grantham.'

'We must stop there,' warned Alec. 'She needs to see a doctor urgently. We can't deliver a dead girl to hospital.'

'Stop worrying. We're goin' to the hospital in Grantham.'

Des drove into the hospital car park and followed the *Accidents* sign. They pulled up near to the double doors and waited until a couple had gone in. Then they placed the rug on the ground in front of the entrance and carefully laid the girl on it folding the rest of it over her. Alec placed his windcheater under her head.

'You'll be alright now,' he whispered.

They drove around the corner and stopped out of sight of the double doors. Alec got out, walked back and watched the entrance through some bushes. Soon a man came out and stopped in surprise. He ran back and a returned a minute later with a nurse and a doctor. The boys went home.

No matter how hard he tried, Alec couldn't get the girl out of his mind. His mates had obviously decided to forget about it but her fate troubled him. It was the not knowing. Did she recover or did she die? If she was still unconscious, the authorities might not know who she was. Her family must be so worried. He had scanned the papers for news but found no mention of her.

They had done their best but he knew they should have told the police at the time. Three weeks later, he walked into the local police station and told them the whole story.

As soon as the Grantham police were informed of Alec Gorman's testimony, they realised that the woodland where the injured girl had been found came within the jurisdiction of the Peterborough force. They made immediate contact and the inspector in Peterborough suspected that the girl could be April Saunders, who had last been seen at Wansford Services. He sent for the file on her disappearance and the case of the van driver who had been stabbed in the same wood just off the A1. The times fitted together but he would need to know where she was found. When the van driver had been found there had been no trace of a girl.

He passed on the news to Inspector Lane at Milsham. The girl had been transferred from Grantham to a specialist brain unit at Nottingham Hospital. Lane took down the details and it was arranged that they would meet there the following day. He would also bring a member of April's family to see whether they could identify her.

Later that day, accompanied by Jenny Jones, Lane called at the Saunders' house. When Shirley answered the door her heart missed a beat as she scanned their faces. She had been dreading the awful news that April might be dead. After a month with no new findings her neighbours and friends obviously thought that must be the outcome, although they had never said it. They had been very supportive and hinted to Shirley that she should try to accept that April might not come back. She wouldn't admit that to herself and kept up her hope that April would be found one day, safe and well.

They came together in the front room. Shirley sat wringing her hands in her lap. Jenny was shocked at her appearance. April's loss had taken its toll. She looked thinner and more drawn and her hair was noticeably greyer. Lane nodded and began:

'Mrs Saunders, there is a possibility that April has been found. At this stage that is all we can say. There is a girl in . . .'

'Is she alive? Is she alright?' interrupted Shirley, her desperation getting the better of her.

Lane waited patiently until her questions had subsided then continued:

'There is a girl answering April's description in hospital in Nottingham. She has been there for three weeks and she is in a coma. Until now, no one knew who she was but some information has come to light that suggests that she could possibly be April.'

'She's in a coma in a hospital in Nottingham? I don't understand. How did she get there?'

Lane explained how she had been found lying in a ditch and had finished up in hospital.

'Is she going to be alright?'

'I'm not a doctor, Mrs Saunders, so I can't answer that question. We don't know for certain that this girl is April. Would you be prepared to come with us to Nottingham tomorrow to help with identifying her?'

Shirley nodded and had to wipe away her tears.

'I'm so sorry, Inspector it's been such a strain.'

'I do understand, Mrs Saunders, I have two daughters myself. Could you be ready at eight o'clock tomorrow morning? We can pick you up from here.'

'Of course I'll be ready.'

After the police had gone Shirley struggled to recover her composure. Overcome with the hope that April was alive she wept for a long time after which she felt better. Then she washed, changed her clothes and put on some fresh make-up before hurrying up the road to telephone Carol. She would tell Ron when he returned from work. She knew he would be cautious. 'Don't get your hopes up love,' he'd say. Arriving home she began to fret about what to wear the following day. Apparently, there would be police there from Peterborough, Grantham and Nottingham and they were all relying on her to identify this girl. In her heart, Shirley felt sure it would be April.

The following morning she was out of the front door and into the back seat of the police car as it pulled up. A twitch of the bedroom curtains next door observed her departure. The local police were already waiting when they arrived and greeted Shirley sympathetically. The inspector from Peterborough had already been in to see the sleeping girl and had been able to match her appearance against the photograph he had received from Milsham a month before. He felt sure that she was April Saunders but would keep his own counsel. April's mother would know her own child. They would wait on her verdict.

A doctor ushered Shirley into a small room. Blinds at the windows suffused everywhere with a soft light. In a single bed lay a girl who seemed to be asleep. She approached the bed cautiously until she stood trembling with a hand over her mouth, looking down at the face of her daughter. She turned and whispered:

'Is she going to wake up, Doctor? Will she be alright?'

The doctor explained about April's head injury and how it could have been fatal.

'There is a possibility that she will wake but we cannot say whether she will or when that will be. If she does come back, you should prepare yourself for the likelihood of some memory loss. There are no certainties in this situation.'

. . .

Three weeks went by without any change while Shirley and Carol were constant visitors.

Shirley leant with her face close to April and whispered:
'Can you hear me, dear? Everything's going to be alright.'
Carol smiled at her mother. 'You always say that.'
'I know she can hear me and I'm trying to tell her, that's all,' said Shirley. 'I suppose I'm trying to reassure myself as well.' She stood up and stretched. 'I'm sure she's going to wake up. Remember what the nurse said. Many patients come out of a coma within two or three months.'

She bent over and stroked April's hair gently.
'Mum's here, April dear. Everything's going to be alright.'
'Mum?'

After weeks of silence that small word was manna from heaven.

'You've been ill, love but you're getting better,' breathed Shirley in her daughter's ear. 'I'm here and Carol too.'

She looked up but Carol had gone. She was running down the corridor to the nurse's room. They quickly summoned the doctor and all returned together. Shirley turned to them, her face radiant.

'She's back, Doctor. She spoke to me.'

'That is good news. He went to the bedside and checked April's pulse and temperature, talking quietly to her.

'Can you hear me, April?'

'Where am I?'

'You're in hospital. I'm a doctor. Try and look at me.'

Slowly her eyes moved and eventually came to rest on the doctor's face.

'That's good. You're doing very well.'

From that day, April made steady progress. Her memory was fragmentary. She couldn't remember getting on the coach or what happened afterwards. She recalled bits about living in Cambridge and being pursued by the police. Shirley and Carol were puzzled.

'Has Emily been to see me?' she asked one day.

'Who's Emily?' Carol asked.

'She's my friend.'

'She must mean Mandy,' said Shirley.

On another day she wanted to know:

'Where's Jake? He loves me.'

That will be James, they thought.

The family were concerned about the names until the doctor explained.

'It's not uncommon for people in a coma to dream. If April has been dreaming she could still be confused between dream and reality. These things that she's been saying about Cambridge are obviously from a dream. Don't worry, it will right itself in time.'

When April was well enough, Mandy came to visit with Brian. She was determined to behave normally, although she couldn't escape her feelings of guilt about the lies she had told. When she approached the bed with her bunch of flowers, April had smiled.

'Hello Mandy.'

'Hello April. You look really well. I'm so. . .'

Her voice faltered. Weeks of tension and anxiety caught up with her. She left the room and walked around the hospital garden, then stood and took in deep breaths to compose herself. Ten minutes later, she rejoined Brian at April's bedside. They had brought a large get-well card that had been made in the art class. It included nearly thirty signatures and little messages of support. There was even a scrawled and uneven signature from *Gary*. April was puzzled for a moment until she remembered. It was Fatty Gates.

For weeks, Mandy, Brian and their team of volunteers had scoured every inch of the local area trying to find a clue to April's disappearance. They talked to dozens of people and chased up every lead but it had led nowhere. Mandy became tired but was determined to go on. She and Brian worked as a team and got together every evening to review their progress. They were a support for each other and he was impressed by her fierce determination and refusal to give up. He found himself more and more attracted to her.

The search had brought them closer and Mandy knew that she couldn't have kept it up without his support. When they were out walking he would often hold her hand. She liked that and noticed that he smiled at her a lot, although he never said why. When she cried with frustration and despair, he would give her a hug.

One day when they were walking along the river, she looked so forlorn that he took her face in his hands and kissed her. She had drawn back in surprise. They continued in silence for a while.

'Why did you do that? What were you thinking about?'

'Nothing. I just wanted to kiss you. What's more I'm going to do it again.'

Mandy tried to take this in. Did he think about her in that way? He must do but she hadn't been expecting it. He'd always been fond of April. She looked at him cautiously as they left the river path and headed for home. How did she feel about him?

After a few yards he stopped and took her in his arms, gently drew her to him and kissed her again. Mandy found herself kissing him back. Afterwards they stood with their arms around each other.

'I want you to be my girl. What do you say?'

Mandy felt her cheeks colouring.

'I'll think about it.'

'No you won't. This isn't a time for thinking, I want a straight answer.'

'Are you sure?'

'Of course I'm sure. I really like you. What do you say?'

'Alright then.'

. . .

Alec Gorman was taken by the police to the part of the ditch where the boys had found her. It was about fifty yards north of where the stabbed van driver had been found. April must have crawled along the ditch to get away from her attacker. A detailed search was carried out along the ditch and they found a scrap of April's dress and her watch. Shirley confirmed that they had both come from her daughter.

After her early fragmentary recollections and initial confusion, April's memory improved steadily and, as soon as she was judged to be well enough, the inspector from Peterborough returned to interview her. He was apologetic about asking her to explain what had happened. April told him all she could remember about her meeting with 'Fred' until finally passing out. The inspector was curious about the sharp stick and whether she could remember crawling along the ditch. Finally he asked whether the driver had mentioned anything about the goods he was carrying or where he was going. April thought he had said something about collecting carpets from somewhere and would drop her off in Milsham on the way.

'I doubt whether any of that story is true,' said the inspector. 'He was carrying a consignment of drugs in a large case beneath his seat. I believe that they were destined for an address in London. He was found lying in the ditch on the Tuesday and died in Peterborough Hospital the following day without regaining consciousness.'

April had a strong feeling of déjà vu. She had heard all this before and said nothing.

'When we issued a statement about the van driver after he died,' said the inspector, 'we said nothing about the drugs. We wanted to flush out the gang who had supplied them. Now that you have been found, the criminals involved might think that you know something of their whereabouts. It's most unlikely but one or more of them could show up here. Therefore the local police are placing an officer outside this room to protect you. It's really important that we catch these people.'

Carol, who had been listening, reacted with indignation.

'It's far more important that April isn't placed under threat or the hospital isn't invaded by dangerous gangsters. You have a duty to protect the public, particularly the vulnerable. You should publicise the fact that you have these drugs immediately. If you don't, I will.'

Within twenty four hours, the police had issued a statement about their meeting with April 'at an undisclosed venue'. The statement included details of the drugs seizure and that she had been unaware of them.

On one occasion when Carol and April were alone, Carol broached a delicate subject.

'Did the doctor tell you that you'd had a miscarriage when you were found?'

'Yes.'

'It wasn't James, was it?'

April confirmed that it wasn't.

'The person responsible was much closer to home wasn't he?'

April looked away and bit her lip.

'You won't tell Mum will you?'

'Alright. But when I get home I'll put the fear of God into him. He won't trouble you again. If he ever comes near you, you must tell me straight away and I'll tell Mum. Do you promise?'

'Yes I promise. Does Mum know what happened?'

'The doctor told her that you'd had a miscarriage. She hasn't said anything but I can tell that she's worried.'

'It's my fault. He said I'd encouraged him and Mum would despise me if she found out. I'd probably be turned out of the house.'

'That's a lie. You didn't do anything of the sort. Why do you think I left home at sixteen?'

'What? Surely he didn't … not you as well?'

'Yes. I'm afraid so. I warned him to keep away from you. I should have spoken up but it would have devastated Mum. You were only thirteen at the time. To be honest, I was worried how you would take it. I feared that you wouldn't be able to keep quiet. I was also concerned that you might not believe me. I'll always feel guilty that I didn't warn you. I've had three years to tell you about him and I never said anything. All this, your illness and your miscarriage are my fault.'

'I wish you had told me. When I found out that I was pregnant, I wanted to speak to you but I couldn't.'

That evening when her visitors had gone, April cried with relief that a secret she had borne with so much guilt and anxiety no longer burdened her. She cried for the innocent and naive girl she had been and who had gone forever.

TWENTY-FIVE

April was deemed well enough to return home that July. Her medical details were with her family doctor and Enfield Hospital. After lying in bed so long, her leg muscles had wasted and she needed to do exercises every day to strengthen them. As far as Shirley was concerned, her daughter was far too thin. She needed regular meals and plenty of walks around the garden.

April's return brought a regular stream of visitors bringing flowers and cards.

Jenny Jones from the police station called to bring a welcome home message from the police team and to return her diary.

'I'm sorry we had to borrow it.'

'That's alright. Mandy told me how hard you all worked. I'm really grateful and I'm sorry that I put everyone to so much trouble.'

Jenny explained that Betty, whom April had met on the coach, had worried so much that she had become ill. April promised that she would visit the old lady when they were both well enough.

Her form teacher called with good wishes from the staff. She told April that if she returned in September, she should be able to take her O-levels in November.

Mandy came regularly. They played records, chatted and, when the weather was fine, sat out on deckchairs in the back garden. There was something April had been dying to ask.

'You and Brian have got together while I've been ill. When did this start?'

'It was looking for you that brought it about. Remember I told you that I'd asked Brian to help me search for you in case the police weren't successful. During that time we got to know each other pretty well. One day he kissed me, just like that.'

'And it took off from there?'

'Yes, I suppose it did. I've always liked Brian but I never thought he found me attractive.'

'I can see why you chose him to help you. You look so right together. I'm very happy for you.'

One day they walked up to the High Street. After the shock of seeing it in 1999 it felt to April like she had stepped back in time and it felt friendly and familiar again. Returning to the house, they saw Fatty Gates and his two cronies coming towards them. He sneered as they passed, making a coarse remark to his companions. Mandy bristled and stopped.

'It's alright,' said April. 'I'll deal with this.'

She turned and soon caught up with the boys.

'Gary, I want a word with you.'

Fatty stopped and turned round. He was smirking but he couldn't look her in the eye.

'What d'ya want?'

April turned her attention to the other boys.

'You two go on, I'm going to speak to Gary.'

They hesitated and looked at their leader for directions. Eventually he nodded and they went on. April waited until they were out of earshot.

'You and I have known each other for over ten years and you've always been horrible to me. This is going to stop now.'

Fatty was taken aback. The defiance in his eyes turned to uncertainty as April looked straight at him. He looked down at the pavement.

'It's jus a bit of fun, I…'

'It's not funny Gary and you know it. It's time to grow up and stop this. Let's call a truce.'

She held out her hand. He looked at it and up at her face. She was smiling.

'Come on, how about it?'

He nodded and took her hand.

'By the way, thanks for signing my card. Have you still got your trains? When we were at primary school, I came round your house one day and you had them all over your bedroom floor.

In spite of his embarrassment, Fatty brightened.

'That was ages ago. I got a big shed in the garden now and three engines.'

'That sounds great. Bye for now.'

'What was that all about?' asked Mandy as they walked on.

'We're going to be a bit more grown up,' is all April would say.'

She had spoken of her experience of the future to her mother and Carol during her stay in hospital. They had listened patiently but both assumed that it was a dream as she had been in hospital all the time. As the doctor had said, dreaming was the only possible explanation.

As April grew stronger, she was able to venture further afield. One warm sunny afternoon she walked with Mandy and Brian along the river and described everything she could recall of her 1999 experience. They were impressed by all the details she could remember of life during that period. Brian wanted to know more about the Kendricks. How old were they and did they both come from Cambridge? She told him everything that she could remember.

'You must miss Emily and Jake,' said Mandy. 'They did so much to look after you.'

'I owe them everything,' agreed April, 'and I miss Jake very much.'

As they approached the footbridge, she remembered sheltering under it with James during the storm three months ago. It would always be a special memory but that naive girl had gone together with her crush on him. He had already left school and hadn't made contact since she'd returned but she didn't mind as she knew from his letter in 1999 how sorry he felt for the way he had treated her and how he was suffering from remorse. As they walked on, Brian wondered whether April should spread her story about 1999 more widely. She was unwilling to so as the idea of publicity brought back painful memories.

'Why don't you write it down in as much detail as possible, while it's still fresh in your mind?' suggested Brian.

After some discussion they all agreed that was a good idea.

'We'll start tomorrow,' announced Mandy. 'You dictate and I'll write it. That way I can make sure it's in proper English.'

Brian had to step in quickly to stop April pushing Mandy into the river.

During the following two weeks, April dictated and Mandy scribbled furiously. Finally she needed a break and suggested a day trip to Cambridge as it might trigger more memories.

The next morning, the girls took the train to Cambridge. They walked around the city centre and April was surprised to see how different it looked. It seemed smaller and shabbier than she remembered. The streets were the same but the pedestrian shopping area with the hairdresser, fashion stores and pizza restaurants wasn't there. Like her recent experience of Milsham, she had an impression of slipping back in time. Before leaving they took a bus down Hills Road and walked along Connaught Avenue. It looked familiar although it had a different name. There were fewer trees and none of the modern houses were there. Both the existing houses and their front gardens seemed scruffier. Many, including the Kendrick house, had crumbling brick walls and gateways. Later April was astonished to see that the vast Addenbrookes Hospital complex wasn't at the bottom of Hills Road. There was just a building site.

On returning home, they found Brian waiting for them at the railway station in a state of great excitement.

'I've managed to track down Richard Kendrick and he's coming here for the day on Saturday.'

TWENTY-SIX

Richard stretched out in a comfortable armchair in the Humphries' living room with his back to a large bookcase. Brian sat opposite him and Mandy and April were together on the settee.

The telephone call from Brian suggesting a get together had sounded interesting, particularly as he had been told that he would hear an amazing story that included details about him. He agreed to come as it sounded promising and he was pleased to learn that April Saunders would be there. He had read about her disappearance and subsequent return in the paper.

Although just 18, Richard had finished his A-levels and had a place to study Physics at Imperial College in London that autumn. He lived in North London and had come up on the train that morning; where the trio were waiting on the platform at Milsham to greet him. April seemed pleased to see him, which he found agreeable as she was an attractive girl. She had recognised him although, as far as he knew, they had never met.

'Well. What's this all about?' he asked.

'It's to do with me,' said April.

She began her story, including as much as she could remember. She described her meeting with Richard and Sarah and Emily in Cambridge and finished with her collapse in a field in Norfolk. She went on to describe her bewilderment at the hospital in Nottingham.

'I've been told that it was a dream but it was much too real for that. In 1999 you told me that I hadn't travelled through time, so what's the answer?'

Richard studied the Edwardian bracket clock on the mantelpiece. April had been speaking for an hour and a half and they had all felt the lucidity of her experience. There could be no doubt that in some form she had lived it all. They assumed that he would be able to explain it but he needed time to think.

He sat up straight and surveyed the expectant faces.

'You were right, Brian. That was the most extraordinary story I have ever heard. I don't know about you lot but I need a drink.'

'I'll go and organise some more coffee,' said Brian, rising to his feet.

'No. I mean a real drink. Have you got any decent pubs round here?'

'Not in Milsham,' said Brian. 'Hang on a minute.'

He returned almost immediately.

'We're in luck, Dad's car is available. There's a nice little pub out at Goff's Oak. The beer's good and they do decent sandwiches. Mandy and I have been out there a couple of times.'

Fifteen minutes later the car bumped onto a small stony parking area and stopped.

'I've been here before with Emily and Jake,' said April. 'It's definitely the same place. It was after that disastrous visit to Milsham. The pub was okay though. There's a good patio and garden at the back.'

She walked up to a fence and peered over it on tiptoe at the area behind the building. There was a jumble of pub detritus and rubbish in a concrete yard and an area of weeds and scrubby bushes. She turned back to her companions with a rueful smile.

'They obviously haven't got around to doing that yet.'

They found a corner table in the smoky bar and sat with a large plate of sandwiches. The boys were plying April with questions about computers and the internet. Eventually Brian rose and went to the bar to get another round of drinks.

'As there were a number of unfamiliar words, I made a list with a brief description of the meaning of each one,' said Mandy.

She produced a sheet of paper from her bag and Richard studied it with astonishment.

'If you're interested, I can make a copy for you,' said Mandy. 'However what we are hoping for today, Richard, is some plausible explanation for April's experience.'

'Is that all? I'm still trying to absorb what is going on here. Promise me that this is all on the level and you're not having me on.'

It went quiet and he was aware that April was looking at him. Their eyes met.

'It's my experience, Richard,' she said. 'Every word.'

They smiled at each other and Richard nodded.

'You have been through so much. I can't imagine what it must have been like.'

'I'm just relieved to be back and it's reassuring to see you again because now I think others will think twice before they insist that my experience was only a dream.'

Brian returned with a new round of drinks and they all turned to Richard, who took a long drink before putting down his glass. He looked at the expectant faces.

'Well, I suppose it's possible that it was just a dream but I find that hard to believe. The technical developments in 1999 that April has told us about are amazing. Some of them are already planned but I don't imagine that you could have known about them, April, let alone project them forty years ahead in operational form.'

He helped himself to a sandwich and munched it thoughtfully.

'What caught my attention at first were the discrepancies between their version of 1959 and ours. The disappearances are totally ridiculous. According to Roger Venn, they began in this country in 1958 and were big news. That hasn't happened. Second, Venn claimed Mandy didn't exist in their records, which is also untrue. Mr Venn told you that April Saunders disappeared in 1959 and was never found. Wrong again. On the same line of thought April, the assertion that your dad isn't your real father may also be untrue. It's far more likely that he is your dad.'

'How do we know that Venn was telling April the truth?' asked Mandy. 'I've been thinking about it and he could have told her anything to suit his own purposes.'

'True enough. I wouldn't trust him,' said Brian.

'There's another thing that's nagging me and I can't remember what it is,' said Richard.

He sipped his beer and closed his eyes in concentration.

'Yes. I've got it. When you took the tube to that publicist Marcus Clarke's office, what was the name of the tube station there?'

'Finsbury Square. I remember seeing the name on the wall along the platform.'

Richard reached into the inside pocket of his jacket and withdrew a slim diary. He turned to the back page and studied a London Underground map, tracing the stations with his finger. He put the diary back.

'There's no such station on the underground. From your description, I think it should be Moorgate.'

'There were a lot more lines and stations in 1999,' said April. 'Perhaps they changed the name.'

'That could be the answer,' admitted Richard, 'or it's yet more evidence that things are not quite the same.'

'Can you explain these differences?' asked April.

Richard paused, scratched the side of his nose, looked around and drew a deep breath.

'If it wasn't a dream, the only plausible explanation is that you passed into a parallel universe.'

'How does that work?' asked Brian.

'There is an idea that there are other universes that may be very similar to our own but which might have a number of differences. If April's accident somehow tipped her into an overlap with a similar universe, things could be almost the same as here, but not quite.'

'That sounds like science fiction,' said Brian.

'Yes it does but the maths isn't new. Charles Dodgson, the mathematician writing during the last century as Lewis Carroll, used a mirror as the portal to another universe in

Alice through the Looking Glass. Today physics refers to such portals as wormholes that can provide a shortcut between two points. When the path of a wormhole passes through a black hole it enters a different universe.'

Brian leaned forward, his eyes shining.

'Perhaps there's a portal in that ditch April was in. We could go out there and see if one of us disappears. I'd love a visit to 1999.'

'No you wouldn't, Brian. Take it from me. I never knew what real loneliness could be like until I found myself there. It was like being an exile in my own country. All I wanted was to return home but I never dreamt that I would ever be able to come back. I've thought about it and reckon we all live enclosed by familiar walls – family, friends, school and recognisable people we see in the street and around the town. We never think about it but we're comfortable surrounded by these people and places. Now, imagine you wake up one day and they've all gone for good. You're completely on your own. It's terrifying.'

'It sounds dreadful and you're not zooming off to another universe, Brian, just as we're getting to know each other,' said Mandy.

'There's no reason to believe that portals are fixed in time or space,' said Richard. 'I'm sure a visit to April's ditch would be a waste of time.'

'You wouldn't be able to persuade me to go back there. Just the memory of it frightens me,' said April.

'You've lost me with all this talk of wormholes and black holes Richard,' said Mandy. 'Why was April forty years in the future and not in the present?'

'I have no idea. I suppose it could have been 1970 or any other year.'

'The thing is, it seemed so real,' said April.

'It *was* real, April. It was every bit as real as we are sitting here now.'

They all reflected on this in silence.

'I earned a lot of money in 1999. If it was real, then I should be able to collect it when I'm fifty-six,' said April.

Richard helped himself to the last cheese sandwich and grinned.

'I'm afraid you won't get that money because, when we all get to 1999, April Saunders isn't going to turn up. That happens in a different universe.'

'Does that mean that my experiences there and all the people will be different?'

'Similar perhaps but not the same,' said Richard. 'For example, I might not be a Cambridge professor. I could marry someone else and be living in Bexhill with six children.'

They all laughed. Even the landlord grinned as he collected up the empty glasses from their table.

'Will you be wanting anything else, gents?'

'We're not all gents here,' said April.

The landlord paused. He glanced at April who was looking straight at him.

'No of course not, sorry Miss.'

As April turned back she caught Richard's eye. She knew that smile so well. It was him without a doubt.

'Richard, your theory of parallel universes only stands up if there are an infinite number of them.'

Richard stared at her in surprise.

'Who told you that?'

'You did.'

TWENTY-SEVEN

Ron came into the bedroom carrying two large full mugs. It was their Sunday morning routine to sit in bed and enjoy their tea before getting washed and dressed for the day. Shirley sipped her drink, deep in thought. Ron was about to ask what was on her mind when she spoke:

'I'm worried about the miscarriage April had in that wood.'

Ron took a long drink and seemed to be studying the end of the bed.

'Yes love?'

'Someone was responsible. Don't you want to know who it was?'

'It was the boyfriend James.'

'I'm not so sure. The doctor thought she was probably about three months gone. That takes us back to February. She only met James that month.'

Ron sat studying his tea.

'It must have been someone else. I'm afraid she was raped and couldn't bring herself to talk about it'

'I can't believe that. You're getting yourself worked up over nothing, love. If April doesn't want to talk about it then that's probably for the best.'

'Oh is it really? Don't you care who was responsible?'

There was a determination in her that unnerved him. He hadn't seen her like this before. He remained silent finishing his tea, put the mug down and made to get up.

'It was early this year that April stopped confiding in me. She's been bottling it up but it's got to come out sooner or later so I'm going to ask her about it.'

'I wouldn't do that, love. If April doesn't want to talk about it, we should respect that.'

'She doesn't talk about it because she can't. You don't know what it's like for a girl. I'll ask her when I feel she's ready. Since she's been back, she's talking to me much more. I feel I've got my old April back.'

The door closed. Ron had gone to the bathroom. Shirley sat clutching her tea frowning.

Two weeks after her meeting with Richard, April went to visit Carol in London. Arriving at Liverpool Street Station, she looked up at the great gloomy cathedral with its smoke blackened glass roof. The place was grimy with the smells from the fumes of noisy steam and diesel engines that hissed and rumbled. She remembered how bright and clean it had been on her previous visit with Emily a few weeks ago. She soon saw Carol waving and the sisters came together with an affectionate hug. April looked around at the dingy concourse.

'They're going to fix this old station up a treat in the future,' she said.

They took the tube straight to Oxford Circus. Walking along Oxford Street reminded April of that afternoon when she had made the same journey with Emily and how she had felt being out of her depth. There had also been that unsettling experience of seeing someone else in her reflection in a shop window.

They enjoyed browsing through the great department stores where Carol bought a number of things for both of them before finishing with lunch in a basement restaurant near Marble Arch. April laughed at Carol's amusing stories of life in the hospital but after a while the conversation lapsed and Carol looked thoughtful.

'The fact is, April, I've decided that nursing isn't for me so I'm leaving the hospital in a couple of month's time.'

'What are you going to do instead?'

'I'm thinking of going into the music business. It's growing rapidly and there are plenty of opportunities there.'

'Do you know anything about the music business?'

'No, but I have a friend who knows a lot. I'd like you to meet him.'

'Okay. When will I be able to do that?'

Carol looked at her watch.

'In about twenty minutes. Let's go.'

They emerged into the noisy brightness of Oxford Street and Carol hailed a taxi. It took them to the Hyde Park Hotel and fifteen minutes later they were seated in the comfortable reception area. Carol waved away an approaching waitress. She's changed, thought April. She's much more worldly and confident.

'Here he comes.'

Carol rose and greeted a smart looking young man with dark crinkly hair. He smiled broadly, they kissed and April was introduced.

'Hello April, I'm John. I've heard all about you from Carol. It's a pleasure to meet you in person.'

They left their bags at the hotel and set off for a walk in Hyde Park. Although just twenty-two, John was already a successful businessman, managing several pop singers and was in the process of setting up his own record label. He'd returned from New York that morning after a series of business meetings there and had just had lunch with an important television executive. These had all gone well, it seemed. April was impressed.

'I've heard about your experience of the future,' said John. 'You've had a terrible time but you must have the same resilience as your sister as you're looking so well.'

April was beginning to understand what Carol saw in this young man. He was fascinated by her recent experience and plied her with questions about the world forty years on. He was particularly interested in the increased wealth and the growth in the number and types of shops. When April told him of the proliferation of pizza restaurants and how she would miss them, he raised his eyebrows and looked thoughtful. After a while they stopped at an open air cafe by the Serpentine for a cup of tea.

'What do you think about my 1999 experience, John? Carol thinks it was just a dream.'

'If it was a dream, it was a remarkable one. I find your revelation of conditions in the future totally believable and yet it must have been some kind of vivid dream. I've talked about it with Carol and we think that it must be similar to the experience some people have when taking certain kinds of drugs. I'm no psychologist but I gather that in dreams we try symbolically to deal with our conflicts and innermost fears.'

He glanced at his watch.

'I'm sorry but I'll have to leave this to Carol as I must get back to my office. It's been great to have met you April. I'll see you again soon as we're coming down to Milsham in a couple of weeks.'

He and Carol rose and embraced each other. After a few quiet words he kissed her and set off with a cheery wave towards Kensington Gore to find a taxi.

'Has he got any younger brothers?'

'I'm afraid not, he's an only child.'

April gazed across the park where John was almost out of sight.

'So what have you got to tell me about my dream of being in 1999 and my innermost fears?'

Carol sat quietly gathering her thoughts. She looked at the people walking along by the Serpentine. It was a beautiful afternoon.

'Don't take this to heart but I've told John everything. We have no secrets from each other.'

'You don't mean *everything*. Like what happened at home.'

'Yes, that too.'

April glared at her sister.

'You had no right to speak to him about me. I suppose everyone in his office knows now that I've had a miscarriage.'

'Of course they don't. John and I are close and I trust him. Neither of us would ever speak about that to anyone else.

We've been trying to unravel what's behind your experience.'

'Alright then, what's your diagnosis?'

'Okay. Now in your account you speak about the 'disappearances' and about the Home Office as some kind of oppressive organisation acting above the law. Both of these things are unreal and suggest strongly that you've been dreaming. Then there are a number of specific clues. The first was when the doctor assured you that you were still a virgin. We know that you're not, so this was an attempt within your dream to reassure yourself and take away your feelings of fear and guilt. The second clue is the revelation that Dad is not really your father. Perhaps that was an attempt to separate yourself from what had happened.'

'Is that it?'

'Not quite. What had happened to you beforehand was very demoralising,' said Carol. 'You were brusquely rejected by James on top of what you were going through at home. Your fear of being used and treated as worthless manifests in the dream as someone recognised and worthy of everyone's attention, a star. You even became the 'Blessed April' for a while although that collapsed under its own improbability. Finally, I see your friends Emily and Jake, who went to extreme lengths to take care of you, as representing a need you felt for close support and intimate friendship.'

April tried to absorb these new ideas. Like Richard's explanation it seemed plausible but deep down it didn't feel true. If it had been a dream, it was one that hadn't evaporated and was still very much a part of her. She looked at Carol who was smiling.

'I'm not sure whether you find this analysis helpful or that I believe it myself. The way you described your experience is more like the description of an exotic story. I don't seem to be finding April in any of this psychology. We know that you were lying in hospital during this time. If there was someone walking around in 1999, it couldn't have been you.'

'I understand that but how do you explain Richard Kendrick? I met him in 1999 and he wasn't a figment of my imagination because we've met again recently. I recognised him at once.'

'I can't explain him. That's where my theory breaks down.'

'By the way, Richard wants to see me again, just the two of us. He's keen to check out my story in more detail.'

'I'm sure he is, as well as checking you out in more detail I should imagine. Take care of yourself, April. Remember you haven't been out of hospital very long.'

'Don't worry Nurse Saunders. I'll be fine. I also had a letter from Alec this morning. When he can afford it, he wants to come down to Milsham on the train to see me. He's a nice boy and I'd like to meet up with him sometime. I just want to relax and have some fun.'

'You deserve that after all you've been through.'

'Tell me about John. How did you two meet?'

'It was at the hospital in May. He'd caught his fingers in a door and I was given the task of dealing with it. He asked me out on the spot.'

'Golly, he didn't waste any time.'

'No he didn't. We've been together ever since.'

She paused, her face serious for a moment. There were sparrows hopping around their feet, searching for crumbs. She brushed some off the table and looked up.

'Can you keep a secret?'

'Yes of course. What is it?'

'We're planning to get married.'

'That's great. Are you quite sure about him?'

'Yes. I've never been more certain of anything. We love each other and I want to spend the rest of my life with him.'

'I can see now why you're going into the music business. I won't breathe a word but promise me that I'll be your bridesmaid. When's the wedding going to be?'

'We're planning to marry in the spring of next year and of course you'll be my bridesmaid. We're coming home in a couple of weeks to tell Mum and Dad. I've mentioned to them about John but they've never met him. I could have an engagement ring by then.'

They rose and walked arm-in-arm back through the park to the hotel.

'I don't know what you've decided,' said Carol, 'but if I were you I would return to school in the autumn and take your O-levels in November. Who knows, next year there might be an opening in the music business for you too if you're interested.'

'Really? That's amazing.'

'When I finish at the hospital in September, I'm moving into John's apartment. He's buying a large house in Hampstead at the moment. He should have completed the purchase by then. After that it will need extensive alterations, including central heating, two more bathrooms and a new kitchen. There's also space for a recording studio and an office for the business. As soon as it's ready, we'll move in. There will be some spare bedrooms and one could be for you. I'd like you to come and stay as I still feel responsible for what happened to you.'

'You weren't responsible. It was the man who took advantage of his own daughters and who it seems is going to get away with it.'

'I know. I feel the same but think of Mum. She's been so happy since you returned. She doesn't deserve to have to face this. Milsham is her home and her life. Exposing him could end up destroying everything, including their marriage.'

'I'm not sure that keeping quiet is possible anymore. She knows I had a miscarriage. If she asks me about it, I won't be able to lie to her and why should I? She has a right to know and, although I no longer fear him, I don't think I can face living at home for much longer without telling her. I know she is waiting for me to speak about it. Harvey told me to be myself and not to be afraid so although I'm dreading telling Mum, I'm ready to go through with it.'

'Alright. Promise me that if you do decide to tell her, you'll make sure that I'm there. We'll do it together. After that, it'll be up to Mum and Dad to sort things out. It will be a terrible shock for her but they may decide to soldier on. It'll be up to them.'

April nodded but she couldn't see how she could go on living at home once the truth was out.

'Good, that's agreed,' said Carol. 'Now all your descriptions of Italian food seem to have influenced John. We're having a few days away next week and I was looking forward to seeing Paris but when he left he said he wanted to go to Rome instead. It looks like becoming Mrs Bernstein is going to be an exciting ride.'

'Did you say Bernstein?'

PART 4

APRIL REMEMBERED

TWENTY-EIGHT
Melbourne. November 2019.

The rate of disappearances had started to fall during the last twelve months after being constant during the last sixty years. The radio station followed this cheery announcement with a noisy rendition of the national anthem. The journalist winced at the strains of *Waltzing Matilda* and turned the car radio off.

On arrival she took the lift in the luxury apartment block to the fifth floor as arranged. The smartly dressed blonde woman who greeted her at the door seemed to be in her late thirties. She led the way into a spacious living room that had glass doors at one end that opened onto a balcony with a view of the shoreline and the ocean. The room was tastefully furnished with an attractive flower arrangement on a side table. After seating her guest, Anna went to the kitchen and returned with a tray of teas and small cakes. They sat opposite each other with a polished coffee table between them. A small recorder was placed on the table and in response to the journalist's opening questions Anna began to speak about herself.

'As I told you on the telephone, my name is Anna Stewart. I'm married to Graham and we have a daughter Emily. We came here from England in 2000 after getting married.'

She took a sip of her tea and continued.

'I'm Australian by birth, being brought up near Sydney by a single mother. She died when I was eighteen. I wanted to get away so I went to London to make a new start.'

'When was that?'

'Twenty years ago in 1999.'

'So that was when you met April Saunders?'

'That's a tough question. Strictly speaking I would say that we never met.'

'I see. So in spite of not meeting this girl you claim to have the true story?'

'Yes. Perhaps I should continue.'

'Very well. I shan't interrupt again, please carry on.'

'On arrival, I found a flat in Earls Court in West London and worked for a temp agency doing clerical stuff. One night I went with three others to a rave in a field somewhere in the country. I can't remember much except I was quite out of it. Returning in the early hours we stopped by a piece of woodland on the A1 road and wandered into the trees for a pee. One of the blokes tried it on and, as I fought him off, I fell back and went crashing down a steep slope. I banged my head in a ditch and passed out. The next thing

I remember is waking up four weeks later in a hospital in Norwich. I subsequently found out that the people I was with that night had searched the wood, but couldn't find me in the dark. They decided that I must have run off so they gave up and went back to London.'

She picked up a cake and nibbled at it.

'When I never returned to the temp agency they crossed me off their list. The three girls I had shared a flat with for a few days assumed that I'd moved on and found someone else.'

'Do you mean that no one reported you missing or was looking for you?'

'Too right. It's easy to slip through the cracks in those conditions.'

'So what happened during those four weeks and where does April Saunders come into this?'

'That's the story. I was April Saunders. I thought you weren't going to interrupt?'

The Journalist jumped up, walked across the room and stared out through the balcony windows to the sea, her body rigid with tension. After a couple of minutes she returned slowly to her seat and looked at Anna with an expression of incredulity and disbelief on her face.

'Okay, so you turned into April Saunders. I won't interrupt you again but I should warn you that you're beginning to strain my credulity.'

'I'm not surprised. How much do you know about April?'

'I read her book.'

'Good. I woke up in the hospital in Norwich after an operation for a brain tumour and was puzzled that everyone was calling me April. I protested that my name was Anna and eventually managed to convince them. My most frequent visitor was Emily Kendrick who had been with me during the four weeks of my 'lost' period. I had even been living in her house. Gradually she filled me in on what had happened during those four weeks. It was unbelievable. To convince me, she brought along her mother who was a doctor and who had found me lying on the road with a head injury and taken me to a hospital in Cambridge. Emily's boyfriend Jake came once but he didn't say much except to confirm everything that I'd been told. Jake and Emily it seems had protected me from being picked up by undesirable elements.'

'Who were they?'

'Home Office people. They were using the police to find me and bring me in.'

She finished her tea and looked thoughtful.

The journalist put down her cup and leaned forward looking into Anna's eyes.

'How do I know you're not just making this up?'

'Perhaps you should hear me out before making up your mind. What finally convinced me that people around me weren't lying were the newspaper reports about April and a recording of her being interviewed on television. She looked like me but behaved like someone else. I would never have been able to fake that. She spoke English without my Aussie accent and as for quoting that poetry at the end, I couldn't have done that as I'd never heard of the poem. Another amazing thing was the swimming. Apparently April had gone to the pool regularly with Emily in the early days before the newshounds came after her. She proved to be the stronger swimmer.'

'Aren't you a strong swimmer?'

'No. I can't swim a stroke. I got out of my depth as a kid and nearly drowned. I've been scared of deep water ever since. Of course, there were some things that didn't add up. April claimed to be sixteen years old whereas I was two years older. Several people had commented on that. When April first appeared she was convinced that she was pregnant. She must have been surprised to be told that she was still a virgin, as I was at the time. Also a DNA test showed that she wasn't related to her own father, which is no surprise. In all these years I still haven't been able to figure out what happened and no one has investigated as my existence has been a secret.'

'Let's get this straight. You're saying that the girl claiming to be April was actually you. She was a returnee from 1959 who was in your body and never realised it.'

'That's about right.'

'This is unbelievable. Apart from April's own book, I read the one by Emily Kendrick, *April's Story* It was clear that she really was a close friend.'

'She was and she gave all the royalties from that book to the Great Ormond Street Children's Hospital in London. She'd obviously been loyal to April and was very supportive of me during my recovery. The earnings April received from her book and media appearances went into a subsidiary bank account of Emily's. She wanted me to have it all but I insisted that she keep it as she was starting her studies in London that autumn and would need it. In the end we agreed to split it and I finished up with a substantial sum.'

'I see. But why haven't you told this story before?'

'While I was in hospital I had regular meetings with a Mr Venn from the Home Office. He explained that the story given to the public was that April had become one of the disappeared (which in a way she had). He organised a private room for me and arranged for my eventual return to Australia without any red tape. In return, I had to sign a piece of paper promising never to speak about April Saunders. However he crossed out 'never' and wrote in 'for twenty years' and initialled it.'

'Strewth. Why do you think he did that?'

'I don't know but he must have had his reasons for wanting the story to come out. He was about fifty so he'll be retired now. I was grateful to him for this arrangement as after the operation I was completely bushed and couldn't have coped with the world's media descending on me. Mr Venn protected me from all that and also squared it with Jake, the Kendricks and the hospital staff. He did an efficient job. Would you like some more tea?'

'Yes. Thank you.'

Anna disappeared into the kitchen and soon returned with two more steaming cups. She continued:

'The shocking way that April was treated by the authorities in England led to a storm of protests and resulted in changes in the law. The Home Office lost the power to pick up people claiming to be returnees and hold them in secret interrogation centres. Then there was the Pendleton Hotel scandal, where an assassination squad took April away. It's just as well she escaped or we wouldn't be having this conversation now.'

'I don't recall that. I was too young.'

'The police investigation at the time discovered that

the woman in the hotel who delivered April to the assassins was employed by MI5. This proved a direct link between the Home Office and MI5 and caused a right barney in parliament. The Home Secretary had to resign and so did a bloke called Sir Harold something or other, a high up civil servant. The reputation of the hotel was shot to bits. In the following years the owners put in new management and a proper security system and after a year or two it recovered.'

'Thanks for all that. Now tell me about your husband.'

'We met by accident while I was recovering in hospital. Graham had been visiting his mother who was terminally ill. One day he lost his way in the maze of corridors and entered my room by mistake. He's still not much good at spatial things and relies entirely on his satnav to drive to places around the city. Anyway, in spite of my daunting appearance after the operation he seemed to like me. I was glad of his company as I was by myself much of the time. He used to call in every evening after visiting his mother and we got on very well. When I left hospital I decided to stay on in Norwich and we saw each other regularly. After a while I moved in with him and on Millennium night he proposed. We married the following summer and shortly afterwards we came here to Melbourne and purchased this apartment. Graham carried on with his writing career and I took a course in Floristry before starting my own business. Two years after we arrived we had a beautiful daughter Emily.'

'Did you name her after Emily Kendrick?'

'Yes, I suppose so. She saved my life by calling the rescue helicopter after I collapsed. My arrival in hospital was just in time.'

'Was there no indication that you had a tumour beforehand?'

'There was but April had kept quiet about the symptoms. I have no idea why as the condition must have been evident and it's clear she was becoming increasingly worried. Only when they became serious did she speak about them, shortly before she collapsed. Dr Kendrick suspected a tumour and was coming to examine her that very afternoon. Fortunately she had confided her suspicions to Emily.'

'Have you kept in touch with Emily and Jake?'

'They seemed to drift apart during that summer. Emily went up to London in October to begin her medical studies. Jake was awarded his doctorate that year and took up an offer to do research at MIT in the United States. I'm still in touch with Emily. She's a paediatrician now and married to a doctor. They have two children, a boy and a girl. I understand that Jake is now a professor in the States and is also married with a young son.'

The recorder was switched off and the journalist rose to leave.

'Thanks for all this. I'll go and type it up and will go through it with you afterwards. I have a feeling that there will be a lot more questions. I should also like to talk to Emily in England. I'd be glad if you could email me her details. I assume she will be able to verify your account. I will also try to track down Mr Venn. If we decide to go ahead, can I arrange for a photographer to call and get a current picture of you?'

'Yes that'll be okay. I'll send you Emily's email address.'

'Have you thought this through? Once this story comes out you could be besieged by the media. Are you prepared for that?'

'I don't think it will amount to much. There isn't anything I can tell them in addition to what I've told you. I'm betting they'll soon lose interest.'

Anna sat on the balcony looking out at the ocean. The road below hummed with the late afternoon traffic. The parkland beyond the road stretched for 200 yards before becoming dunes and a sandy beach. The brightness of the day had gone. Something was nagging at the back of her mind. It was in April's book. She retrieved it from the bookshelf, returned to her place and leafed through the pages until she found the passage:

When I looked at myself in the mirror for the first time in the hospital I saw with a shock that I was looking at someone else. I assumed that it must be a side effect of my injury.

She closed her eyes and thought about it. After a while she dozed off and was woken suddenly when a door banged.

'Hi. Are you there, love?'

'Of course. I'm on the balcony watching the sunset.'

'How did the interview go?'

'It was fine. I'll tell you all about it. What about your meeting?'

'We had a useful discussion. I should get some work there. Fancy a drink?'

'Yes please. The usual will do very nicely. Come and join me out here.'

They carried on the conversation at a distance while Graham organised two gin and tonics in the kitchen.

'You know, Graham, I've been thinking about April Saunders. People were obsessed at the time with whether she was a returnee. Now at last I have realised that she was, but not in a way that anyone had expected. I've finally understood it. Do you believe that someone can be in two places at the same time?'

Graham emerged into the living room bearing the drinks.

'Sorry, love. I couldn't hear you properly in the kitchen.'

He put the drinks down. Anna wasn't there. She wasn't anywhere any more.

April Saunders, *My Journey* (Unicorn Press 1999)
Emily Kendrick, *April's Story* (Hooper & Day 2000)